TURNPIKE
CONFIDENTIAL

TURNPIKE CONFIDENTIAL

NEAL SAVAGE

Brandylane Publishers, Inc.
Publishing books since 1985

Copyright © 2025 by Neal Savage

1950s map of Richmond courtesy of the Library of Virginia

This is a work of fiction. Certain names, places, characters, and incidents are either the work of the author's imagination or are used fictitiously. Any resemblance to actual persons, living or dead, events, or locales is wholly coincidental.

All rights reserved. No part of this book may be reproduced in any form or by any electronic or mechanical means, or the facilitation thereof, including information storage and retrieval systems, without permission in writing from the publisher, except in the case of brief quotations published in articles and reviews. Any educational institution wishing to photocopy part or all of the work for classroom use, or individual researchers who would like to obtain permission to reprint the work for educational purposes, should contact the publisher.

ISBN: 978-1-962416-56-6
Library of Congress Control Number: 2024915210

Designed by Sami Langston
Project managed by Andrew Holt

Printed in the United States of America

Published by
Brandylane Publishers, Inc.
5 S. 1st Street
Richmond, Virginia 23219

Brandylane Publishers, Inc.
Publishing books since 1985

brandylanepublishers.com

for Nancy,
my first and best reader

SHERWOOD
CUMMINGS DR
HARDY
DURHAM
OVERBROOK
HERMITAGE
BROAD ST. STATION
20
21
22
23
BROAD
MONUMENT
ALLISON
MARSH
TERMINAL PL.
MYERS
KENSINGTON
STUART
HANOVER
GROVE
FLOYD
CARY
MAIN
ROSENEATH
TILDEN
CLEVELAND
SHEPPARD
BOULEVARD
COLONIAL
CUTSHAW
GRACE
FRANKLIN ST.
PARK
PATTERSON AVE.
WYTHE
ALTAMONT
SUMMIT
HIGHPOINT
NORFOLK
CLAY
MOORE
LEIGH
MAXWELL
10
11
12
13
6
STADIUM
7
8
9
24
27
32
33
MAPLEWOOD
ROSEWOOD
IDLEWOOD
BEAUMONT
GRAYLAND
PARKWOOD
DOOLEY AVE.
AUBURN AVE
BELLWOOD
BELMONT
CRENSHAW AV
MULBERRY
ROBINSON
DAVIS
STAFFORD
ADDISON
SHIELDS
ROWLAND
LAKEVIEW
Boat Lake
Swan Lake
Shields Lake
MEADOW
GRANBY
ALLEN
VINE
LOMBARDY
PLUM ST
TEMPLE
JACQUELIN
KEMPER
CLAIBORNE
BLAIR
WINDER
POWHATAN
APPOMATTOX
AMELIA
COLORADO
DAKOTA
NEVADA
PENNSYLVANIA AVE
NEW YORK ST.
KANSAS
GEORGIA
GREEN
CARTER
TEXAS
HAMPTON
SOUTHAMPTON
MT. CALVARY CEMETERY
RIVERVIEW CEMETERY
HOLLYWOOD
GILBERT
WALKER
GATES ST.
SUMPTER
NEADE ST.
TOBACCO
WORMLEY
MAYMONT
PARK
WILLIAM BYRD
PUMP HOUSE DRIVE
SHIRLEY
WEST
BERKELEY
SPOTTSWOOD
BRANDON
DOVER RD.
BLANTON AV
WALPOLE
HUXLEY
GARRETT
DOUGLASDALE
CONDIE
FRENCH
MCCLOY
GRANT
SUNSET LANE
BUTE
THOMPSON
CAMERON
LAFAYETTE ST.
ELLWOOD
FLOYD AV
KENSINGTON
STUART
MALVERN
ANTRIM
HAMILTON
REVEILLE
BROMLEY
SAUER
SHENANDOAH
QUEEN CHARLOTTE
GUN CLUB
PORTLAND PL.
TOMACEE
ROTHESAY
ROTHESAY CIRCLE
MARSTON LANE
R.F.&P.R.R.
A.C.L. R.R. BRIDGE
RIVER
RIVERSIDE DRIVE
EVELYN RD
BYRD
BOULEVARD
KENT
PRINCE EDWARD RD
CALEDONIA
KING
SYLVAN
DEVONSHIRE
PETERBOROUGH
PRINCE ARTHUR
WILLIAM
FOREST
ROAD
NEW KENT
PRINCE GEORGE RD
ARCHER AV.
NEWWOOD
CEDAR LANE
STONEWALL
HILL
SPRINGHILL
SMITHDEAL ST
HILLCREST
FOREST CIRCLE
FOREST HILL PARK
CHESTERFIELD
CLARENCE
DORCHESTER ROAD
BOXCODEL
A.C.L.
HILLS
48TH ST.
45TH
44TH

ESSEX ST.
HANES
GARLAND
FENDALL
GRIFFIN
EDGEWOOD
HOOPER
HAMMOND AVE.
NORTHUMBERLAND
SEMINARY
EDGE HILL RD.
HAWTHORNE
NORWOOD ST.
LANCASTER
ROAD
OVERBROOK 39
GRAHAM RD
GRAHAM
WICKHAM
ROBERTS
UNION UNIVERSITY
BROOK
WELLINGTON ST.
GROVELAND
CUSTER
FOUQUREAN LANE
CRAFTON
PELHAM
HOUSTON
HAROLD
HENRICO
CLIFTON
HARVEY AVE
VICTOR
PULASKI ST.
MAGNOLIA
MYRTLE
SPRUCE
JUNIPER
WILLOW
CYPRESS ST.
ALTHEA
CHESTNUT
ALDER
TRIGG ST
CALL ST.
FIRST
SECOND
THIRD
FOURTH
FIFTH
SIXTH
RICHMOND
MONTROSE
ALTHEA
DOVE ST.
BATTERY
BARTON
LAMB AV
VALE
LAMB
ROAD
WYNDALE
WICKHAM
ROBERTS
HOME
YANCEY
POE
MINOR
WELLFORD
KING
FELLS
MONTEIRO
SEWELL
BEALE
DANIEL
TAZEWELL
TYLER ST.
SCHOOL ST.
SLEDD
QUICKSALL LANE
FELLS
FRITZ
BACON
MITCHELL
WEBSTER
CREEK
CALHOUN
CHAMBERLAYNE
HICKORY
FENDALL
GREENWOOD
MILLER
JOSHUA ST.
ROSE
GENTRY
SCHOOL
ST. JAMES
COUTTS
ORANGE
BACON
HILL
J. STUART BRIDGE
VALLEY
ROAD
STONEWALL JACKSON BRIDGE
HOSPITAL
SHOCKOE CEMETERY
84
ADMIRAL
CURRIE
SCHOOL ST.
LOUIS
SLEDD ST.
BROOK
OAK
ATTUCKS
CATHERINE
HANCOCK
GOSHEN
GILMER
MUNFORD
SMITH
BAKER
DUVAL
PRICE
CAMEO
ST. PETER
ST. PAUL
ST. JOHN
FEDERAL
CHARITY
BATES ST.
PRESTON
BAKER
DUVAL
JACKSON
LEIGH
CLAY
MARSHALL
BROAD
GRACE
FRANKLIN
MAIN
CARY
CANAL
BYRD
ARCH
43
40
41
42
28 MONROE PARK
HENRY
MADISON
JEFFERSON
ADAMS
FOUSHEE
49
48
50
51
52
53
54
55
56
57
58
59
60
61
62
63
64
65
66
67
68
69
70
71
72
73
74
75
76
77
78
79
80
81
85
CAPITOL SQUARE
BANK ST.
GOVERNOR
COLLEGE
BALLARD
CLAY
ABIGAIL
ELLETT
TURPIN
CROUCH
FEDERAL
BATES ST.
SEABOARD YARDS
C. & O. RY.
WHITCOMB
MECKLENBURG ST.
LEBANON ST.
CHELSEA
SUSSEX
CONRAD
GLENLEA AVE
WOOD
HOSPITAL
FERRELL
RAVEN
GAY ST.
FORD
FAIRFIELD AVE.
CHESAPEAKE
BURWELL
RICHMOND
SALE
LOWNDES
AVERY
LITTLEPAGE
BALDING
RICHARDS
CHRISTIAN
WILLIAMS
JAMES
GOODCHLAND
COALTER
BRYAN ST.
WASHINGTON
CARTHAGE ST.
JAY ST
BUCHANAN
CARRINGTON & VENABLE
MECHANICSVILLE
SPOTSYLVANIA
FAIRMOUNT
ROGERS
19TH
DRAPER
AUSTIN
LACROSSE
EARLE
SOUTHERN
LANE
PLEASANTS
90
BURTON
JESSAMINE
TULIP
MOSBY
JEFFERSON AVE
LEIGH
CLAY
MARSHALL
BROAD
GRACE
91
92
86
87
88
89
DOCK
CARY
MAIN
LIBBY TERRACE
93
CHIMBORAZO
VIRGINIA
14TH
FRANKLIN
DOCK ST.
BYRD
9TH ST. BRIDGE
R.R. BRIDGE
A.C.L.
SOU. RY. YARDS
MAYO'S ISLAND
MAYO'S BRIDGE
47
S.A.L. RR. BR.
BRANDER ST.
MANCHESTER RD
BRANDER
46
45
ROBERT E. LEE BRIDGE
RAILROAD AVE
SEMMES
McDONOUGH
PERRY
PORTER
BAINBRIDGE
HULL
DECATUR
STOCKTON
COWARDIN
LEWIS
NICHOLSON
DENNY
PEEBLES
WATER
MAIN
PEAR
DETROIT AVE.
FIFTH AVE.
FOURTH
LAUREL
PINE
BELVIDERE

"'At this moment' is a rare thing because only sometimes do I step with both feet on the land of the present; usually one foot slides toward the past, the other slides toward the future. And I end up with nothing."

– Clarice Lispector, *A Breath of Life*

CHAPTER 1

The City on the River

Richmond, Virginia

Friday, October 26, 1956

I was alone inside my shop, cutting a key and pondering the fate of the world when the kid walked in. I glanced up and saw he had freckles, big teeth, and a western shirt one size too large. In profile he was like a chinless Howdy Doody. While he stood there fidgeting and double-checking the address, I finished the key and killed the motor to get another blank.

"Can I help you?" I asked.

"You Bostic?" he asked.

"What if I am?"

"I'm supposed to give you this," he said.

He extended the envelope toward me and placed it on the counter. In the old days I might have thought he was a process server, but not so much anymore. I wiped both hands with a rag and picked up the envelope. It was addressed to me personally, and not my shop, which was odd. I cracked it open and found a single business card inside. On the back in red ballpoint was written *Today 12:45 Key Needed.*

"What's this?" I asked.

"It's from Mr. Gettle, sir," he said.

"I can see that. I can also see that he's with the Turnpike Authority, which I guess means you are too. What I don't know is why you're giving me this. Unless Mr. Gettle needs a duplicate key, I'm afraid I can't help him."

"I don't know nothing about it," the kid said. "They didn't tell me to do anything other than make sure I give it to you personally. Those were my only instructions."

"Mission accomplished," I said. I gave him a look to let him know we were done. He paused and reached for the door, then turned to face me.

"I heard the Authority is taking your building," he said.

"So you do know something after all," I said. "Sayonara."

The door closed behind him with a shush. I studied both sides of the card once more, then stuck it in my shirt pocket. I eyed my cutter, a dingy green Keil, sitting idle on the counter. It was my backup. It was on its last legs and none too quiet, but it was also keeping me in business. My main cutter was already packed. On the keyboard wall behind me was a full display of blanks and a handful of locks for sale, both keyed and combination. I knew I should be doing more to move, but I just couldn't make myself.

I decided I'd finish the order later. I rolled down my sleeves and buttoned the cuffs, untucked the tie from my shirt. As I did, two official-looking men in suits and hats paused outside my front window. One of them plastered a notice to the glass with a brush and glue, while the other scribbled notes on a clipboard. The brush man did a sloppy job, all that glue streaming down. Not that it mattered. I put on my suit jacket and went outside to them.

"That's bad for business," I said.

The man with the clipboard looked at me, then scribbled something down.

"Just a few preliminaries, Mr. Bostic," he said. "I trust you are packed and ready to leave."

He handed me a yellow copy of the notice that told me what I already knew. The place was technically still mine until a week from Sunday, but after that it became the property of the Richmond-Petersburg Turnpike Authority. I double-checked the address to make sure they hadn't made a mistake, but there it was bold as day: 1523 East Main.

"You getting everyone on the row?" I asked.

"Not quite," he said. "Mr. Viola at the sock shop has been spared, as has the Belting and Supplies building, Turpin's Barber, and Sardi's."

He took a step back and pointed with the clipboard down the line of storefronts. "But City Diner, Al's Grill, and Merchants Supply are all condemned by the Authority. So is your next-door neighbor the jeweler, and the women's clothing store next to that. And you, of course, Bostic Lock & Key."

"Of course," I said.

After they left, I stood on the sidewalk and watched a train roll in along the elevated tracks of the Seaboard rail line. Above that, the train station's clock tower rose into the sky, affording me an unobstructed view of exactly nothing. For the time being anyway. Glancing back at the notice on the window, I caught sight of my pale reflection. Condemned or not, I needed a haircut and shave.

I flipped the sign on the shop door from open to closed and walked down the block to Turpin's. It was an old-timey place with a striped wooden post, straight razors, strops, and combs in jars of blue Barbicide. Their radio was tuned to the Alden Aaroe show on WRVA. Once I was inside, there was no waiting. I reclined in one of those heavy Koken barber chairs with a footrest while Bobby Jesse spruced me up. Like me, Bobby had something of a sideline. His was more respectable though. He called local square dances on the weekends.

While he worked, I glanced at the morning's *Times-Dispatch*. A John Doe had turned up in Shockoe Bottom just blocks from here, shot to death, and a Jane Doe had been fished out of the river. A St. Patrick's student named Jane Wynant, who'd gone missing a few weeks ago, was still missing. And on page twenty-eight was a short article on the movie page about Daisy Williams, a local girl who'd made good. In Hollywood, no less. She was in town to promote a new movie; the premiere was Sunday. Maybe I'd run into her. I turned the page and looked for the funny papers.

* * *

Back at the store I rang up Gettle. It was a short conversation, but I told him to expect me at the requested time. He didn't say where or how he got my name. But in my line of work, if a man needs a key, you give him a key.

CHAPTER 2

The Turnpike

Most everybody in Richmond agreed we needed an interstate, but almost nobody agreed where it should go. The idea had been kicked around for a decade, studied, debated, and put to popular vote. It lost. Then more study, more debate, and another vote. It lost again. Tired of the impasse, the General Assembly created the Richmond-Petersburg Turnpike Authority in 1954 and granted it eminent domain. Two years later, the interstate was happening whether we liked it or not. At the moment, Richmond still looked like it did a decade before, when I came here. But big change was on the way, most especially to residents of the city's Black section, Jackson Ward.

The RPTA's downtown office was on the ninth floor of the Southern States Building at Seventh and Main. The building was only a few years old, positively new by Richmond standards. Its twelve floors were occupied not just by the namesake company, but by the insurance agents, lawyers, accountants, and secretaries of its tenants. Ironically, it did not contain the offices of my former employer, Southern States Investigating Agency, which still had its offices at The Jefferson Hotel. On the ride up, everybody stared at the elevator door in silence until someone coughed quietly into their hand. A rowdy bunch.

I got out on the ninth floor and found Suite 916. The receptionist pointed me in the direction of Conference Room F. I went down the hall, knocked twice, and was told to come in. Inside was a large rectangular room with three long windows that looked out on the James River and beyond into the area of south Richmond called Manchester. At the far end of a conference table, two men in gray suits sat in leather chairs. One was around sixty, the other in his mid-forties with salt and pepper gray.

"You must be Bostic," the younger one said.

"In the flesh," I said. "I understand you need a key."

"Of sorts," the older man said.

We shook hands. The younger man was D.W. Malone, from Chester. The older man introduced himself as Albert Gettle of Petersburg, whose business card was in my pocket. We sat at the conference table across from each other. A worn manila folder sat on the table in front of Gettle. He opened it and put on a pair of reading glasses.

"We don't need a locksmith, Mr. Bostic," he said. "We got your name from a colleague of yours, a man named Mike Wells."

"A former colleague, in my estimation," I corrected him. "But I know him."

"He tells us you have an interesting sideline," Malone said.

"It's not that interesting," I said. "In fact, the less interesting it is, the more I like it. Locksmithing is my living, or at least it was until the Authority decided my store was in the way of the interstate."

The silence was audible. I looked around for a clock on the wall so I could watch the seconds of my life tick away. There wasn't one, so I made a mental note to get my watch fixed. Gettle covered his mouth with his hand, trying to hide a frown. Malone cracked his knuckles and cleared his throat. "Care for something from the bar?" he asked, gesturing toward a pewter tray in the middle of the table that held an assortment of liquors.

"Not before lunch, most days," I said.

"Good," Gettle said. "Alcohol dulls the senses. I hate a man with dull senses on the job."

I lit a Lucky and clicked the Zippo closed. "I'm not on any job yet," I said.

Gettle pulled a red ballpoint from his pocket and peered into the folder in front of him. "According to this, we reached a settlement with you with regard to your property. Is that not the case?"

"That's correct," I said. "It was better than nothing, which is what the folks in Jackson Ward got. Certainly not enough for a deposit on a new one."

They exchanged a dubious look.

"If you are willing to listen to an offer," Gettle said. "We can set you up with enough capital to reopen your enterprise elsewhere."

"I'm listening." I studied the lighter in my palm, ran my thumb along the red and black insignia of the army's Twenty-Seventh Infantry.

Malone rose from his chair and started pacing in front of the long windows. "Mr. Gettle and I sit on the board of the Richmond-Petersburg Turnpike Authority. Work has been underway in our districts for some time now, since the summer, as well as in Dinwiddie and Colonial Heights. Crews clearing land in rural and heavily forested areas along the route. It's brutal work." He paused and looked at me as though trying to read my expression.

"Sounds like," I said.

Gettle lifted the file and started reading. "Says here you served in the army in WWII. Is that correct?"

"It is. I was a rifleman in the Pacific."

"And then with the Richmond Police for a few years after that?"

"Until February of '51, yes."

"Why'd you leave the force?"

"Philosophical differences."

"We heard it was because you were soft on coloreds."

I exhaled some smoke with a sigh and shook my head. This again.

"I'm soft on a lot of things," I said. "Just last week I rescued a litter of kittens. But if you're referring to the Martinsville Seven, then yes. That's why I left policing."

They exchanged another look. I was starting to think it was in their job description. Malone cleared his throat again.

"The Richmond police had nothing to do with Martinsville."

"Maybe not, but the executions happened right here at the state pen. I was on duty that weekend and had to walk each of those men from their cells to the chair. You'd quit too if you saw what I saw."

Malone considered this, then changed the subject. "Mr. Wells told us you're not afraid of a little work."

"I'm not," I said. "But I'm out of the excitement business and I'm not trying to get back in it. It's hazardous to my health."

"There's some money in it for you," Malone said.

"That I could use."

Gettle scoffed. "That's hardly the attitude to have if you want to succeed in life, son. A man needs passion in life, a goal, something to strive for beyond mere money. Maybe that's your problem. Maybe that's why you make your living as a locksmith and not as a detective with the RPD."

"Let me guess," I said. "You pitched this idea to Wells, but he turned you down flat because he's too busy with the Wynant case. And he was your last resort until he referred you to me. I'll be sure and thank him the next time I see him."

"He merely said you might be willing to listen."

"Which is all I'm doing."

"Mr. Wells indicated you were merely . . . selective about the cases you'll take."

"Putting it mildly. The most dangerous thing I'll look into is insurance fraud, and that's hardly ever dangerous. Anything more than that is a hard no."

"What would you say if I told you that one of our contractors is defrauding us?"

"I'd say you need to vet your contractors more carefully. Which one?"

"That's what we're trying to find out."

"Look, I don't want to take up any more of your time." I stubbed out my cigarette in an amber ashtray and reached for my hat. "Thanks to you I have to move out of my store, and I have nine days to do it. I have customers with orders they've already paid for and a pretty steady walk-in. So, unless what you're offering is worth more than the inconvenience, I need to be getting back."

Most of that was a bluff. Business wasn't great.

They were both silent again before Gettle spoke up in his raspy voice. "Tell us about the Pacific, Mr. Bostic."

"Not much to tell," I said. "I survived."

"Get your hands dirty there?"

"You could say."

"I hope you retain some of that same spirit for this assignment."

"Like I said, I'm trying to stay out of the dirty hands business. So why don't we cut to the chase?"

"The crews clearing the land between Petersburg and Richmond, our contractors," Malone said. "There have been . . . rumors."

"Such as?"

"You know the sort of man who does this sort of work for a living," Malone said. "The roughneck, the itinerant, the uneducated. The work they do is not difficult mentally, but physically is another story."

"Sounds like the army," I said.

"Yes, well," Gettle said. "These rumors about the crews need to be investigated and quashed. The Authority, through no fault of our own, doesn't get the best press locally. Heaven knows we've tried. If these rumors prove true and word gets out, it could be disastrous."

"I still don't know what these rumors are," I said.

"Well," Malone said. "The sort of man working out there is, um . . ." He left off and raised his eyes at Gettle.

"They're base," Gettle said. "Prone to animal urges and impulses that are... animal in nature."

"At least they're consistent," I said. "Look, are you trying to say that your contractors are engaged in some sort of prostitution ring?"

The two men made a show of clearing their throats loudly, and Malone pressed a fingertip to his lips.

"Certainly not," Gettle said.

"Merely that there are rumors to that effect," Malone said. "And that is what we need someone to investigate. We think that someone is you."

"I see. I think."

"You could begin however you like. But we would like to arrange a day next week for you to go undercover with a work team, mingle with the workers and blend in. If you go out there as an official investigator asking questions and taking notes, you'll never get anywhere."

"That sounds like a lot of work," I said. I looked at Gettle. I didn't appreciate his dig about me being an RPD detective. "I might have to pass."

Gettle nodded to Malone, who wrote something on a piece of note paper, turned it over, and slid it toward me. I looked at it, found a pen, and crossed out what he'd written. I'd been shopping for new buildings lately and couldn't afford any of them. When a suitable number came to me, I scribbled it down and passed the note back to him.

"For this I get combat pay."

They both looked at the figure. Gettle nodded.

"That shouldn't be a problem," he said. He seemed relieved and I suddenly wished I'd asked for more. "We'll make sure it's reflected in the agreement. We'd like your day at the worksite to be next Wednesday if that's agreeable."

"As much as it'll ever be," I said.

"You will have to ride the bus there just like any other worker," Gettle said. "Which is the whole idea. Blend in, keep your eyes and ears open. The men assemble at the Bellwood Drive-In parking lot at 5:00 a.m. Check in at the desk."

Malone continued. "It is important to note that you will not be working directly for the Authority, but rather for one of our subcontractors, Drewry Brothers. We'll have an employment application to be processed in your name, so you don't need to worry about that. If you'd prefer it under an alias, we think that might be a good idea as well."

"That's fine," I said. "As long as the check's made out to the right guy."

CHAPTER 3

Model Tobacco

I didn't love whoring myself out like that, but it was hardly a first. I'd been doing side work as an investigator the last few months. Nothing much, just a little extra dough here and there and never more than a few hours. If I didn't like the sound of something, I didn't do it. Working for myself gave me the freedom to say no, a luxury I didn't have at Southern States Investigating. I spent two crummy years there after leaving the RPD, mostly tailing cheating spouses and typing case reports for lawyers. That'll burn you out if nothing else will. This job with the Authority was bigger than usual, but the payday meant I could afford a new building. I figured I'd spend a day or two out in the sticks talking to rednecks and that's that. The rumors were probably bullshit anyway.

After the meeting I crossed the street for a grilled cheese sandwich and Coke at the Stumble Inn. When I got back to the shop, I changed into a pair of blue coveralls I wore when I worked on-site. They had my first name stitched on the front and business logo on the back. My company car was a work van, specifically a black 1950 Bedford PC. I was mildly troubled by its resemblance to a police paddy wagon, but it looked legitimate enough with my business name and address painted on the side. I kept it parked around back and was lucky to have it. My usual ride was a '49 Mercury 8, but it had been in the shop since Wednesday. I'd had it towed to Old Market Auto on Eighteenth Street because they were the closest, but I wasn't convinced they had my best interests at heart. I used to have a mechanic there, a guy named Barney. He'd kept that damn car running the last two years. But then Barney lit out for New Orleans, and now I didn't have a guy there. Now I had a Vince who slicked his hair back with used thirty-weight motor oil and worked on cars in his jeans and black leather jacket. I told him there was something wrong with the starter, then got two days of nothing. Two and counting.

I'd been working a locksmith job at the Model Tobacco building since Monday, changing the locks on the executive offices. It was the last big job I had scheduled ahead of the move, and today was my last day on it. All week I'd gotten there via the usual route, across the Mayo Bridge and through Manchester. But today the bridge was backed up all the way to Cary, so I took the long way up Main to Belvidere. As I crossed the Lee Bridge, the dingy metal sign for Climax soft drink on Belle Isle caught my eye. At night the green and orange neon lights were bright enough to serve as a landmark for planes looking for Byrd Field. The "i" in Climax popped like a bottle of risqué champagne. At the other end of the island stood the radio tower for the city's only Black station, WANT. I tuned the van's radio to 990 and found them playing some Art Blakey, so I turned it up.

I crossed into Southside over the Shops Yard, a grimy snarl of train tracks and cars that lined the banks of the river. I hit Cowardin Avenue and kept south, reaching the Model Tobacco building with a few minutes to spare. It was a long brick Art Deco box six stories high with six lines of windows overlooking Jefferson Davis Highway. Parking was around back near a small open warehouse. I stepped out of the van and was struck by Richmond's signature scent, the smell of curing tobacco lingering in the air. I got my tool kit from the back and entered the building through the loading dock.

Down a long wood-paneled hall I passed a couple of loafing office workers, then rode the service elevator to the fourth floor. I found where I'd left off the day before and realized I only had two more offices to go. The door to the first office was shut and someone was talking inside. A secretary sitting outside it told me to have a seat nearby. A couple of minutes later, the office door opened. A harried looking man in shirtsleeves walked out with a manila folder. A voice called out after him.

"I need those figures first thing Monday, Hal."

His secretary looked at me. "You may go in now," she said.

I collected my tools and went to the door; the nameplate read Coulson. A man in a gray suit and burgundy tie stood behind an oak desk. He was a little older than me, but not by much. He seemed annoyed.

"This won't take long, will it?" he said.

"Not if I can help it," I said.

At that moment, his phone rang. I offered to come back later, but he gestured for me to continue with the task at hand. I pulled the door mostly closed to give him some privacy, then kneeled by the handle and got to work. It was hard not to eavesdrop and easy to see why he might be irritated.

"Mother," he said, "I told you I can take care of it. I *am* taking care of it."

If she didn't believe him, it was hard to blame her. I didn't believe him either. There was some silence as he listened, then he continued.

"I don't want it in the papers any more than you do. I left a message with one of the agencies, but they haven't gotten back. Yes, it was the one you gave me."

More silence.

"I told you," he said. "I don't know who called last night. One of his degenerate friends, probably. Yes, I know. You've told me that a dozen times. I'll go to his place and find it myself if I have to."

I worked as quickly as I could. The process of changing the locks wasn't all that hard, but the building used those old Corbin knobs which could be stubborn. By the time I'd assembled the new lock and reattached the doorknob, he'd been off the phone for a few minutes. I tested the new lock to make sure it worked, then took the key and stepped into his office. He was standing next to a bar cart and staring out a long window. A water tower and brick smokestack stood behind the facility. I heard ice hitting glass and the clack of bottles.

"All done," I said. "Here's your new key."

Coulson didn't bother to look at me. "Just leave it on the desk," he said.

I did as he asked, then turned to go. I knew it wasn't my place to say anything, but curiosity got the better of me.

"You sound like a man in need," I said.

Coulson turned and looked at me like something he'd just scraped off his shoe. "What the hell do you know about it?" he asked.

"Just what I overheard."

He eyed the name stitched on my coveralls. "Which is what exactly, Eddie the goddamn locksmith? Who gave you permission to pry into my private life?"

"Relax, friend" I said. "I do odd jobs now and again," I said. "If you're looking for something, I might be able to help you find it. For a small fee, of course."

"Are you kidding?"

I shook my head no. He sighed.

"It's Friday afternoon," he said. "And I need a drink like you wouldn't believe. How 'bout you?"

"Bourbon," I said.

Coulson poured two glasses and handed me one. "Here's mud in it," he said.

I raised mine. "So you've called someone for help, but they haven't returned your call?"

"Yes. For some reason my mother had the number of the William J. Burns Agency. Probably from when she had them tail my father on one of his escapades. If that's the case, standards there have slipped."

"That's what I've heard," I said. "I used to work for one of their competitors, but now I'm more of a freelancer. This late on a Friday, I doubt you'll hear back. I might be able to help."

Coulson peered at me. "Who are you?" he asked.

"Name's Bostic." I took out one of my cards and handed it to him.

He read it. "Says here you're a locksmith."

"That's correct," I said. "But like I said, I sometimes work side jobs."

"Why's that name familiar?"

"I don't know," I said. "Maybe HUAC, it got some press locally. Believe me, it wasn't a great experience."

Coulson nodded. "That's it," he said. "Yes, I remember now. Not naming names, that took some nerve. It's been a while, but I was impressed."

"You're the only person in town who was," I said.

It *was* surprising. A couple of years before, in my days as a private investigator, I'd testified before the House Un-American Activities Committee about a case I'd worked that spring involving a Richmond writer and social worker named Nedra Tyre. I didn't name names but otherwise told the truth, which was only appropriate since I was under oath and Miss Tyre was not a Communist. But not everyone appreciated it. When I got back from D.C., I found that Richmond was a hotbed of closet McCarthyites. Any of them with an axe to grind about race relations, Communism, or homosexuality enjoyed grinding it on my head. Providing that testimony before HUAC was also my last official act as an agent for Southern States Investigating. After it, I was fired and quietly blacklisted across town.

"I don't suppose you heard about the body found yesterday morning by the tracks in Shockoe Bottom," Coulson said.

"John Doe, from what I saw in the *Times-Dispatch*. Friend of yours?"

He paused for a moment and stared into his drink before taking a swallow. "Brother, actually," he said. "Casey."

I cleared my throat. "Sorry."

"Don't be. I'm not. Growing up, Casey was the blackest of black sheep. His absence from my life will not affect it one iota."

I was starting to regret saying anything to him. "You must be a million laughs at Thanksgiving."

"Don't get me wrong," Coulson said. "I had no reason to want him dead. Hardly ever heard from him, almost never saw or even thought about him much. I freely admit his death might even make my life easier in some respects. I'm the administrator of the trust Casey's been living off since he turned eighteen. With his stipend gone, all that money reverts back to the family. I feel better already knowing it's no longer subsidizing his deviant behavior."

"Deviant, huh?"

"Does that put you off, Bostic?"

"Is it supposed to? What anybody does behind closed doors is their business."

"Our father puts a lot of stock in bloodlines and wasn't happy to learn Casey was homosexual. He holds out hope Casey can be cured, which is the only reason he wasn't disinherited. It's an illness after all and can be cured like any other. But I want to keep it out of the press."

"Was he older or younger?"

"Younger," Coulson said. "I hadn't seen him in months; nobody from the family had. Obviously, he had his own friends."

"How did you hear the news?"

"I was at home last night with my family when I got a telephone call around 9:30. When I picked it up, I thought nobody was on the line. They didn't identify themselves, and when they spoke, all they said was, 'Casey's dead.'"

"Man or a woman?"

"Man, at least I think. Sort of a high-pitched voice."

"And that's all they said?"

"'By the tracks,' I think they said. Then the line went dead."

I thought for a few seconds and took a drink. It was good bourbon, better than the rotgut I was used to. "Any idea what he was doing in Shockoe Bottom?"

"None. He didn't live there. He kept an apartment off Jeff Davis."

"I'd like that address if you have it."

Coulson read off the address, which I wrote down on a spiral notepad. "His trust fund checks go there."

"So he was independently poor?"

Coulson looked at me. "In a sense," he said. "The last time I talked to Casey he demanded to have the stipend raised. Pitched a fit when I told him it wasn't up to me, our father has final say. But Casey never passed up an opportunity for theatrics."

"And your mother is concerned about having the family name dragged through the mud."

"She and my father are not well, and I'd just as soon not subject them to public disgrace. The Coulson name mustn't be associated with this in any way."

"Is that all she's concerned about?"

"There is one other thing. Truthfully, I think she's more concerned about this than anything else. Casey has a particular piece of jewelry that belongs to my mother. It's a ruby necklace that's been in the family since before the Civil War. Casey stole it about two years ago on a visit home, and mother wants it back very badly."

"Have you checked the local hockshops?"

"Impossible," Coulson said. "Mother would have heard."

I didn't even want to ask about his mother's underworld connections. It seemed neither she nor Coulson had any interest in having Casey's killer brought to justice, which should have been odd but wasn't.

"I'll make you a deal," I said. "If I can find the necklace, you pay me for one day's work. That's $25 a day plus expenses. If you'd like me to stay on it, we can talk about it then. As for my fee, it's exactly what you'd pay the Billy Burns Agency. Only I'm here in front of you, and they're not."

"It's a little unorthodox," Coulson said.

"I have one more lock to change here but have some free time after that."

"If you would just go to his place and have a look around, it would save me a lot of trouble."

Coulson stood and went to the window that looked out on the back of the facility. He struck a pensive pose and looked out in the gray afternoon. "Our father is Lloyd Coulson," he said. "*The* Lloyd Coulson, of the Hanover County Coulsons. Perhaps you've heard of us?"

"Naturally," I said, though that was a lie. I'd long since discovered that the quickest way to ingratiate yourself with some no-name Virginia family is to pretend you've heard of them.

"My father's first name is how my brother came to use Casey Lloyd as an alias. Like he was ashamed of being Casey Coulson. One more petty way of humiliating the poor man." He shook his head and kept staring out at the smokestack. "In some ways, it seems like nobody hates you quite like family."

I was starting to get that idea. As I got up to leave, Coulson remembered something. He opened his bottom desk drawer and took out two cartons of Chesterfield cigarettes and handed them to me.

"On the house," he said.

The rectangular boxes were white with red lettering. I didn't have the heart to tell him they weren't my brand.

CHAPTER 4

Blackmail

Digging through a dead person's belongings was one of the things I didn't miss from my days as an investigator. Often I'd picture them leaving their place for the last time. Did they look around with a vague sense of unease at that mess in the living room, or that dirt on the floor? Did they worry about their pet and what might happen to it if they never came home again? Probably not. More than likely they left without a second thought, free of morose premonition. They'd be back in a few minutes or hours or days and could clean up when the time came, only it never did and never will. Now here comes some stranger picking through an entire life's worth of crap looking for clues.

I finished up with the last lock and packed it in. It was late afternoon and Coulson was still in his office, the door open. I nodded to him before I left, then got in the Bedford and kept south on Jeff Davis. The address he'd given me was located in a small compound of brick apartments just off the highway called the Rebel Maisonettes. Down there the necks were red, and the collars were blue. My work van didn't look terribly out of place, so I just pulled into the complex next to Casey Lloyd's former residence. To no one's surprise, the back door was ajar.

I nudged it open with a creak and stepped into a small, cluttered kitchen. Sure enough, the sink was full of dishes. Two empty plates sat on the table, while a built-in ironing board jutted into the room and sagged at an odd angle. In the living room, the curtains were drawn. Books littered the floor where a bookcase sat overturned, and under the window a broken aquarium rested on the floor. Shards of glass lay on the squishy carpet along with some dead fish that were starting to stink. Whoever had been here before me hadn't been gone long.

It looked like a well-appointed poor person's house. A Greek-looking vase lay broken on the floor next to some dead flowers, and a fussy porcelain tea-set had been shattered to bits. I wondered if Casey had ever regretted turning his back on his family and a predictable life of ease and money. Some of the knickknacks from his old life told me he probably did. Dresser drawers had been pulled out and emptied. A jewelry box lay open, its contents spilled onto the dresser and floor. No sign of a ruby necklace. I couldn't know what else was missing, but what was left would have been stolen by any respectable thief.

In the nightstand was a hype kit, a dark brown leather case sealed with a zipper. Inside it was a syringe and a length of rubber tubing, and a spoon with scorch marks. Another pouch held a small baggie with white powder in it and some extra needles. I zipped it up and tucked it into the pocket of my overcoat. J.W. Coulson wouldn't appreciate the police or press knowing that his brother was a junkie.

I sat on the side of the unmade bed and stared at the floor littered with clothes. I produced a flask from the hip pocket of my coveralls and took a bite, then another. Most of the clothes spread around me appeared clean, having sat folded neatly in a drawer until a couple of hours ago. I cleared a space on the floor with my foot and tapped my shoe against the hardwood. It made a solid noise. I went to the other side and did the same thing but heard a hollow sound. I found the edges with my fingers and used a pocketknife to jimmy it open. The craftsmanship of the hidey-hole was better than it needed to be, with a beveled edge and everything. It was a good place to hide a pre-Civil War ruby necklace that was less impressive than I'd imagined. It was an even better place for a Mohawk Chief cigar box filled with black and white photos and a wad of $800 in cash held together by a thick blue rubber band.

The pictures were the sort to spice up any vacation slideshow. Casey Lloyd in the company of various gentlemen in various stages of undress. Most of those being photographed looked surprised, and not in a happy way. There were also non-dirty shots of Casey at a party somewhere in the company of many men. Everyone kept their clothes on in these. In two, the face of the same Black man was caught in profile. It made me wonder who the photographer was. It wasn't hard to imagine the victim of blackmail turning the tables and exacting a little revenge on his tormentor. Probably what all this was about, some squalid little Southside drama.

I'm never above a little thievery. I put everything back in the cigar box and took it with me. Back in the living room I peeled back a corner of the curtain. Near the main office of the apartments, I noticed the faint reddish glow of a phone booth. Inside it was a skinny kid with the receiver pressed to his ear as he wrote something down. I left the way I came and made my way toward the phone booth. The kid saw me and hung up, then sprinted away. I was too tired to follow.

I went to the booth and used my nickel to call the city morgue. This late on a Friday, I was only a little surprised to find the assistant coroner, Dr. Herbert Ivor, still working. It was mostly a nine-to-five gig, but if you ever needed someone to come in early or stay late, he was your man.

"Herb, it's Eddie Bostic."

"Is that so?" he said. "It's been a while. I'd heard you got out of the snooping business."

"I almost did. Say, are you busy?"

"Yes," he said. "I'd be home by now, but we got a fresh one two hours ago."

"Are you done with the John Doe found by the tracks?"

"Yeah," he said.

"How much longer will you be there?"

"About another hour."

I looked at my watch. "Mind a little company?" I asked.

"Sure," he said. "What else have I got to do but go home to but my delightful wife and delightful kids?"

My other call was to Coulson, still at his office. I told him I had the necklace and could drop it off on my way back into town. An easy twenty-five bucks. I hung up and peered into the main office where a man was watching me from behind some curtains. I made my way over. Inside I found him straightening some magazines on a coffee table. He was a squirrelly little guy in a white shirt, green cardigan, and brown pants. He was holding a feather duster with both hands in front of him. I thought for a second he was going to start gnawing on it.

"Hello," he said. "We're almost closed."

"That's fine," I said. "I'm a locksmith and someone called me a little while ago and said they'd been locked out of their apartment. Name of Casey Lloyd in 4D of the Rebel Maisonettes."

"Is he in some sort of trouble?"

"It's possible. His door was wide open when I checked. Have you seen anyone coming or going out of his apartment this afternoon?"

"No."

"What do you know about him?"

"Young, keeps the place tidy. Has nice things. Pays the rent on time, maybe the occasional party."

"What sort of company did he keep?"

"Why do you want to know that?"

"I'll ask the questions. What sort of company did he keep?"

"Oh, I don't like to say."

I flicked a fiver in front of his face. "A lot of the same people, or different ones? Black, white? Commies with little bombs?"

"Different people come and go, but I guess there's a group of three or four men I see fairly often. I remember one of them smoked a pipe."

"Did anyone come to see him earlier today?"

He shook his head.

"When was the last time you saw him?"

"I don't remember," the man said. "Sunday night I think."

"Thanks," I said. I forked over the five-spot, then handed him a business card. "Bostic Lock and Key," I said. "I do residential and commercial, if you ever find yourself in need."

CHAPTER 5

Uaxactun

At night, the Model Tobacco building glowed in its outdoor lighting. The long, clean lines and sharp corners looked like something out of *Dick Tracy*. I met Coulson around back in the mostly deserted parking lot. When I presented him with the heirloom, he was so happy I thought he might burst. He was probably going to run home and tell his mother he'd done it himself like a big boy. Per our agreement, he paid me on the spot. I asked him if he wanted me to stay on it and he said yes. I agreed and told him to skip the retainer. I felt bad about the $800, but not that bad. I didn't tell him about the cigar box or the fix kit. He was paying me, in part, to erase, so I was erasing. He asked where I was off to, and I told him it was the morgue.

"Why are you going there?" he asked.

"You still want this kept quiet, right?"

"Yes, but what does that have to do with the morgue?"

"If you expect me to finesse an active police investigation, I'll have to know what they know. That starts with the body. I also have a friend at the *News-Leader*; I'll contact him and see what he's heard. Believe me, by Monday, all this will be gone."

* * *

Weaving through the city, it took about fifteen minutes to reach the medical examiner's office on North Twelfth. I found a spot on Marshall and walked up the hill to the entrance. Mike Wells was standing outside smoking a cigarette beside a wrought iron fence. I'd known Mike a couple years; he was the private eye who'd given the Turnpike Authority my name. He was looking for the missing St. Patrick's girl, Jane Wynant. Or rather, he was supposed to be. I knew this because I'd given him some help on it not long ago. She had vanished earlier this month after the Tobacco Festival Parade, and the trail had gone cold.

"Thanks for giving the Turnpike guys my name," I said. "That's sarcasm, if you can't tell."

"Evening, Eddie." He looked at my coveralls and shook his head. "How's the locksmithing?"

"Swell," I said. "Any luck finding your girl?"

He took a drag off his cigarette and nodded. "Yeah, all bad."

"Maybe lean on the yearbook staff a little harder. What brings you out?"

"Jane Doe. It was a reach, but I had to check. How 'bout you?"

"John Doe."

"He need an extra key?"

"Hilarious."

He flicked the butt out into the darkness. "I could use a beer," he said.

"I'm working," I said. "Try it sometime."

A grimy concrete stairwell led to the basement entrance, which was unlocked. The morgue was officially known as the Office of the Chief Medical Examiner, or OCME. Whoever came up with that surely had army training. Giving official-sounding names, abbreviations, and acronyms to things that don't need them is an army specialty. The administrative offices were on the upper floors, while the autopsy room was in the basement. It had good refrigeration but poor ventilation. Thanks to the assortment of cleaners, formaldehyde, and embalming fluids, you could barely tell an autopsy was in progress until you were right up on it. And then it was all you could smell, a reek I'd tried to avoid since the war. To my credit, I couldn't remember the last time I'd been here. At the end of a green-tiled hallway, I paused outside a heavy wooden door and lit a Lucky to cover the stench. Then I opened the door and stepped inside.

I'd known Dr. Herbert Ivor since my time with the RPD. He was short and slightly pudgy. In a blood-stained coroner's apron, he looked a little like a butcher. He'd heard all the herbivore jokes he'd ever wanted to hear and a few more that he didn't. But Herb was sharp, and only mildly pedantic. I liked him. He had a grouchy wife Peggy, and a pair of grouchy children, Herbert Jr. and Ivy. Ivy Ivor, who does that to a kid? If my parents had done that to me, I'd be grouchy too.

At the moment, Herb was bent over a metal table that held the bloated corpse of a young woman with brown hair and gray skin. He had made an incision in the torso that released the fetid gases built up inside. He took a step back and looked over at me through a pair of black, heavy framed glasses. He smiled when he saw my coveralls.

"Bostic?" he said. "Yes, I thought I'd heard something about a new line of work."

"Something like that," I said. "Am I interrupting?"

"Not at all. Just getting under way. Yours is in the icebox."

He stepped away from the woman on the slab and pulled a large, heavy drawer from the wall. In it lay the body of Casey Lloyd. Herb opened a manila folder on the counter.

"In life, subject was approximately five feet five, a hundred and twenty pounds. As you can see, the dark hair was cropped short, the fingernails and toenails painted crimson. Both legs recently shaved. Signs of intravenous drug use in the left arm."

I pointed at a patch of purple skin across the right shin. "That's a weird bruise. What do you suppose that's from?"

"Hard to say. Perhaps a restraint of some sort." Herb paused. "Whatever it was, it was not as fatal as the two small bullet holes above the heart. A .22 from the looks of it. The first one did the job, the second was just for kicks. Powder burns indicate close range."

Herb walked to my right and placed his arm over my left shoulder and stuck a finger gun in my chest where my name was stitched.

"Bang, bang," he said.

"Signs of struggle?"

"None," Herb said.

"Personal effects?"

"No wallet or identification, obviously. What's left of the clothes is in a bin if you'd like to see."

Herb gestured to an open cardboard box in the corner and closed the drawer. The box contained a red bandanna, underwear, jeans, and a blue denim work shirt, all heavily bloodstained. In the bottom of the box was a single brown work boot sticky with blood.

"Where's the other shoe?" I asked.

"Still waiting for it to drop," Herb said.

"Any cops been around?"

"Yes," he said. "A detective named Clay, never seen him before. He didn't stay long."

Herb had gone back to work on Jane Doe. I placed everything back in the box and walked over for a look. She looked vaguely like a Chamorro woman I remembered from Saipan, a refugee headed back behind the lines. Our paths hadn't crossed for more than a few seconds, but her face had stuck with me over the years. She'd held my gaze when our eyes met.

"Local girl?" I asked.

"Not unless Uaxactun has been relocated to the state capitol."

"How's that?"

"Look at her. Meso-American features. If I had to guess, I'd say Guatemala. God knows how she got here."

"How long was she in the drink?"

"Some fishermen on the Mayo Bridge found her this morning. I'd say about twelve hours or so."

"Weighted down?"

"Floated from somewhere upriver. It's been a wet month; the James is high."

He was quiet for a moment and looked at the woman for a few seconds as though she'd been an acquaintance. Her coarse, dark hair had been brushed onto the table over her head, and Herb took the opportunity to brush some back a strand from her ear.

"Poor thing," he said. "Part of me wants to stay late and get the whole story, and the other part wants to wait so I can come in tomorrow."

"I know how you hate missing family time on weekends."

"Who doesn't?" He adjusted his glasses and gave me a look. "Do you have a professional interest in this one too, Bostic, or are you just being morbid?"

"Just morbid. But thanks all the same."

My second cigarette was almost done; I used it to light a third. I went to the back of the building where the incinerator was. Nobody was around, so I pulled the heavy iron door open and took Casey Lloyd's fix kit out of my pocket. I stared into the flames for a moment, pondering the ethics of erasure. Then I tossed it in and watched it burn.

CHAPTER 6
Swimming Pools, Movie Stars

Out in the cool night air, I just wanted to keep walking. Away from eviction, away from scheming contractors, away from the morgue stench that lingered on my skin and clothes. I thought I'd walked away from shit like this for good, but somehow it kept finding me. The worst of it was, it was my own damn fault. I pictured the woman on the slab, something to be washed away and forgotten. And Casey Lloyd, or whatever his name was, shot and dumped like a dog. The .22 bothered me. People used those in tight spaces when they didn't want noise or mess. Inside a car, say. Fire a .38 in a car and you'll blow out your eardrums.

I'd wandered onto the Marshall Street viaduct, a motley wood and steel structure that spanned Shockoe Valley. Halfway across, I stopped. The bridge was dark and the city was quiet. I leaned against the railing and stared at the lights stretching south. Directly below was the yard at the city jail at Fifteenth and Marshall. A few blocks past that stood the long rectangular shed leading into Main Street Station and the dingy rail lines of the Seaboard and C&O. Beyond Dock Street and the massive brick warehouses of Tobacco Row, the James River curved south toward Petersburg. I heard a car horn and some kids shouting, then the noise faded. I checked my watch and knew there was no walking away. There never was.

I went back to the van and drove down the hill to my shop. As expected, I hadn't missed much, just some junk mail. I changed out of my coveralls and back into the suit I'd worn earlier. Then I closed up for the day and drove west in the direction of Windsor Farms.

* * *

The prospect of seeing Daisy again had me uneasy, as did the thought of a somber gathering among the stifling, wood-paneled rooms of Richmond's well-to-do. That's what Archie's birthday was last year, except Daisy wasn't there. Just me and Mort and a few of his buddies from the neighborhood. Quiet voices and hushed tones, reassurances. I stopped at Joe's on my way and sat at the crowded bar in my coat and hat for a few minutes. Thanks to the city's idiotic liquor laws, beer was the hardest thing available. No liquor by the drink unless you did it at home, and lots of people did. I drank a mug of Richbrau and had a smoke. Static played on a TV over the bar.

I'd last talked to Daisy a few years back when she was in town for her mother's funeral. Other than that, it was a letter here and a postcard there. I'd tried to move on from her, and had in most ways. But when her career took off and she started getting roles, that got a little more difficult. I'd go alone to the Colonial or State and look at her in glorious black and white, the way that face was meant to be seen. Against the odds, she'd made her Hollywood dream a reality. One day you're a receptionist at a talent agency, and the next you're the talent. She'd been right to believe in herself, and I'd been wrong not to. The wrongest I'd ever been about anything. Other than her three-year-old son, Daisy didn't mention her home life much and I didn't ask. But something about her last letter disturbed me. When I'd brought it up, she never responded.

When I pulled up in front of the Williams residence on Canterbury, I wondered if I had the right house. The windows of both floors were brightly lit; loud music and voices could be heard from the street. I doubt the neighbors approved. The brick front walk was damp and covered with leaves. As I approached, the door sprang open, and two men flew down the stairs and past me onto the lawn until one tackled the other. They grappled briefly then broke into a fit of laughter side by side on the wet ground.

"I'll kill you!" one of them said, to more laughter.

From the door, Daisy Williams called out to me. Her small dark silhouette against the yellow light of the doorway was unmistakable. It was the exact size and shape of the hole she'd left in me a few years back. Coming out of the house behind her was a song, Mercer Ellington's "Things Ain't What They Used to Be," which was true enough. We'd danced to it once upon a time at the Tantilla, and whenever I heard it now I could only think of her. The moment was stupid and surreal, as though it had been scripted. I placed my foot on the first step and paused, her face still in shadow.

"Friends of yours?" I asked.

She laughed. "They're just young and drunk, don't pay them any mind."

I reached the landing and Daisy turned her face toward the light. It was still the most beautiful face I'd ever seen, one I'd studied and even memorized back when I was a fool. Not that I wasn't one now.

"Dearest," I said.

She stood on tiptoe and straightened my hair and fixed the knot in my tie. The tiptoe always killed me. Then she kissed me on the cheek. The music and voices faded until it was just the two of us. It was a ridiculous moment; reunions like this always are. You think about them from time to time, script what they will look and sound and feel like. But when they finally happen, it's never anything like you'd imagined.

Reality intruded in the form of another drunk who clapped me on the shoulder. "All new faces must pay the toll," he said. I recognized him as the actor Paul Eggar. He smelled like a distillery. He looked at me unsteadily and then at Daisy.

"Is he with the company?" Paul asked.

"No, Paul," Daisy said. "This is Eddie, he's an old friend. Eddie, this is Paul Eggar."

We shook hands. "Pleasure," I said.

Eggar looked me up and down and laughed out loud. "Cheap suit!" he said.

He wasn't wrong, but I wasn't in the mood.

"Great to meetcha!" Eggar said. He clapped me on the shoulder again. I looked at the hand.

"Paul," Daisy said. "Why don't you go look after Blair and Hoke? They're in the front yard."

"Yes, I've been looking for those scoundrels," Paul said. He touched two fingers to his forehead. "Seeya round, pal."

"No doubt."

When he was gone, I gave Daisy a look.

"I think he feels a little more uninhibited so far from home," she said. "Everyone seems to."

"What's happening here?" I asked. "I thought this was a solemn birthday commemoration, not some Hollywood bacchanal. I'd have come sooner if I knew it was a bacchanal."

"It's a little of both," Daisy said. "Yes, it's Archie's birthday. That's why I'm here. But the premiere of our new movie is Sunday afternoon. That's why everyone else is here."

"At the National, right? I saw the article."

"Yes," Daisy said. "It's called *Shadow of Tomorrow*, starring Paul Eggar, Cleo Nichols, and me. Well, mostly them." She bit her lip. "Anyway, you're escorting me. It's at one o'clock. Don't forget."

"I'll clear the calendar," I said, taking her in. "You're blonde now?"

"I had to," she said. "How else can I compete with the Monroes and Mansfields of the world? Honestly, it's exhausting."

"It suits you better than them."

She smiled. "Could we make time to talk this weekend?"

"That depends," I said. "What about?"

"Oh, you know," she said. "Things."

"Like your last letter?" I asked.

"For starters, yes," she said. "But later. For now, let's join the party."

Daisy laced her arm in mine and we stepped into the noisy living room where there had been a spontaneous outbreak of attractive people. The record player had gone silent, and someone was at the piano with an up-tempo improvisation. In the center of the room, a crowd of partygoers clapped in rhythm to a woman dancing atop a coffee table. She looked smaller in person than she did in the movies, but there was no mistaking bombshell actress Cleo Nichols as she danced an energetic Moulin Rouge that was at once completely ridiculous and strangely erotic.

She had the sort of face that got men in trouble and a body that kept them there. In tight white pants and a snug, low-cut yellow sweater, she shimmied and dipped to the music, then finished with a brief one-woman can-can. It was an impressive display. After the laughter and applause died down, she curtsied. A pair of young men whisked her off the table, and her momentum took her across the room toward Daisy and me.

"Whew!" she said, taking a glass of champagne from a passing tray. An artfully applied hint of perspiration did little to dim my appreciation. She brushed a curl out of her eye.

"Some show," I said.

"You ain't seen half of it," she said.

"I saw at least half."

Cleo laughed. "Where'd you dig this one up, Daisy?"

"He's local, believe it or not," Daisy said. "An old friend. Eddie, this is Cleo Nichols."

Like royalty, Cleo presented me with her right hand. Like her dutiful subject, I kissed it. I also caught an eyeful of cleavage and a whiff of Chanel No. 5.

"Charmed," I said. "Or something like it."

"You damn well better be," she said. Cleo had light blue eyes, long eyelashes, and dark, dramatic eyebrows that contrasted with her dyed shoulder-length blonde hair. There was a hypnotic directness to her gaze, something that probably withered most men in her path and was doing a fair job on me.

Cleo glanced at Daisy. "Does he know he looks like Tom Neal?"

"I doubt it," Daisy said. "As long as he doesn't act like him, we're safe."

"What is it you do, old friend Eddie?" Cleo asked. She eyed my face. "Let me guess. Attorney?"

"Nope."

"Groundskeeper?"

"Warmer."

"Undertaker?"

"Bingo," I said.

"Cleo, don't let him fool you," Daisy said.

From across the room, Daisy's father called out for help. Mort had both sleeves rolled up and was carrying a tray of hors d'oeuvres, bouncing from one chair to the next taking drink orders. I was starting to think he'd missed his calling in life. Daisy narrowed her eyes at me, then excused herself and went to Mort's aid. Over the hi-fi, a needle dropped onto vinyl with a hiss before side one of Elvis Presley's debut album started with "Blue Suede Shoes." The living room filled with noise and dancing.

Cleo downed her champagne in one gulp. "Fool me about what?" she asked.

"Nothing," I said. "It's an in-joke."

"I hate those," she said. "I never get 'em!"

"I'm happy to explain it to you, but not here. Let's go downstairs and get a drink."

I led the way through a small door to the basement. The music and noise still thumped upstairs, but it was quieter here. I found the right amount of light, some ice cubes, and a bottle of Mort's most halfway-decent bourbon. I poured us both a snort and raised my glass to hers.

"Chin-chin," I said. "What's the name of your movie?"

"*Shadow of Tomorrow*," she said. "I play Lorna, a suicidal, down-on-her luck former waitress. After I get arrested for trying to drown myself, I end up spending the night with a condemned man on death row, played by Paul."

"Makes perfect sense. Paul's a killer, you say?"

Cleo smiled. "He's quite good in it, you know."

For a few moments the only sound between us was the ice in our drinks. We stood facing each other in Mort's den in all its wood-paneled glory. Dusty law books filled the shelves, and official certificates, diplomas, and awards filled the walls. Above us the party raged in a muffled roar.

"How long have you known Daisy?" Cleo asked.

"Ten years now, I guess."

She paused. "Anything I need to know about?"

"Once upon a time, yes. But not now. She's a married woman."

"Are you married?"

I shook my head. Cleo pondered this for a second. "So seriously, what do you do for a living?"

"I'm a locksmith," I said. "I own a shop on Main Street." I fished out one of my business cards and wrote my home number on the back, then gave it to her.

"'Bostic Lock and Key'? Well, ain't that a kick?" She had a slight Southern accent I'd never noticed in her movies. "You don't look like any locksmith I ever saw."

"I do cut a dashing figure in my coveralls," I said.

She didn't deign to respond. Instead, she asked, "Why don't you explain your in-joke to me now that we can hear each other?"

"About not letting me fool you?"

"That's the one."

"If I had to guess, I'd say Daisy doesn't think much of my new line of work. She thinks I'm wasting my time and should go back to doing what I used to do."

"Which is?"

"Being a cop or a private eye. It's a long story, but that's the gist. Say, why are we talking so much about me? You're the famous Hollywood actress."

"I already know everything there is to know about me. But also because I asked. I like getting to know my fans."

"There's not much else to it, so we may have no other choice but to talk about you."

"So you used to be a private investigator, but you're not anymore. I bet there's a story there."

"Not really. It's like Goldilocks. Being a cop is too dangerous, and the detective agency is too boring. But being a locksmith is just right."

"Did you carry a gun when you were an investigator?"

"Sometimes," I said. "Depending on the job."

It seemed like an odd question. Cleo was quiet for a moment as if thinking something over. She milled around the dimly lit room, looking at Williams family photos. There was Archie as a boy in the back yard; Archie on the baseball team at Trinity; Archie's senior portrait; Archie with his fraternity brothers at Cornell; Archie on the front porch in a crisp army uniform, posing with Daisy, then barely a teenager.

Cleo stopped at another frame nearby. In it a group of about a dozen soldiers in ragtag army uniforms posed together in a jungle clearing. In the front row center, three men held the top edges of a rising sun Japanese flag. I walked over to where she was standing and leaned in. I knew the picture well and could remember the bright and bloody day it was taken. I'd survived to that point through no particular skill of my own, just good timing and dumb luck. I never talked about it much but would make exceptions in certain situations. And this was certainly a situation.

"That's Nafutan Point on Saipan," I said. "That's Archie in front on the right. I'm in the back row, second from left."

She looked closer at the photo and then at me as though trying to reconcile the two. She faced me and took a step closer.

"You're full of surprises," she said. Her husky voice had found the right frequency as she brushed back a lock of my hair. I hate seeing a perfectly good neck go to waste, so I stepped closer and pulled her to me with my right hand on the small of her back.

"Not really," I said. "Instead of a gun, I carry a set of lockpick tools. I could show you if you'd like."

"Not really," she said softly. She looked me in the eyes and I felt a little powerless as her sweater worked its magic.

"I've got a wafer jiggler," I said. "Some hooks and rakes. And a tension tool."

"What's your tension tool do?" Cleo asked. If her hand drifted any farther north up my leg, she'd find out for sure.

"It turns the, uh, core of the lock while I work the pins. There's competing schools of philosophy about the proper amount of tension to apply when picking a lock."

"Are there?" she said. Her hand drifted farther still. I was starting to get the impression she wasn't all that interested in lockpicking.

"Some people say you should use very light tension, but I myself believe in using the heaviest tension possible."

"Is that so?"

"It is," I said. "Ask around."

"It feels tense enough to me right now," she said.

I ran my left hand through her soft blonde hair and kissed her. Then I pulled her head back and nuzzled her neck.

"Say," I said. "I don't suppose you like jazz, do you?"

"Not particularly," she said. "Some Dixieland, maybe. Why?"

"I have an extra ticket for a show tomorrow night in Jackson Ward. We could make a night of it."

"Well," Cleo said. "I know there's a radio interview in the afternoon. And I believe Daisy has some sightseeing and shopping planned."

"Are you staying here at the house?"

"No," she said. "The studio is putting us up at the Hotel King Carter."

As I took in this information, the sound of a door opening came from the top of the stairs. Suddenly the quiet space was flooded with noise and light.

"I bet she's down here," a voice said.

Two sets of footsteps descended the stairs and peeked into the room. I was surprised to see the two young men from the front yard. Hoke and something.

"Cleo!" one of them said, bounding down the stairs and into the room. Other partygoers followed suit, and suddenly the space was flooded. Someone opened the sliding glass doors that led out onto the patio, letting in the cool night air. Cleo looked at me, her eyes wide.

"I know just the thing!" Cleo said. She took my hand and led me out onto the patio.

To my surprise, there was now an in-ground swimming pool in the back yard. Mort hadn't mentioned it to me, and it seemed odd that a widower in his sixties living on a fixed income would need a pool of any size, much less one with a diving board. At present it was covered by a tarp snapped into place at the edges. I peeled back a few buttons. The water was clear, but I wouldn't say it was terribly inviting given the cool mist falling around us. Cleo lifted the tarp until most of the pool was exposed, then kicked off her shoes and stripped to her underwear. With a squeal, she jumped in.

After a few seconds, she resurfaced. At the lip of the pool, she swept the wet hair away from her face and smiled. Elsewhere, revelers pulled more of the tarp away and jumped in. Most everyone in the pool was younger than me, and it seemed that another generation was on its way, another one more carefree. They wanted to forget the war, forget The Bomb, and move the hell on. It was hard to blame them; I wanted to do all that too. The problem was, I couldn't. Cleo splashed the leg of my pants.

"Come on in," she said. "The water's fine."

"Looks cold," I said.

Cleo gave me a look and treaded water for a few more seconds, then lifted herself with both hands onto the lip of the pool. Her wet bra was fighting a losing battle.

"Help me out, fool," she said.

I didn't move. "Now why would I go and do a silly thing like that?" I said.

"Typical," Cleo said. She hoisted herself up out of the water and stood beside me, shivering and squeezing the water from her hair. "You could at least lend me your coat," she said.

Shamed into gallantry, I took my coat off and placed it around her shoulders. "Better?" I asked.

"Maybe," she said.

Mort and Daisy walked out onto the patio through the sliding glass doors. Neither seemed surprised at much of anything by now. As we made our way over to them, Cleo turned her ankle on one of the slick slate tiles on the pathway. She let out a slightly comical yelp and would have fallen if not for yours truly, Prince Valiant.

"My ankle!" she said, closing her eyes in what I took to be pain. She leaned her weight on me and hobbled the rest of the way to a metal chair on the cement patio, an Oscar-worthy performance. Daisy gave me a look.

"How's your accident insurance, Mort?" I asked.

He smiled nervously and swallowed, but said nothing.

I knelt down in the pale light and gave the ankle a look. I could only imagine the adorable bruise that would be there in the morning.

"You'll survive," I said.

"But it hurts," Cleo insisted.

Around this time the rest of the leg, still damp with beaded water, caught my eye. Well, the calf mostly. But also the dimpled patella and a little dipper of birthmarks on her pale, plump thigh. If she'd been a chicken, I'd have eaten her then and there.

"Daisy," I said. "Where might we find some ice and a towel?"

"I think we have some in the prop department," she said. "This way."

It wasn't a two-person job, but I followed Daisy back inside the house through a door that led to the garage. She clicked on a light. On the far side of the room was a freezer next to a shelf with some towels and rags.

"I swear," Daisy said. "That woman can't stand to not be the center of attention for two seconds."

"A prerequisite for anyone in Hollywood," I said. And then after a pause, "I hear you'll be on the radio tomorrow."

"Yeah," Daisy said. "Ray Schreiner's show on WRNL."

"The big time," I said. "How's Mort holding up?"

"Surprisingly well," she said. "I couldn't have him wallowing today of all days. I hope that's all right."

"And you?"

"And me what?"

"It's not every day your dead war hero brother turns thirty-six," I said.

Daisy spread a hand towel across a table, then took a metal ice cube tray from the freezer and cracked it open with a lever. Daisy wrapped some of the cubes in the towel and gave me a look.

"You know how I feel about that," she said. "Archie's gone, and he's been gone. All the tears and all the sadness in the world aren't bringing him back."

"I reckon not," I said.

She laughed. "Since when do you reckon anything, Mr. Upstate New York?"

I grinned. "You live here long enough, you pick up a few Southernisms. But if I ever say *y'all*, you can deport me."

Daisy handed me the ice pack. "Here you are, Dr. Kildare," she said. I could tell she wanted to say something. Instead, she just smiled at me in that same old way.

"What are these mysterious things you want to talk about?" I asked.

"My marriage mostly, or lack thereof."

"I'm sorry," I said, though I can't say that I was.

"I think I'm finally ready to do it. Leave him."

"Are you sure?" I said. "That's a change from your last letter."

"I know," she said. "Look, can we talk tomorrow?"

"I'm working, but I'll be around."

We started back outside and encountered Cleo with a young blond idiot who was helping her up the stairs. They stopped, and the kid gave me a smirk as I pressed the ice pack into his palm.

"Vulture," I said. They left so fast I felt lucky to get my coat back.

Mort called out for Daisy again. Outside on the patio, the onslaught of walking popsicles had commenced as people realized that going for a swim fully clothed on a damp fifty-degree night hadn't been the best idea. Mort had towels for a lucky few, but for the rest there was only suffering. Suddenly everyone had sobered up. I took a towel from the stack and handed it to a sullen young woman with dark hair who took it from me and walked away without a word.

"When did you get the pool, Mort?"

"Last spring," he said. "I thought it might be nice for Daisy and her family when they visited."

"Has it been?"

He smiled. "Not really," he said. "I think this is the third time it's been used this year."

We were both quiet while the last of the swimmers made their way back inside. "How have you been?" I asked.

"Good," he said. "I'm glad Daisy is here. And you too, Eddie."

I put my hand on his shoulder and gave it a squeeze. "Archie's birthday," I said. "Wouldn't miss it."

I looked him in the eye and I could see that Daisy had been right to keep him busy. More than a decade after Archie's death, tears were never far from the surface. I wondered how one of the city's toughest prosecutors had been reduced to this, but I knew he had never recovered from his son's death. No matter what was happening around him, Mort was only concerned with what wasn't. He wanted to see Archie growing older, happily married by now with a brood of kids and a successful career. What he had instead was the lack of that, a succession of empty picture frames on the walls and dressers where his son's life should've unfolded.

We went back inside and Mort closed the sliding doors behind us. Up on the main level I excused myself and went upstairs to the second-floor bathroom. I could hear people saying their goodnights at the front door and car doors slamming outside as they streamed out. I gave myself a pat on the back, knowing I'd killed another party just by showing up. It almost made me feel like a cop again.

I didn't mean to snoop, but old habits are hard to break. I passed the bathroom and made my way down the hall to Mort's room where a lamp burned on a table next to the bed. Beneath it in a small circle of pale light sat a stack of yellowed V-Mail letters Archie had sent during the war. On top was a telegram from Western Union, yellow strips of tape with blue lettering saying the Secretary of War regrets to inform you.

Atop this was a single plain white envelope that was all too familiar. With one ear open to the voices downstairs, I went over for a look. The envelope was open now, of course—that was the whole point. I'd carried it with me from July '44 to April '46 without knowing what was in it. I hadn't seen it in over a decade; it was still gently crumpled, the right edge light brown with a thumbprint in dried blood. I took the letter out and unfolded it. It was a single paragraph on a single page, handwritten in blue ink, deeply personal, and exactly none of my damn business. A few simple lines that were the last words of a son to his parents, a brother to his sister. I was an outsider looking in.

> Father, Mother, and Sister–
> Do not mourn me for I am not gone. When you remember me, when you need me, I am there with you. Honor me as you will, less with words, and more with the everyday acts of your life. Love others as you loved me and remember me with neither sadness nor regret. Live the best lives you know how, and I love you always.
> -Archie

Flowery words for a man in the middle of the Pacific, but not all that surprising. Archie had been a theology student at Cornell. I turned the letter over but that was it. Having carried it around all that time, I think I'd been expecting something more. The meaning of life or a nice recipe. I tucked it back in its envelope and left it where I'd found it. As I was leaving, a legal-sized brown envelope on Mort's dresser caught my eye. I checked to make sure I was still alone, then picked it up. The return address was for an outfit named Admiral Security. Their logo was a blue anchor attached to a length of yellow chain.

The envelope's seal was broken, so I took a peek. Inside was an employment agreement between Mortimer A. Williams III and Admiral Security, Inc., for him to serve as in-house counsel. For a handsome sum, I might add, signed, and sealed. That helped explain the pool, at least in part, but it was odd he hadn't mentioned it. I put the document away and went back downstairs to look for Mort but couldn't find him or Daisy. After a few minutes I left without a word to anyone. I wasn't Irish, but it was the only kind of goodbye I was good at.

CHAPTER 7

Backfill

I served in the Twenty-Seventh Division, Second Battalion, 105th Infantry. From the time we waded ashore on Saipan on June 16, 1944, to the time I was wounded almost one month later, I spent a total of twenty-nine days in combat. That was all, and that was enough. Since then, I've met men who served longer or got hurt worse, and while I was there, I met some who never came home at all. Up to then, my experience of violence had been limited to gangster movies and westerns. Blood was shed in tidy black and white, and death was quick and painless. As a city boy and the son of a Baptist minister, I'd never hunted for food or sport. In the chaos of combat, the effect of flying lead, explosions, and shrapnel on the human body was a nightmare in full color.

Archie Williams had been an officer, one of the good ones, but in truth we weren't close. He knew me to the extent he knew any of his men, but the only time we ever spoke at length was the night before we came ashore. A bunch of us were sitting on the deck of a troop ship about three miles off the island. The Marines had landed that morning and established a beachhead. Other than that, none of us knew what was going on, but there were plenty of rumors. The island appeared to be completely aflame, rocked by explosions and gunfire. It was hard to understand how anyone on it could still be alive. We were all afraid we'd never see home again, but nobody said so. Archie went from man to man, trying to calm us down. He found me at the end of the group as we leaned on the railing in the Pacific night and looked out at the raging island.

"Scared, Bostic?"

"No, sir."

He smiled. "A man in your position should be afraid. It keeps you sharp. Where we're headed, you'll need that."

Several large explosions shook the island, their flashes lighting the night.

"I promise you, you'll get off the island," Archie said. He looked over and offered me a cigarette from his pack.

"Don't smoke, sir."

Archie smiled and nodded. "Yeah, neither did I. Until Makin."

He lit it with a Zippo and exhaled.

"What makes you think I'll live?" I asked.

"You have to," Archie said.

"Say again?"

"I can tell," Archie said. "With some guys I just get a sense that they're going to make it. But besides that, I need you to do me a favor. And if you don't make it off this rock, how can you do me the favor?"

I tried without success to follow his logic. In the blackness ahead of us, the island continued to roil and burn. Archie shook his head.

"I'd give anything to be back home with my family," he said. "Richmond is so pretty in June, before the real heat sets in. I'd give anything to be back there now with my family. My folks, my bratty little sis."

"A Virginia boy in the New York Division?" I said. "What would Bobby Lee say?"

"It's not that unusual," Archie said. "We've got boys from all over. Texas, South Carolina, Michigan, Wisconsin."

"You're the only Virginian I know of."

Archie exhaled a lungful of smoke and shrugged. "I was a junior at Cornell when Pearl Harbor happened and I rushed down to enlist with the rest of my friends. It turned out the army wasn't so picky about where I was from as long as I wanted to serve."

"I was at Cornell too," I said.

"I heard," he said. "That's not the whole reason we're having this talk, but it's part of it."

"What's the rest?"

"I need you to do something for me," he said. "If I don't make it off this rock, there's a letter I wrote for my family. It's in my footlocker. I need you to deliver it."

"I barely know you, sir."

"That doesn't matter, Bostic," he said. "What matters is I'm asking you to do it. The army will fuck it up, and my family will never get the letter. And I can't have that."

"Isn't there someone else you've known longer or trust more?"

"It doesn't matter," he repeated. "You're the one. Which means that now you have a reason to make it off this island. Well, another one."

A Klaxon sounded behind us and we assembled to go below decks. It was a noise he seemed to have been waiting for. This time it was no drill.

* * *

The telephone rang. I looked up from what I'd been doing, cutting a flathead steel key for a client. It was a service I could provide that many of my competitors could not because they didn't have the right machine. Fortunately I did, thanks to the man who'd sold the business to me in June of the year before. Irv had a little of everything in his shop; it was the first thing I noticed about it. Yet another reason I was dreading the move. I let the phone ring itself out, then went back to the key. Cool, muggy air drifted in through the open door, along with the whistle and clatter of a train pulling in on the C&O. I'd grown used to the noise and had even come to like it.

My building was little more than a storefront with a back room. Its former owner was a man named Irv Binnix who'd operated his locksmith business in that same location since 1930. I'd gotten to know him back when I was a beat cop and once responded to a robbery there. We made friends and stayed in touch, an unlikely pair. After I left law enforcement, I needed a job. We talked it over and I apprenticed under him for six months. My final exam was a box filled with all manner of locks that I'd had to pick in one hour. I passed. Irv had a good book of business. When he retired not long after, he'd sold the whole thing to me. Eight months later, he was dead from a heart attack.

I finished the rest of the order and turned the machine off, then washed up and found my suit jacket. Out in the damp and gray Saturday morning, Shockoe Bottom bustled with the usual crowd of neatly attired shoppers: men in suits and fedoras, women in dresses. Outside the First Market building, Black vendors in denim overalls, hats, and flannel shirts sold an assortment of fresh fruits and vegetables from the backs of battered pickups. I bought an apple from one of them and ate it as I made my way north a few blocks to the Seventeenth Street train yard where Casey Lloyd had been found shot twice and dumped.

The train yard itself was a large open rectangle of land stretching north. I passed under the Marshall Street viaduct and came to a two-story brick warehouse where an empty boxcar sat idle. Farther on was a repair facility for passenger cars, and a small wooden stock pen with a handful of cattle milling around in the mud. One mooed at me as I walked toward the roundhouse where two workers were struggling with a length of heavy chain.

"Excuse me," I said.

It was a couple of guys in their sixties. They looked up and dropped the chain as if it had burned their hands. They wore grease-stained overalls and conductors caps and looked like railroad lifers.

"Goddamn it, JR," one of them said.

"Why don't we use the wagon, Hank?" the other said.

"Because the fuckin' wagon is all the way over there, and it's got a busted wheel."

"Perhaps if we took a minute to address the wheel situation."

"Excuse me," I said again. I felt like I'd stumbled across vaudeville's worst comedy team. "Either of you working yesterday morning?"

"Naw. We're both retired, but they still let us help around here and there on weekends."

"For free?"

"I guess," Hank said.

"So you haven't heard anything about a body that turned up yesterday morning?"

"I wouldn't say that," JR said. He was smaller and had a raspy voice. "It were right o'er there," he said, gesturing to a spot farther up the tracks.

"Mind showing me?"

Neither spoke, but we started walking up the sandy access road littered here and there with patches of gravel. A dump truck carrying dirt passed us and kept left toward the base of a massive mud hill.

"See much construction traffic here?" I asked.

"Yup," Hank said. "This is an access road to the interstate worksite up the hill."

We stopped at a place on the tracks where a tiny yellow flag marked a patch of stained ground.

"You a detective or something?"

"Insurance investigator," I said.

On the ground was all manner of oil, brake fluid, and industrial runoff. Slightly fresher on top was a large, dark red stain sticky to the touch. I took out a pack of Luckys and offered both of them one. We stood there a moment smoking when something caught my eye a few yards away. I went over and found a chewed-up cigar stub with its colorful red and yellow band still intact. It was a Mohawk Chief. I gave it a sniff and took out a handkerchief and wrapped the stub in it.

"Either of you guys smoke Mohawk Chief cigars?"

JR gave me some side eye.

"Y'all," I said. "Do either of *y'all* smoke Mohawk Chiefs?"

They shook their heads. It wasn't much to go on, but it was something. I went back over and showed them the pictures and asked if they had seen any of the people in them. All I got in return was a pair of heads shaking no.

"Where can I find the station agent?"

"Up yonder if he's here."

I thanked them and followed the path to a stout brick building. The door was locked. I checked the window and saw only a wooden desk cluttered with timetables. I went around back and tried that door but it too was locked. My question about arrival and departure times would have to wait.

A light drizzle fell. I looked west to the big muddy hill that would soon be part of the Turnpike's foundation. It had been smoothed but not graded, its bumpy outline rising into the gray sky. The rutted tire tracks of work vehicles curved west toward Jackson Ward. Rumor had it the Authority was using backfill from Navy Hill to build up this area, once a slave burial ground. The stark ziggurat of the MCV building loomed above all.

I spotted a couple of workmen farther up the hill near an earthmover. Neither it, nor they, nor the earth were moving. I climbed up behind the station agent's building past a couple of scrub trees to a smoother section of hill curling west. My shoes and pant legs were slathered in mud. As I approached the two workers, I slipped and fell on a patch of mud that was slick as ice. They had a good laugh.

"Might wanna try you some work boots, boss," one of them said.

"Thanks," I said. "Which contractor you guys with?"

"Winkelman," the other said.

"You fellas working yesterday morning?"

"Yessuh."

"See anything out of the ordinary down on the tracks?"

"Body covered with a sheet and some cops."

"Seen any of these people hanging around lately?"

I took the pictures out to show them. I shuffled through them slowly like flash cards but got only shaking heads in return. I was about to put them away when one of the men spoke up.

"Hold up," he said. "Let me see that last one again."

He touched his index finger to the picture. "I seen this dude up by the trailers," he said. He gestured with his left hand to a point on the hill's horizon.

"When?"

"Last week sometime."

"He work here?"

"Don't think so, but . . ." he trailed off.

"But what?"

"The guy looked out of place up there when I saw him. But when one of the construction managers confronted him, the manager got chewed out by one of the higher ups."

"Do you know his name?"

"Naw, man," he said. "I mind my own."

I thanked them both and started up the hill when he called out after me.

"I wouldn't fuck with him if I was you," he said. "Man's stocky." He waved his hand around his head like a claw. "And he's got some sort of skin condition. You can't tell from the picture, but the other side of his face is all pink like a strawberry."

CHAPTER 8
Admiral Security

I made my way to a flat stretch of ground at the top of the muddy slope. A small fleet of dingy yellow earthmovers stood idle, alongside a pair of trailers. A handful of cars sat parked at random angles nearby, but there was no one around. Construction debris littered the area. Farther out along the periphery stood the dilapidated remains of Navy Hill, a neighborhood of one- and two-story homes soon to be wiped from the map. The battered landscape was dotted here and there with bare trees.

I came to the first trailer and knocked. No answer. It was unlocked so I went in for a look-see. At my feet was slippery linoleum. The walls were wood paneled from floor to ceiling. Dirty cream-colored curtains covered the glass jalousie windows. Apart from the calendar above a desk showing a naked Marilyn Monroe sprawled atop a red blanket, there wasn't much to see—contracts and subcontracts, technical specs, and blueprints. I went through some of them but was quickly bored. I made for the door and stepped out into the misty gray morning.

"You there!" a voice barked.

I looked over and saw a tallish older white man in a dark suit, overcoat, and hat marching toward me. He was a hard-faced old fucker and none too pleased to see me.

"What the hell are you doing in there?" he asked.

"Federal safety inspector," I said.

He glared at me. "Bullshit."

"I don't know what sort of operation you think you're running here," I said. "But I can see at least half a dozen violations just from where we're standing." I pointed at the long iron neck of a crane sitting abandoned atop a mound of dirt and started walking toward it. In its maw was a piece of jagged and rusted scrap metal jutting into the footpath. "This alone is a substantial fine."

"I don't give the first goddamn about your Washington regulations," he said.

We stopped and faced each other again. He put his hands on his hips, making sure I got a good look at the Colt revolver tucked into the waistband of his pants.

"Mister," I said. "That might work on a construction worker afraid of losing his job, but it doesn't work on me."

I stood still, waiting for him to call my bluff. He reached for the gun but was too slow. As he found the handle, I grabbed his wrist and wrenched his arm back with a twist. His hat flew off as he cried out in pain. The gun arced through the air and landed a few feet away with a splat. I knew immediately I'd dislocated his shoulder, the right arm hanging useless. I let go, then watched him back away and take a knee. I found the gun at the base of a scraggly bush and held it on him as he grunted and groaned. He had a full head of short, brushed-back white hair. He was trying hard not to scream but he really wanted to.

"You work for the Turnpike Authority?" I asked.

He spat into the mud and shook his head. "No," he grunted. "A contractor, Admiral Security."

"There was a Black man hanging around this worksite earlier this week," I said.

"So what else is new?" he said.

"This one doesn't work here," I said.

I took the picture out of my pocket and showed it to him. The old man spit on it.

"You know," I offered. "I could help with that shoulder if you'd like. A quick tug and it's right back in place." I cleaned the picture off with the sleeve of my raincoat.

He kept trying to work it himself, but it was strictly a two-person operation. I pocketed his gun and watched him a moment, then lit a cigarette. As the old guy gritted his teeth and moaned in the mud, I gazed east toward Church Hill and could make out the spire of St. John's Church. I myself was a pretty crummy Christian, but my father had been a minister when I grew up in Troy. Now was hardly the time to start making amends.

"What do you say, old man?"

"Do it," he said. His forehead had broken into a sweat, his face ashen.

"Gladly," I said. "Who's this man?"

"I don't know. I've seen him, but I don't know his name."
"Strawberry on his face?"
"Yeah."
"What's he do here?"
"Something to do with the trailers," he said. "Jesus Christ!"

I grabbed his right arm with both hands and pulled hard, and the joint crunched back into place.

"What's your name?" I asked.

He was rubbing his shoulder and breathing hard. "Buford," he said.

"It's your lucky day, Buford."

As I made my way down the hill, I took his revolver from my raincoat. I emptied the bullets onto the ground and tossed the gun back in his direction.

Back at the shop, I changed out of my wet and muddy suit and into some coveralls. I was packing some things in the workroom in back when someone came in and closed the door. A man's voice shouted a hello to no one in particular; I told him I'd be right there. The voice was familiar. When I reached the front counter, I saw a man holding a large leather portfolio suitable for drawings. It was a face I hadn't seen in twelve long years.

* * *

If you've never seen a man beg for his life before, I can't say I recommend it. In this particular instance, it was on Saipan and the man in question was a young private in the Imperial Japanese Army, or IJA. He'd surrendered after a firefight in which one of our men had been killed. The interpreter ordered the soldier to strip to his skivvies and come out showing his hands. The man emerged after a minute holding a white cloth in his right hand and a sheaf of papers in the left. He was wearing what appeared to be a diaper, a tattered cloth hat, and that was it. From behind their cover, some of the men laughed. Lt. Archie Williams looked at me.

"You up to it, Bostic?"
"What's that, sir?"
"What else?" he said. "Your first prisoner."

Taking prisoners wasn't common on either side in the Pacific, but I'd seen it happen once on Nafutan Point. The man in front of us now had advanced to an open area in front of the small, crib-like house where his machine gun team had been hiding. He was crying and his legs were shaking so hard he dropped to his knees.

"Shouldn't an interpreter be involved?"

"That's the thing, Bostic," Archie said. "We have to send someone out there to make sure he's not hiding a grenade up his ass before we send in the interpreter."

"My lucky day," I said.

I advanced on the man, my M1 trained on him. He just sat there quivering and holding his head in his hand and weeping. Behind me, our interpreter told him in Japanese to take his cap off and then carefully hand me the papers. I crept up and took them. No sooner had I done that then shots rang out behind me, BAR rounds. They hit the surrendering soldier across his torso, nearly bisecting him in a hail of blood and shredded intestine. The front of my uniform was covered in gore.

"Goddamn it," Archie shouted. He emerged from cover to find the source of the shots.

"Fuck him," the shooter said.

"Who said that?"

"I did," the voice said. "We're here to kill these bastards, not play patty-cake."

I looked back and saw the soldier and knew he wasn't our regular BAR man, but someone from another company.

"What's your name, soldier?" Archie asked.

"Janus," the GI said. He took off his helmet to reveal a short blond crew cut. "Teddy Janus."

* * *

"Eddie Bostic," Janus said. "So that really is you?"

"In the flesh, Teddy. It's been a few."

Reluctantly, I shook his extended hand. Immediately, I wanted to wash it.

"Twelve years," he said, nodding. "I saw your name on the front window and I thought, 'No, it couldn't be.'"

"What are you doing here?" I asked.

"I was getting ready to ask you the same thing."

"Be it ever so humble," I said.

"You're joking," Janus said. "Since when?"

"Came to Richmond in '46 and just kinda stayed. Got a job."

"Doing what?"

"This and that," I said. "What about you?"

"Still in good ol' Troy," he said. "In fact, my train's about to leave without me. Look, I've started a security firm, name of Admiral Security. I don't guess you've heard of it?"

My tussle with Buford still fresh in mind, I shook my head. Mort's new employer was popping up everywhere these days.

"Well, the short version is we're expanding into this area. Say, how are you set for work?"

He lost his grip on the portfolio and some of its pages spilled to the ground. I helped him collect them but didn't get much of a look. One of the sheets appeared to be blueprints and technical specs for a ship.

"Believe it or not I'm doing fine," I said. "Don't judge by the shop—I'm in the middle of a move. Richmond is getting an interstate, and my building is in the way."

"The whole country is getting the interstate," Janus said. He handed me his card. "It's going to need people to build it. That's my business."

"Thanks."

"Always on the lookout for good men," he said, holding out the portfolio with a grin. "Look, you have my card. Give me a call. I'll see you around Eddie."

We shook on it again and that was that. He paused for traffic, then crossed toward Main Street Station with the portfolio tucked under his arm.

It was weird though. Janus himself hadn't changed much, apart from the fact that his once blonde hair had gone stone white.

CHAPTER 9

Little Bird #1

I spent a few hours packing up the shop. I took a break in the early afternoon and called my friend Art Lynn, an editor with our afternoon paper, *The Richmond News Leader*. He was not in the office, which, on a Saturday afternoon, was not unusual. When I rang him up at home, his wife answered. I waited a moment while Art came to the phone.

"I rang you at the office earlier," I said. "Now I'm not sure why."

"Why on earth would I be there on a fall Saturday when I could be at home listening to the Cavaliers and Gobblers?"

Ah yes, the big rivalry. It was at this point I remembered that I lived in a state where one of the major colleges was nicknamed the Gobblers.

"Where's the game?" I asked.

"Roanoke," Art said.

"Say Art, I need a favor."

"When do you not?"

"It may require a little actual work."

"I try to do as little of that as possible," Art said. "How am I ever going to write the great Confederate novel if I have to work all the time?"

"Let me guess," I said. "It's Reconstruction and the South will rise again?"

"Something like that, blue-belly."

Art's mood darkened when VPI scored a touchdown to make it 7-0.

"As much fun as this is, Bostic, it may behoove you to come to the point."

"The John Doe from the Seventeenth Street tracks. What have you heard?"

"Not real dead, but dead enough. Other than that, nothing. Why, what have you heard?"

"Nothing fit for a family newspaper. Or yours."

"Coy is not your strong suit."

"He lived on Jeff Davis south of the city line. Your old stomping grounds, right?"

"When I was a reporter, yes. But I haven't been there recently, and I can't say I've missed it. What's it to you anyway? I heard you quit the private eye business."

"Favor for a friend," I said.

"Some friend," Art said. "There is one person who might be able to help you out. Rita Kizzie, a reporter with the *Richmond Afro-American*."

"She still plugged in there?"

"Whenever something bad happens in Southside, she's the one they send."

"Fair enough. Got a number?"

Art put the phone down and rooted around on his desk as the radio play-by-play droned in the background. Then he came back on and gave me the number which I scribbled in my notebook. I thanked him, hung up, and dialed Rita's number at the *Afro-American*.

"Hello, is this Rita Kizzie?"

"Speaking," she said.

"Miss Kizzie, I'm glad I caught you," I said. "My name's Eddie Bostic, I'm an insurance investigator. A little bird told me you were a good source for all things Southside."

"Oh, a little bird huh? What else did it say?"

"That you might be able to recognize someone if I was to show you a picture."

"And let me guess, this someone just happens to be Black?"

"That's right."

"And I'm supposed to jump at the chance to help some random white man play Find the Negro. What'd the brother do, jaywalk?"

"All I need to do is talk to him. I was told you could help."

"Well, I can't now, Mr. Bostic. I'm late for an interview."

"Who with?"

"The President of the Virginia Teachers Association about next week's conference at Virginia Union."

"Who's he?"

"It's a she. Mrs. Irma Thompson."

"What conference?"

"The VTA, the one for Black teachers. The white ones in the VEA are holding their conference at the same time over at The Jefferson. But that's fine, I'll take our keynote speaker over theirs any day."

"Who's that?"

"Dr. Martin Luther King, Jr. Surely you've heard of him? The Montgomery bus boycott?"

"Sorry," I said. "It didn't get much press here."

"It did if you looked in the right places."

"Look, can we meet somewhere after your interview? It won't take long."

"You can meet me at the Turnpike Relocation Authority on North First at 3:30. Do you know where that is?"

"I know the street, but I can't say I've been to the office."

"It's easy," Rita said. "It's in Jackson Ward. Do you know the part of First Street that's about to get plowed under for the interstate?"

"Sure."

"Well, it's right there," she said.

* * *

The Turnpike Relocation Authority was housed in a squat white cinderblock building on First Street. It was surrounded by a scattering of other doomed structures, part of a swath of land through Jackson Ward set to be cleared for the interstate. These were the abandoned remains of a once-vibrant Black neighborhood where generations had lived and died. Now decayed and condemned, the lots were choked with weeds and trash as the buildings waited to be razed.

I pulled up across the street and parked beside a bare tree, its bony limbs stark against the gray sky. Piled high to my right stood the debris of a wrecked Franciscan convent, twin brick pillars surrounded by a mound of jagged wood. Amid the rubble was a piano keyboard, the line of black and white keys intact somehow. The rest of the piano was nowhere to be found. I poked around and killed a few minutes. Three other cars were parked nearby. An elderly Black couple walked out of the office and over to an old Ford, then got in and drove away.

A few minutes later, another car pulled up and parked. A young Black woman was at the wheel. She got out and started walking toward the building. I called out as she was about to go inside, and she stopped. She gave me a funny look when she saw the coveralls.

"You Bostic?" she asked.

"Yes, thanks for meeting me."

"Got a card?"

I dug one out and handed it to her.

"I'm confused," she said. "Says here you're a locksmith, but you told me over the phone you were an insurance investigator."

"I'm moonlighting," I said. "How did it go with your teacher's conference president?" I asked.

"She's very excited about the conference and Dr. King."

"Happy to hear it," I said. "What made you choose this delightful place?"

"Researching my next story, about the projects in Whitcomb Court and Fairfield Court."

"What's that?"

"Subsidized housing. They're going up in the east end to hold all the people displaced by the turnpike."

"Maybe they'll save a spot for me."

"Doubtful," she said. "The interstate will essentially dam up all the Black people in projects to keep them outside of the city. A prison without bars."

Rita pointed inside the Turnpike Relocation Office. It had a large front window with its name stenciled across it and a glass door to the left. Inside, a young Black couple was speaking with someone behind a counter.

"Anyway, what can I do for you, Mr. Bostic? You said you were looking for someone?"

I took out the pictures I'd taken from Casey Lloyd's apartment, minus the dirty ones, and handed them to her.

"Anyone in here look familiar?"

Rita had expressive, dark brown eyes that scanned the images quickly.

"Where did you get these?"

"A place off Jeff Davis," I said.

She stopped and looked at one of them closely.

"That looks like him," she said.

"Him who?" I asked.

She looked me in the eye. "Give me your word this isn't a set-up."

"You got it," I said. "I just need to speak with him."

"It's hard to say for sure in profile. You can't see it in the picture, but he has vitiligo that takes up half his face."

"Vita-what?"

"A strawberry," she said. "On the right side of his face. If it's who I think it is, he runs a trailer delivery company in Chester. Supplies them to construction companies and whoever else needs them. His name is Lamar Clemons."

CHAPTER 10

Round Midnight

Clemons's company was, of all things, Dixie Trailer & Hauling down in Chester. I found a payphone and called the number, knowing they wouldn't be open this late on a Saturday and wouldn't pick up if they were. I let it ring six times and hung up. It was too long a drive to get there before dark, so I resolved to check it out tomorrow after the premiere. I also rang Cleo at the King Carter, to no avail. She and Daisy were probably still out doing whatever it was they were doing, so my spare ticket for the show would go to waste. I went back to the shop and boxed up a few more things for the move, then went back to my apartment on N. Morris. There I spruced up for a night on the town.

I was headed to the part of Jackson Ward affectionately known as The Deuce, Second Street, specifically the Eggleston Hotel at the intersection with Leigh. The show was in its lobby restaurant, Neverett's, where a jazz quartet from Kansas City named The Freddie Francis Four was on the bill. Freddie was a young alto sax player, and if you bought into all the magazine hype, the heir apparent to the late Charlie Parker. Freddie's nickname was Chick, diminutive of Bird, something Freddie supposedly loathed. And like Parker, Freddie allegedly had a smack habit. Sad, but hardly surprising.

I had no choice but to take the van, which I parked a few streets away. Out front of Neverett's, a growing line of well-dressed Black folks waited, spilling out onto the damp sidewalk. They were couples mostly—in overcoats, shiny suits, and dresses—filling the cool night air with cigarette smoke and easy patter. Along Leigh Street, tires rolled through puddles of shimmering light, while one or two cars idled in front of the hotel, releasing passengers.

I knew the doorman, Maurice Fenton. He was an ex-welterweight I'd seen fight a couple of times at The Arena. Maurice was dark and wiry, with one of the best left jabs I'd ever seen. He was a better bouncer than doorman, so I tried to stay on his good side. He stood at the front of the line beside the orange neon sign in the window. He knew me by sight. I greeted him and pressed a ten-spot into his palm. He worked the toothpick in the side of his mouth and glowered at me.

"Perhaps you haven't heard who's playing here tonight," he said.

"I've heard," I said, fishing out another ten. "Blackmail."

"An ugly word, Mr. Bostic. I prefer extortion."

Maurice unhooked the velvet rope as a collective groan went out from those waiting in line. Inside, the club was intimate with good acoustics and low lighting. It had parquet wood-paneled walls decorated with a series of stylish handcrafted mirrors. The floors were of black-and-white marbled tile. There were some tables and a long bar to the right as you walked in and some booths on the left. Toward the back was a small stage with round tables clustered around.

I was greeted by the quiet murmur of diners and one or two stares as I walked in and took a seat at the bar. I wouldn't say I'd gotten used to it exactly, but I also had the privilege of not letting it bother me. If you'd reversed the situation and I was a Black man walking into an all-white restaurant anywhere south of the Mason-Dixon, a few hostile looks would have been the least of my concerns.

The gray-haired bartender, Henry, made his way over. He wore a white dress shirt with the sleeves rolled up, black pants, tie, and vest. He was friendly enough, but I'd never seen the man smile. Maybe it was me. I took off my hat and coat, ordered a beer, and started a tab. On stage, the warmup act was a young torch singer in a slinky silver dress that was just tight enough. She was finishing her set with "My Funny Valentine" accompanied by a piano. She'd improved since the last time I'd seen her and was more comfortable in the club's smoky spotlight. It was a smoldering rendition to the very end, and when the song faded, there was applause as the singer took her bows.

The lights went up. Between sets, tables were cleared, and people stood, milled around, and chatted. I found a spot in the corner with a clean tablecloth and a good view of the stage. I made myself comfortable, enjoyed a cigarette with my beer, and tried not to worry about all the things I was supposed to be worrying about. Not one woman took notice of me now that I was there alone. I closed my eyes and tried not to worry about that too.

After a few minutes, I got up to use the men's room. The aqua and white tiles were vaguely mesmerizing as the sound of flushing toilets filled my ears. In the mirror, my shave was not as close as I'd thought, my face not as dashing, my hair not as thick. I washed up and took the plush white towel handed me by the rest room attendant, who was better dressed on that one night than I'd ever been in my life. On the way back to my table past the kitchen, over the smells of cooking food, I caught a vague whiff of something I used to bust guys for.

I pressed through the swinging doors of the kitchen and into the bustling clatter of cooks, porters, and waiters. Outside the rear door I found a couple of young waiters toking up at the base of the steps under an overhang. A cloud of sour smoke filled the space. When they saw me, they both turned and faced away, one of them cupping the joint.

"Busy night, fellas?" I said. I started down the concrete steps.

"Oh shit, bruzz," one of them said.

"Go easy," I said. "I'm here for Tony."

Tony looked at the other waiter and nodded.

"Beat it, man," he said. "I'll catch up with you later."

The waiter stumbled past me up the steps and back into the noisy restaurant.

"I hope the boss doesn't catch him like that," I said.

"What do you want, Bostic? Talking to you is bad for my image."

I took the pictures out of my pocket and handed them to him. "Recognize any of these cats?"

"Cats, huh?" Tony said. He shook his head slowly and took a puff off the joint. He held the smoke in and offered me a hit. As he leafed through the pictures, I took a drag that burned the back of my throat. I held it in a few seconds but was soon coughing more than I should have.

"Jesus," I said. "What is this shit?"

"Just some Mexican," he said. "Town's dry, it's the best thing going. And no, I never seen any of these people. I'm insulted you even asked." He handed me the pictures back.

"Any H around?" I asked.

"I don't deal that shit, you know it."

"I didn't ask if you did. Do you know anyone who does?"

"Not in the Ward," Tony said. "Not to say there aren't new players in town. Why don't you ask some of those art students and professors down on Grace?"

"I just might at that," I said. "What about Southside? Jeff Davis area?"

"C'mon, man," Tony said. He extended the joint to me again. "You looking to buy or not? It's two bucks."

I took another drag, held it in, and handed it back.

"This shit?" I said. "Maybe next time."

"Asshole," he said.

Back inside, my mood began to improve. The band was setting up, and at my table sat two attractive young women, likely coeds from VUU. They had turned the chairs to face the stage and weren't paying me any attention, but their perfume was still change for the better. Freddie Francis walked on stage to light applause and strapped on his alto sax. He ran through some scales, then smiled. The piano player banged a few notes and the drummer tested the snare. The bassist played a stand-up. He tuned a key and played a snaky scale, the strings like rubber at his fingers. With a flourish, an emcee stepped up onto the stage in full tuxedo and grabbed a mic.

"So this is where all the pretty people went," he began, his breathing audible through the mic. "How you folks feeling tonight?"

There was a squeal of feedback through the PA. The wan response from the audience only egged him further. He shook his head.

"Ladies and gents, y'all making me sad," he said. "Now, I'm gonna ask one more time: how you *feelin*?"

This time, a more enthusiastic answer.

"That's more like it," the emcee said. "Now we get a lot of special talent here at Neverett's, but none more so than this man here on the stage tonight. Please give up a warm Jackson Ward welcome for Mr. . . . Freddie . . . Francis!"

The emcee left the stage, and after some applause the lights went down in the smoky room. In the chair in front of me, the young woman in the black dress turned her head to me and asked for a light. I gladly gave her one. She was all-right looking, if you found Dorothy Dandridge types all-right looking.

Freddie counted off the band's first number, a tight, high-energy "Bernie's Tune." The opening sax riff was challenging but Freddie nailed it. This was followed by the up-tempo "Milt's Tune" and then "Crescendo Blues" which gave Freddie two long solos. The band was tight. The pianist kicked off a lovely version of "My Old Flame" that closed the short set and showcased Freddie's ability to hit precise, off-kilter notes. As the tune faded with a shimmer, the lights went up to applause, and Freddie announced a quick break.

I got up and went to the bar. As I waited for my order, I saw Freddie

Francis emerge from the men's room. He brushed past a slightly older woman who'd been waiting outside, then made his way through the crowd to the bar beside me. He looked a little green in the gills but ordered a beer which I was happy to pay for.

"Thanks, friend," he said, looking me up and down. "You a cop?"

"Just a fan," I said.

"Izzat so?" he said. "Chicago I get white fans. New Orleans and Kansas City, some. But Richmond? You may be the only white person here who's even heard of me."

"I like your style," I said, which felt wildly inadequate. So I added, "Your phrasing is very unique."

"Oh, my phrasing?" he said, laughing. "If you're not a cop, you're a music critic."

"Neither," I said.

Then, in the far corner, I noticed a group of four Black men seated in a booth. The one in charge was stocky and well-dressed. All I could see was the left side of his face in profile, but when he turned his head to speak to a waiter, I saw a strawberry that took up the right side of his face. Across from him in the booth was a younger kid, lean with short hair and a pink scar on his right cheek.

Freddie took a swallow of beer and looked a little unsteady. The woman he'd brushed past a few moments earlier came over to where we were talking. She raised her voice to be heard over the crowd.

"Freddie," she said. "I see you have a new friend."

"Eddie," I said.

"Freddie and Eddie," she said. I extended my hand, but she ignored it.

"Well, we don't need no white police friends, Eddie."

"Jesus Christ," I said. "I'm not a cop already."

"It's okay, Shug," Freddie said. "Man here says he likes my phrasing. Ain't that something?"

"Yeah, it's something all right. Straight bullshit is what."

Without warning, Freddie Francis collapsed. His momentum took him into me, and I caught him more out of instinct than design. His glass shattered against the floor and the restaurant was instantly quiet. Freddie was shorter than me and portly, a dead weight damp with perspiration.

"Hold on," Shug said.

I tipped him forward and she inserted herself under his arm. Freddie's head lolled forward, and he mumbled something through a string of drool. Shug looked at me.

"I got him," she said.

"The hell you do."

"You think this is the first time I've done this?"

"If you try it alone, neither of you is gonna make it."

"We'll take the elevator."

"There isn't one," I said. "Let me take him."

"Fine," Shug said.

She took the lead through a short hallway that led to the back of the hotel lobby. Unsteady Freddie was out on his feet, dragging one and then the other behind and mumbling the whole time. We went through a door and crossed the carpeted lobby of the Eggleston, getting our share of double-takes along the way. By the time we reached the room and Shug opened the door, I'd broken a sweat.

"In here," Shug said, leading the way to the bedroom.

I set Freddie on the side of the bed sitting up while she loosened his tie and took off his coat, hat, and shoes. Shug took a leather pouch from his suit pocket and stuck it in the nightstand drawer. Freddie had stopped mumbling by this time and his breathing was shallow but steady, like a bear ready to hibernate. I lifted his legs onto the bed as Shug guided his head to the pillow and pulled the covers up. We both caught our breath in silence and looked at him in the room's pale-yellow light.

"Getting busted might not be the worst thing that ever happened to him," I said.

Instead of snapping with righteous indignation, she just looked at him and wrung her hands. Then she sat on the edge of the creaky bed beside him.

"Would you mind bringing me a cool washcloth out of the bathroom?"

I did as asked, then watched as she ran the damp cloth over his forehead. She folded it lengthwise and draped it over his brow.

"I'm sorry about downstairs," she said without looking at me. "Thank you for helping me with him. This is all so stressful. Another blown gig."

"Are you Mrs. Francis?" I asked.

Shug turned her head and looked at me through wet eyes.

"She doesn't like the road," she said softly. "She's the one pushing all that 'next Charlie Parker' shit in the newspapers, but she can't stand to see what that pressure does to him."

"The smack ain't helping either," I said. "If he's gonna use, at least get decent stuff."

"And how do you propose we do that? Most of what he makes goes back home, the rest to gas, food, and hotels. He scores what he can when he can."

"Where'd this fix come from?"

"Durham. Played there last week, couple of good shows too. Thought he was on the upswing. Guess it was too much to ask."

"A junkie's never on the upswing for long," I said.

We left him there with the door ajar and walked into the main sitting area. Shug sat on the couch and lit a cigarette with a trembling hand. After a pause she looked up at me.

"Who are you, anyway?"

"Eddie Bostic," I said. "I'm a fan."

"You look like a cop, Eddie."

"I'm not. I just like jazz."

"You in the wrong town for that," she said.

"I get by," I said. "How long are you here?"

"We leave for D.C. tomorrow afternoon," she said. "Hopefully we'll get something for tonight's set even if it was supposed to be two with an encore."

"Good luck with that," I said. She'd need it.

CHAPTER 11

Pink Scar

My overcoat and hat were still in the club, so I made my way back down. The crowd was milling around as though expecting the show to resume at any moment. The men in the booth I'd seen earlier while talking to Freddie Francis were gone. At my table, the two young women were also gone, the night an official bust. I put on my coat and made for the door but decided to stop at the bar for a nightcap. I asked Henry if he'd seen the four men at the corner table or knew where they'd gone, but he was as mute and unsmiling as an oak.

I finished my beer and was ready to call it a night. In the mirror behind the bar, I noticed the young woman from my table who'd asked me for a light. In her purple coat she made her way over to me as if to say something, but kept going for the exit. As she passed, she brushed the finger of her left hand from my left shoulder to my right. Then she opened the door and left by herself without a word, heading west on Leigh. I put on my hat and followed her out.

She took an immediate right on Second toward Jackson Street, her high heels echoing in the night. Against the long shadow of the Eggleston, I lost sight of her in a flickering streetlight. I slowed, and when it flickered on again, I caught her about twenty feet ahead as she ducked into a cobblestone alley behind the hotel. Just as it occurred to me this might be odd behavior for an unaccompanied woman late at night, from behind me came the clicking hammer of a pistol jammed into my lower back.

"Keep going, lover boy," a man's voice said. He gave me a nudge with the pistol into the cobblestone alley, then a foot to the ass that sent me sprawling. I landed in an oily mud puddle near some trash cans. I got to one knee, my clothes soaked with dirty water.

"I just had this dry cleaned," I said.

I looked up and was blinded by the beam of a flashlight. I covered my eyes and was struck from behind with a length of metal pipe. The blow landed on my left ear. I'd been hit in the head with a pipe before and could tell it was mostly an attention getter, this guy's way of shaking hands. If he'd meant business, I'd have been out cold or worse. My face reacquainted itself with the alley, its grit and filth some of the finest in the city. I gave it three Michelin stars.

From behind the beam of light a voice boomed, "Who are you and what the hell are you doing here?"

I got to all fours and tried to clear my head, then smelled the pungent smoke of a cigar I was willing to bet was a Mohawk Chief. I could only assume this was Lamar Clemons holding the flashlight. I counted three of them in total, including the gunman behind me and my friend from the pipe fitters union.

"Name's Eddie," I said. "And there are ways of finding that out that don't involve caving in my skull."

A dropkick landed in my ribs, knocking me onto my side.

"How's that?"

I caught my breath. "Better, thanks."

"Why were you at the Eggleston?"

"Taking in some Southern culture."

"Whitey, you better stick with Sunshine Sue."

I picked myself up and was trying to stand when I saw the pipe man again out of the corner of my eye. He took another swing at me. I ducked and punched him in the gut and landed an uppercut that knocked him silly. The gunman behind me tried to pin my arms back, but I broke free and flipped him over my head onto the alley floor. The man with the flashlight used it to clock me on the back of my neck. On the ground once again, I decided to stay there. I was tired of being hit.

"If you know what's good for you, you'll stop following me around," he said.

"All I want to do is ask you a few questions. Like where you were last Thursday night."

From the alley entrance came the squeal of brakes and a pair of headlights from a black-and-white RPD cruiser. In the bright flash, the kid with the pipe picked himself up, the pink scar on his right cheek illuminated. Then they were gone, sprinting down the alley. The trail runner knocked down a succession of metal trash cans to discourage pursuit, but he needn't have bothered. The red and white lights of the siren angled against their fleeing shadows.

From the patrol car, two cops finally emerged. The driver approached me with his service revolver drawn.

"Well, if it ain't Izzy and Moe," I said.

"Who's there?" the uniform asked.

I sat up against a trash can and got to my feet. Another flashlight in the face.

"Bostic?"

"Yeah," I said. "Who's that?"

The cop holstered his gun and laughed. "Look Haywood, it's our resident crusader."

The voice was familiar. I looked down at the nameplate pinned to his brown jacket and saw that it was Howard Braxton. Howard had joined the RPD in '46, one of four Black patrolmen who had integrated the force. He was pushing forty now, his short mustache tinged with gray. His partner, Wilson, was unfamiliar to me though it was common practice to pair up older, more experienced officers with younger ones. Their beat, of course, was Jackson Ward because heaven forbid a Black officer should arrest a white criminal in a white part of town.

"Hiya, Howard," I said. "What brings you two out?"

Braxton looked over at his partner. "Haywood, tell the citizen what we're doing here."

"Report of somebody smoking reefer behind the Eggleston," Wilson said. "Know anything about it?"

He didn't wait for me to answer but instead wandered up the alley, flashlight in one hand and gun in the other. Behind the hotel on the other side of the alley stood a series of brick row houses. Wilson looked like he was itching to shoot a hophead, which I thought was funny. I shook out a handkerchief and wiped my face, then found my hat and put it on.

"It was me," I said. "Only my friends didn't like it so they did a tap dance on my balls."

"That's a shame," Braxton said. "Prefer a soft shoe myself. So what are you doing out here?"

"Why does everyone want to know what I'm doing tonight?"

"A simple question," Braxton said. "And Bostic?"

"Yeah?"

"You stink on ice."

"Tell me something I don't know," I said. "Look, I was at Neverett's to hear some jazz, and things got out of hand."

Braxton smiled. "Jazz, huh? Was that the musicians bookin' it up the alley?"

"I don't know who that was," I said. I felt kinda bad lying to Howard. We'd joined the force around the same time, and I knew what he and the other three Black patrolmen had gone though. But that was then, and this was now.

Wilson made his way back toward us, his gun finally holstered. He stuck the beam of the flashlight in my face. "Jazz," he said, "is the music of degenerates."

"That's why we have better funerals," I said.

CHAPTER 12

The Hotel King Carter

Braxton bought the whole shabby story and even offered me a lift, but instead I took a painful, limping walk to clear my head. I'd left the van outside Dave's Market at Fourth and Leigh. They were almost closed, but I got there just in time for a pack of Luckys. Back at my place on N. Morris, I took a shower to wash the night off. It wasn't late and I wasn't tired, but I was sore and knew I could use the extra shut-eye. I took a pack of frozen peas from the ice box and stuck it behind my ear. People always told me I had a hard head like it was a bad thing, but it had its advantages. I went to the record player and put on some Max Roach. As the music started up, my phone rang. I picked up.

"Is this Bostic Lock and Key?" a woman's voice asked.

"Sort of," I said. I turned the music down. The voice was familiar but I couldn't quite place it. It was my favorite kind, though, soft and breathy. Especially at 10:30 on a Saturday night.

There was another pause. "I have a lock," she said at last. "But I seem to have misplaced the key."

"I may be able to help, Cleo," I said. "But I'll have to see your lock before I know what kind of key it needs."

"Can you possibly see to it tonight?" she asked. "I hate to impose, but the need is rather pressing. You can bring your tension tool."

It was the damndest job offer I'd had in some time.

* * *

The doorman at the King Carter nodded as I passed under the red-and-yellow striped awning. I made my way through a spacious lobby with shiny marble floors and Ionic columns. The coffee shop and cigar stand were closed, but plenty of people milled around under a smoky haze. I detoured up the carpeted stairs to the exposed second-floor mezzanine where many offices were located. The Virginia Road Builders Association was among them, as was Mort Williams's new employer, Admiral Security. I made a mental note and continued on to the elevator.

The operator was a cheerful old guy in a red jacket, gray pants, and a matching red and gray hat strapped to his chin. The name of the hotel was stitched on the front of the hat, and his nametag identified him as Sam.

"Floor?" he asked in a raspy voice.

"Eleven," I said.

He closed the doors manually and ran his finger up the buttons until he reached the one at the top and pressed it. The mechanism engaged with a lurch. Sam stepped back and stood beside me with his hands clasped together in front. We were quiet for a few seconds.

"Mint?" he said.

I looked over and he produced a round green tin of Bowers Mints. I hadn't seen one of those in a while, so I took one.

"You must not be from around here," I said.

"Pennsylvania," he said.

"Upstate New York, myself," I said. It was always surprising to encounter another northerner in Richmond, especially one as old as Sam. Looking at him felt a little like looking into a mirror from the future. I wondered how I'd look in the hat.

"Union spies," Sam said.

"Carpetbaggers," I said.

We reached my floor and Sam stepped forward to pull the doors open. "Good night, sir," he said.

"Night, Sam," I said.

I stepped out into the carpeted hallway, took a left and then a right down a quiet corridor. Cleo's room was at the end. I knocked lightly and heard rustling behind the door. When it opened, I found her standing there barefoot in a powder-blue lace teddy. The idea of lingerie had always struck me as ludicrous. I could only assume its purpose was to stoke the flames of desire, as if any man needed more of that. The truth is, men are not complex animals and never have been. The nude female form does not require a great deal of embellishment, apart from proper lighting and a dab of perfume. Lady Godiva had it right all along.

"Well, are you just gonna stand there and drool, ya big dope?" Cleo said.

The Lord might have hated perfume-smellin' things, lacy things, things with curly hair, but I myself was a fan. I stepped inside and closed the door. Any self-respecting private eye would have been jumped by a thug hiding in the bathroom, or menaced by a tough guy sitting in a chair by a lamp. Fortunately, I was a locksmith, and the most threatening thing in the room was a nearly naked female whose painted toenails had rendered me mute. She backed into the room maintaining eye contact, one arm behind her back.

"I've had enough surprises for one evening," I said.

"I hope that's not true," she said.

Cleo brought her hand forward and produced a highball glass that had an ice cube in it and a couple of fingers of whiskey.

"Room service," I said. I took the glass from her with my left hand and took a sip.

A male's voice spoke up behind me. "Yeah, room service," it said.

"Oh, what now?" I said.

I felt a nudge in my back. When I turned there was a young man in a loose-collared shirt and jacket holding a small pistol on me. "I knew I should have checked the bathroom," I said. I looked closer at his face and realized it was the same young man I'd seen carrying her up the stairs at Mort's house the night before. "Wait," I said, "aren't you Blair, or Hoke?"

"Blair," he said, though he looked a little unsure about it.

"Are you an actor, Blair?"

"Yeah."

"Have you been in anything I might have seen?"

"I haven't had any speaking parts yet," he said.

"Well, Blair," I said. "From what I've seen of your tough guy act, it needs work."

I reached down with my right hand and took the gun from his sweaty palm. He seemed relieved. I took another sip of my drink and set it down. The pistol was a Beretta M34, an interesting weapon and something of a collector's item. It had a rough finish and was nicked up pretty bad, probably late war. I worked the slide and found nothing in the chamber, but when I checked the magazine, it was full. I looked at Cleo.

"Was this your idea?"

"I thought you were working for my fiancé."

"What on earth?"

"In our travels today, Daisy reminded me you used to be an investigator, and that sometimes you still moonlight as one."

"I do," I said. "But I'm not working on any case where you're concerned."

She bit her lip. "Well now that you say it, it just sounds silly."

"Silly enough to give Blair here a loaded gun and have him sweat me. Thanks a lot."

I turned to Blair, who wasn't quite sure what to do. I tucked the gun into my back waistband and put my arm around him as we turned toward the door.

"Look, son," I said. "I oughta settle your hash right here. But the minute I raise a fist to you, that's assault. And when I hit you, well, that's battery. Let me ask you, does all that commotion sound like good press for your movie?"

"No, sir."

"It's not. So in the interest of not having the police show up and wake the other guests, I'm going to let you off with a warning."

"I could mess you up, sir," he said.

I shook my head. "You'll just hurt your knuckles, Blair. Look, if you wanna look tough, you gotta narrow the eyes and jut your chin. Give it a shot, let's see your mean face."

He turned and narrowed his eyes at me and jutted his chin. The look wasn't much; he kept moving his jaw back and forth until his lips pursed. He looked confused.

"Like that?" he asked.

"Work on it," I said. I opened the door and nudged him into the hallway. "Go back to your room and practice in the mirror. Tomorrow at the premiere I'll look for you, and we can go over it again."

"You'd do that?"

"Sure," I said. "But I have one more thing, and it's something I want you to remember."

"What's that?"

"You only point a loaded gun at someone you're prepared to kill. If you ever pull a gun on me again, it will be the last thing you ever do. Understand?"

"Yes. I'm sorry."

"It's okay, sport. Now go get some rest. And remember: the chin. Jut it."

I closed the door in his face, locked it, and set the chain. Then I turned and went back into the room and found my drink.

"Nice kid," I said.

"Don't be sore," Cleo said.

"Me? Why would I be sore?"

"I believe you now," she said. "My fiancé didn't hire you. But he's hired private eyes to keep tabs on me before."

"What sort of life do you lead that would make him do that?"

She paused and looked at me. "The exact life I want and nothing less."

She came over to me and stood on tiptoe, then put her arms around my neck and kissed me. Being a gentleman and perhaps too quick to forgive, I kissed her and pulled her close. She made a convincing case for the lifestyle.

"Can we just forget it?" she asked.

"Definitely not," I said.

"Suit yourself," she said. "You could at least stay long enough to finish your drink and keep me company." Then she smiled and turned, showing me that her teddy had been lovingly tailored by God himself. I watched her walk toward an ironing board set up in the middle of the room where she was smoothing the wrinkles out of a pink dress. Across from it on a wheeled stand was a television. It cast a blue glow into the room that mixed with the dim yellow light from a beside lamp.

"What's on?" I asked.

"Million Dollar Movie," Cleo said. "*Berlin Correspondent.*"

"I've seen it," I said, which was true. All I really remembered about it was Dana Andrews's silly mustache and the Nazi with the weird face. It'd played in some second-run theater in Troy a couple of weeks before I shipped out to basic. I'd spent that time being nervous and scared and looking for anything to take my mind off it. It felt like a lifetime ago.

"I love Dana Andrews," Cleo said. "I was almost in a movie with him once, but they cast Carolyn Jones at the last second."

"Their loss," I said.

"Have you seen any of my movies?" she asked.

"I've been thinking about that all day," I said. "I saw *Angels Without Wings* at the Capitol, and *Open and Shut* at the Bluebird."

The TV screen started to roll, so I gave it a whack with the flat of my hand and it stopped. I sat down in an overstuffed chair and felt almost useful until the screen started rolling again. I never got WXEX worth a damn anyway. Cleo gave the dress a few final strokes with the iron, then held it at her side for me to see.

"There," she said, eyeing the dress. "Isn't it precious?"

"It sure is," I said, though I wasn't talking about the dress. The light from the lamp behind her filtered through the lacy material and outlined her shape perfectly. She brought the dress over to the closet and placed it on a wooden hanger, then clicked the TV off. She poured herself a drink at the makeshift bar and downed it in one gulp, then came over to the chair where I was sitting. She plopped down in my lap and put her arms around my neck.

"So how was your day, dear?" she asked. She began planting little kisses on my face and neck.

"Oh, you know," I said, "the usual—peeping through keyholes at cheating spouses and taking dirty pictures."

She stopped and looked at me. "Is that supposed to be funny?"

"You tell me. I flunked Ethics at Locksmith U. And besides, you're not married yet. But now that you mention it, I *did* get conked on the noggin earlier if you'd like to see."

"I would," she said.

I craned my neck and she ran her fingers gently over the lump. I drew back with a wince and she apologized, then gave it a little kiss.

"You should be more careful," she said. "The Almighty doesn't just go around handing out nice faces. Who knows what you might look like next time around?"

"I'll keep that in mind," I said. I gave her neck and ear a kiss. "And how was your day?"

"It was perfect," she said. "Daisy took me sightseeing and we went shopping. Richmond is adorable. I found some stockings and a pretty dress for tomorrow at Miller & Rhoads. I signed some autographs."

"How was the radio interview?"

"It was grand; Mr. Schreiner is a delight. Oh, and I got my hair done at Wooten's in the hotel lobby. Don't you love it?"

"I do," I said, catching another whiff of Chanel. "Richmond won't know what hit it."

"Neither will you," Cleo said.

CHAPTER 13

Liquor Store Holdup

Her lingerie ended up exactly where it belonged, crumpled in a heap on the floor next to my undershirt. The earth didn't move at any point, but the bed certainly did. Cleo was taken aback at the scar on my chest, but didn't let it slow her down. When I showed her a smaller scar near my temple from an accident in boot camp, she was less impressed. Which was fine, it didn't impress me either. After we'd caught our breath, I lit a smoke to share as we lay there staring at the ceiling. In the silence that followed I was sure I'd bored her to sleep. Then she nestled into the crook of my arm and traced her finger on my chest along the scar's pink edges.

"So how'd you get it? The truth."

"A bad combination," I said. "A Japanese bullet and an American surgeon. I'm still not sure which one did more harm."

"You're lucky to be alive."

"I was careless," I said. "We were mopping up after the island was secured. We'd just finished clearing out a pillbox when one of those little bastards popped up out of a spider hole."

"A what?"

"It's a narrow little hole barely big enough for one, with a hatch cover made of grass or leaves. They were all over that island. The men hated them. You could pass one and not even know until it was too late."

"What happened then?"

"He shot me. With an officer's pistol, no less. Turned out he was only a private so he must have scrounged it from somewhere. He also shot and killed the man next to me. He squeezed off those two rounds before the rest of the guys cut him down."

"And after that?"

"Battalion aid, then a hospital ship and a trip back to Pearl. There the wound got infected and nearly killed me a second time. That was what got me sent me home, not the bullet. It was my million-dollar infection."

We were both quiet for another minute. I felt like changing the subject.

"Anyway, thanks for the Beretta," I said. "But tell me, why would a pretty girl like you have a nasty thing like that?"

"Protection, I guess," she said.

"Ever use it?" I asked. "I mean, before tonight when you gave it to Blair?"

Cleo glared at me and shook her head. "Not once," she said.

"Where'd you get it?"

"My brother Eugene brought it home from Italy. A souvenir."

"Doesn't he miss it?"

"I'm afraid not," she said. "He's dead."

"I'm sorry," I said. "May I ask how?"

"He couldn't adjust to civilian life," Cleo said. "He was like a different person from the one who went to war. Nightmares. Couldn't hold a job. Started drinking. One night he got drunk and held up a liquor store in Baton Rouge. The owner was ready with a twelve gauge."

"Sorry," I said again.

"Don't be," she said. "We all make our choices. Eugene made his."

We were both quiet for a bit before she continued.

"My father gave it to me. Said any woman who traveled by herself as much as I did needed to defend herself from prowlers and intruders."

"And shady types like me."

"Among others," she said. "But truth be told I don't like carrying it around. I've never used it and I never will. And the association I have with it is quite unpleasant."

"You could have sold it. Or dropped it into the nearest body of water," I said. "The James has enough small arms in it to field an army."

"How would you feel about holding on to it for me?"

I laughed. "I was planning to."

"That's not terribly gallant."

"Neither am I." I grinned and shook my head. For all I knew the Beretta was evidence in a multi-state killing spree or a string of bank robberies. I didn't have a permit for it or any gun. Maybe the whole thing was a set-up, but probably not. "I'll sign something if it'll make you feel better."

"Of course not," she said, "but that reminds me."

She reached over to the table on her side of the bed and picked up a large envelope. She settled back down beside me and pulled out a glossy black-and-white publicity shot. In it, she was wearing a lacy halter and leaning forward showing the camera her left profile, her lips parted in a slight smile, the dramatic eyebrows arched perfectly.

"Do you like this one?"

"How could I not?" I said.

She took a magic marker and signed it "To Eddie, All My Love – Cleo Nichols" and drew a little heart.

"All your love, huh?" I said. I pulled her back on top of me roughly as the envelope fell to the floor. "Are you sure?"

"Well," she said. "There might be a little bit left."

But just then, the damn phone rang. Cleo sprang up and slapped my hand away as I reached for the receiver.

"No, you cretin!" she said. "What if it's my fiancé?"

She picked it up and told the operator to put the call through. She rolled off me and listened for a moment, then made a face and handed me the receiver.

"For you," she said.

She got out of bed wrapped in a sheet and disappeared into the bathroom.

"Eddie, it's Daisy. I tried you at home but you didn't pick up."

"I generally don't when I'm not there. Is this a social call?"

"Not exactly. I need a favor."

"I'm busy," I said. "Is this a work favor, or *favor* favor? My rates go up after two in the morning."

"Shut up," she said. "Paul's in jail. I need you to bail him out and keep it quiet."

"Daisy, this is Richmond, not Los Angeles. The only people who know about it are you, me, and the switchboard operator. The list of people who care is even shorter."

"Well, I care," she said. "Paul's on thin ice with the studio as it is. I need you to get him out and back to the King Carter as soon as you can. I'll meet you both back there."

I hadn't agreed to anything, but as far as Daisy was concerned, I didn't need to. The line went dead as Cleo emerged from the bathroom in a fluffy white hotel robe and flopped down on the bed beside me. I hung up and sat still for a moment on the edge of the mattress.

"Duty calls," I said.

"But how am I supposed to keep warm?"

She was saying the right things, but I could tell her heart wasn't in it. Cleo had slathered some sort of green muck onto her face and put her hair in curlers.

"I'm afraid you'll have to suffer," I said.

I got dressed. I found the Beretta and chambered a round, then put the safety on.

"There's one more thing," she said, "about the pistol."

I was almost out the door when I turned to look at her.

"The liquor store owner reported that it jammed during the robbery. It's the only reason Eugene was killed and not the owner."

"Rotten luck," I said. "For one of them, anyway."

"You said it," Cleo said. "A split second where one person dies and another lives, and all thanks to random chance. Whoever heard of such a thing?"

"That's funny," I said. "It happens to me all the time."

CHAPTER 14

The Hotel Graybar

This was hardly my first trip to the City Jail, but it would be among my last no matter what. Located at Fifteenth and Marshall, the jail was now the subject of potential litigation between City Council and the Turnpike Authority. The dispute was, as always, over money. Like most buildings in the area, including mine, the jail was in the path of the toll road. The city wanted $573 large to replace it with a building of similar size and quality; the RPTA countered with $171 small which they argued was fair market value. In truth, they could pay nothing at all for the site and simply take it via condemnation. City Council refused to even negotiate and claimed the RPTA lacked the authority to condemn the building. It was a little like listening to *The Bickersons,* except everyone knew who would win.

The lockup itself was an L-shaped, white-brick building on Marshall with a couple of squad cars parked in front. I found a space at the curb in front of the city pound. I sat in the van for a moment beneath a flickering streetlight as a train crept along the Seaboard Air Line overpass, screeching and hissing its way into Main Street Station. The noise woke every miserable mutt in the city pound next door, and another hundred or so that happened to be in the neighborhood. I got out and lit a cigarette, then made my way to the jail accompanied by the racket of every goddamn dog in the city barking at nothing.

The attendant sat in a small office behind a window. He was a cop in his mid-sixties with thinning gray hair and a heavily lined face. He didn't look happy to be there—probably wasn't happy to be anywhere. Without looking up, he shoved a clipboard toward me and told me to state my business.

"Bail for Eggar," I said.

He found a form and slid it under the window. "Fill it out and sign it."

I did and slid it back to him. He studied it for a moment, then arched an eyebrow. The chair creaked and groaned beneath him.

"Seventy-five dollars," he said.

"The going rate is going up."

"Especially for sodomites."

I took out my wallet and forked over the cash, which left me with exactly five bucks. The attendant gave me a receipt, nodded toward a row of wooden chairs in the lobby, and told me to take a seat. After five minutes in one of them, I began to wonder if this was how people got hemorrhoids. After ten minutes, I was sure of it. I joined four chairs together and stretched out with my hat over my face. It was a far cry from a soft hotel bed next to an even softer movie star, but it would have to do. If someone came along and wanted to roll me, I was okay with it.

I was jolted awake when the attendant kicked away the chair supporting my feet. It was almost four in the morning. I followed him to a heavy wooden door which he unlocked with a jangling set of keys. I walked into a green cinderblock hallway with black tiles and a barred door on the far side. Next to this door was another old cop sound asleep on a stool. The attendant handed me a yellow form.

"Your copy," he said. "If Mr. Eggar fails to show up for trial, your money is forfeited to the court. Officer McMahon will assist you from here."

He pointed at a cop asleep on a stool at the end of the hallway. I walked over and recognized him from my time with the RPD. Pat McMahon was one of those guys you'd have to cut the uniform off of. I didn't know him well, but he was a decent enough cop from what I remembered. No family to speak of, bit of a drinker, not much ambition beyond wearing the uniform for as long as they'd let him.

"Hey, Mac," I said.

He jerked awake with a snort but kept his balance on the stool. I was guessing he'd had a lot of practice.

"Who's that?" he said.

"Doesn't matter. I'm here for a prisoner. Eggar."

He stood up, and I showed him the yellow slip. He picked up a clipboard off the floor and mumbled as he ran his index finger down a handwritten list of names. We walked down a wide, dimly lit corridor lined with cells on either side. The city jail was the one place in Richmond where "separate but equal" actually meant something. The cells were no more integrated than schools, restaurants, or hotels, but accommodations for both races were equally terrible. It was in here that the astringents used to combat the stench fought and died, overcome by that sour *eau de jail* reek of puke, piss, and desperation. White or Black, that all smelled the same. At this hour, most of the prisoners were sleeping one off. Not mine.

"Cell D-7, Eggar comma Paul," Mac said.

Paul got up from his bunk where he'd been sitting nervously while his sleeping cell mate—dressed in work boots, denim overalls, and a plaid quilted jacket—farted loudly. Paul came to the cell door and put both hands on the bars.

"Please tell me you're here to get me out of this shithole," Paul said.

"Cheap suit, at your service."

He didn't seem to remember my name, but he knew who I was. His pencil-thin mustache was a little worse for wear, but it went nicely with the busted lip and shiner. The key ring jingled in the lock, and the heavy iron door squeaked open. Paul stepped out into the corridor as the door slammed shut again. Around us, inmates grumbled at the noise.

"What the hell took you so long?" Eggar said.

"Paperwork."

We were about to make for the exit when a voice I recognized called my name. I looked over and saw Randy Daigle in the cell beside Paul's. I'd known Randy for a couple of years; he was a source for reliable (if not always useful) information. He was looking a little rough too, disheveled and bloodied. I asked Mac to take Paul down the hall while I went over for a chat.

"Randy, I'm surprised at you," I said. "This is no way to spend Saturday night."

"Can you bail me out, Eddie?" he asked.

"Afraid not," I said. "I'm busted."

"I'll pay you back," Randy said. "You know I'm good for it."

"I definitely don't. If memory serves, you still owe me from the last time I bailed you out."

"Oh bullshit," he said. "What's ten bucks?"

"The cost of a hand job?"

"Oh please," Randy said. "I won't go near a dick for less than twenty."

"Oh yes you will!" someone chimed in from a nearby cell.

"Speaking of which," I said. "Why are you in here?"

Randy nodded in Paul's direction at the other end of the corridor. "Ask him."

"Paul?" I asked.

"I didn't catch a name," Randy said. "But the mustache is cute."

"Classy. What happened?"

"He was cruising the basement at Broad Street Station. I offered to take him back to my place, but the horny fucker couldn't wait. The cops caught us fogging up the windows of some random car in the parking lot."

I studied the marks on his face. "Looks like you both resisted arrest," I said.

"That's what it will say in the report," he said. "Bum a smoke?"

I gave him one and lit it. "Say, Randy," I said. "Do you know a Casey Coulson? Or a Casey Lloyd?"

Randy smiled and blew some smoke through his nose. "Slick, Eddie," he said. "No dice."

"All I got left is a fiver."

"Let's have it."

I got my wallet, took the bill out, and handed it to him.

"I know the name," Randy said. "Different circles and all, but he was Casey Lloyd when I met him. Moved to a not-very-nice part of the Southside last year sometime, got into some rough trade."

"Hey!" Paul shouted from down the corridor. "Can we get the hell out of here?"

"Shut up!" someone shouted. Other inmates made kissy noises.

"Keep your shirt on," I told him. I turned back to Randy. "So far you haven't said much I didn't already know."

"What do you expect for five bucks?"

"How about something I can use?"

"What can I say? Casey's not in the scene anymore."

"He's even less in it now. Found by the tracks not far from here early Friday. Not feeling so good on account of the two bullet holes in his chest."

Randy didn't look surprised. "I'll keep my ears open," he said.

"You do that," I said. I turned to leave and reached the end of the corridor.

"Hey, I got problems too!" Randy shouted after me.

"Shut up!" someone else shouted, as the heavy cell door closed behind us with an echo.

CHAPTER 15

Nails

On the way back to the hotel, I had to listen to Eggar bitch about Richmond cops, the Richmond jail, and Richmond generally. I could hardly blame him. Everybody's got their gripes about the place—I had mine when I first moved here. But it's funny. You live in a new place long enough that you start to call it home, suddenly you don't like hearing somebody else run it down. But I kept my mouth shut and drove. It was either too late or too early to argue with someone who'd never been here before and almost certainly wouldn't ever be back. I made a U-turn at Eighth and wheeled around to the front of the King Carter where Daisy was waiting under the awning. Paul got out without another word and vanished through the lobby doors. Daisy stuck her head inside the car through the open passenger window.

"We still haven't had that talk," I said.

"Looks like you were too busy. With work, was it?"

"Give me a break," I said. "The last time I checked you were still married and I still wasn't."

"You need to be better than that," she said.

"Tell me something I don't know."

Daisy shook her head and stepped back from the car. "Two o'clock tomorrow afternoon. Don't be late."

***

In bed the next morning staring at the ceiling, I could only think of how much I didn't want to go. My watch on the bedside table didn't seem right, so I gave it a shake. I swung my legs out and sat on the side of the bed. The lump behind my ear felt directly related to the headache swelling my brain. In fairness, it could also have been the beers, the cigarettes, or the two hits off a joint. I'd enjoyed myself at the time, but in retrospect it might not have been the best idea.

I found a crumpled pack of smokes on the dresser and dangled one from my lip, staring at the Zippo in my palm. *What if I didn't light it?* I'd been a smoker since Saipan. *What's the worst that could happen?* I crumpled the cig onto the floor and shook my head to clear it. I opened the window for some air and the first thing I could smell was tobacco curing. I made breakfast, got cleaned up and dressed. By the time it was all said and done, I looked as good as I was going to look, and the headache had ebbed to a dull roar.

Thankfully, it was a quiet fall morning in the city. I found the van and drove to the National. As I walked up, a kid with a buzz cut stood on a rickety ladder and finished up the lettering on the front marquee.

PREMIER
S H A D O W O F T O M O R R O W
PAUL EGGAR
CLEO NICHOLS
& RICHMOND'S DAISY WILLIAMS

"Hey, kid," I said, "what time you got?"

"A little after one o'clock, sir," he said. Seeing the confused look on my face, he added, "Time change."

So I was an hour early for something I didn't want to do to begin with. I thought about going down to my shop but wasn't feeling the walk. Nothing was open, including Pat's Records right next to the theater, which had a new Sonny Rollins release in its front window. I wandered down to the state capitol and watched the pigeons crap on George Washington. Since he couldn't tell a lie, I asked him what sense it made for Lamar Clemons to kill Casey Lloyd. The father of our country didn't have any better answers for that than I did. I could also ask Lee, Jackson, or Stuart, whose monuments stood elsewhere in the city. But they'd just tell me the same old thing: when in doubt, blame the Black guy.

I didn't want a cigarette in any way, which is to say I would have murdered someone for one. A smattering of tourists milled about, taking pictures, but I didn't dare bum a smoke for fear of being asked directions to a Confederate this or a Civil War that. I thought about going to the hotel to check on things but dismissed the idea. In this life, there few things more futile than telling a woman she needs to hurry up. Instead, I sat and watched the leaves change through the insides of my eyelids. Birds sang. I may have snored.

A few minutes later I awoke and circled back to the King Carter just as the entourage was leaving. Dressed to the nines and perfumed to the hilt, Daisy, Cleo, and Paul were all chatter and laughs. Surrounded by assorted hangers-on and one or two members of the local press; I'd heard quieter mobs. All the same it was a little bit of Hollywood glamour in the heart of gritty old Richmond, and it was all right. I waited for the excitement outside the theater to die down. The front was roped off with red velvet. The marquee was lit up, and the red carpet had been unfurled and cleaned. It led from the sidewalk in front of the box office through the lobby doors. On it at the moment stood Daisy Williams in all her glory while a photographer from the *Times-Dispatch* crouched at her feet, flashbulbs firing.

The first time I'd ever seen her was in the backyard of her house in Windsor Farms in April of 1946. She wore a white dress patterned with bright red flowers, similar to the one she had on at the premiere. Back then, on a warm spring afternoon with Mort's azaleas in bloom, Daisy had been the first splash of color and life in a world turned gray. In my crisp army uniform, I was just another rube from nowhere who'd served overseas with her brother. As I spoke with Mr. and Mrs. Williams on the back patio, my hat in hand, it was all I could do to not stare at Daisy. All these years later, she still had that spark, that color, that face. Part of me was still dumb enough to dream of the day we would end up together, living a life that was all present and no past.

"Eddie!" she said, beaming at me. "Get over here!"

I stood on the sidewalk for a moment, my shabby shoes one with the concrete.

"Right now!" she said.

I took three steps forward and there I was, part of the same Hollywood elite as the Three Stooges. I remembered to stand up straight and look as much like a soldier as I could. The photographer made a face and lifted the camera. Daisy laced her arm in mine and smiled as though I was about to be stuffed and mounted. The bulb flashed one final time, and we moved off to a corner of a lobby.

"Thanks again for last night," Daisy said. She tilted her sunglasses down and gave me a look. "Mostly."

"What mostly?"

"Just don't ever let me catch you in Cleo's bed again."

"A man's gotta eat," I said. "And besides, that's unlikely. I haven't gotten so much as a sideways glance from her. Or Paul, for that matter. I'll be surprised if either one of them remembers anything that happened here in a week's time."

"Bum a smoke?" Daisy asked.

I patted the pockets of my suit jacket knowing full well I had none.

"I'm out," I said, feeling vaguely stupid. "Vending machine?"

"Be a dear," she said.

Inside the foyer and to the left was a Philip Morris cigarette machine. I put in a quarter and pulled the lever, and out spat a pack of Marlboros in the tray. Back outside, Daisy was at a velvet rope next to the crowd, autographing a program for a young fan.

"Smoke, your highness?" I said.

"My hero," she said. I gave her a light with the Zippo and she blew out a lungful of smoke. "You're not trying to quit, are you?"

Before I could answer, a man in a tuxedo stepped out from the lobby onto the sidewalk. Daisy took one puff and let it drop at her feet.

"Ladies and gentlemen!" he exclaimed. "Welcome to the Richmond premiere of a new Hollywood classic, *Shadow of Tomorrow*, starring Miss Tobacco Harvest 1947, Richmond's own Daisy Williams!"

The crowd clapped politely. On Broad in front of the theater, traffic moved at rubbernecking speed. Daisy stuck her tongue out at me and joined the man in the tuxedo. I looked down at the cigarette she had dropped, nearly pristine with just the slightest hint of lipstick. I wanted to pick it up and start puffing away, but I knew there would be at least one person in the crowd who'd see and mistake me for a hobo. I crushed it out with my shoe instead.

"And Daisy's co-stars, Paul Eggar and Cleo Nichols!"

Hand in hand, Paul and Cleo stepped forward. Neither showed any signs of wear from the previous evening's exertions. Paul's fat lip and shiner were things of the past thanks to artfully applied ice and makeup. His pencil-thin mustache was flawless, the envy of tough guys everywhere. Cleo looked as though she'd slept a good eight hours, and maybe she had. The photographer went to work again.

"And now, ladies and gentlemen, please join us inside—we will get to the main event without further ado."

The manager led the charge into the lobby. I wasn't sure who or where I was supposed to be, so I lingered in a quiet niche as the movie's cast and crew made their way to the front. My grumbling stomach and the fresh pack of smokes in my pocket felt like part of a test, but I wasn't sure if I was passing or failing. I eyed the smoky auditorium and wondered how much I'd be missed if I just vanished. My eyes drifted up toward the ellipse in the ceiling, one of the theater's quirks. It allowed people on the second floor to see down into the lobby and concession area. The thing is, hardly anyone in the lobby ever notices it. Why would you if all you're expecting to see is the ceiling?

Just then, Daisy appeared at the auditorium entrance with her hands on her hips and told me the whole theater was waiting. As unlikely as that seemed, my seat did have a cardboard placard with my name on it. Better yet, it was on the aisle next to Daisy. The short man in the tuxedo took to the stage and clasped his hands together.

"How about a warm Southern welcome for our stars?"

Daisy, Paul, and Cleo stood, in turn, to polite applause. In her dress from Miller & Rhoads, Cleo got the most applause and a few wolf whistles. Attaboy, Richmond. Daisy gave me a funny look, as though she'd just remembered something. Then the noise died out as the lights went down and the movie started.

CHAPTER 16

Pink Scar Redux

The opening credits ran over a sequence of Daisy driving a car through Los Angeles as filmed from the back seat. From time to time, her eyes caught the camera in the rear view, but we did not see her full face until the credits ended and she stepped out of the car for a close up. It captured something about her I'd last seen years ago when I was too dense to realize how she felt about me. I hoped I was less dense these days, but I doubted it.

The story unfolded pretty much like Cleo said. Paul Eggar is a condemned man on death row in an unnamed country, spending his last night on earth behind bars. Daisy's character is killed in a flashback, the crime that landed Paul on death row. Cut to Cleo spending some time depressed on a beach, showing some skin before deciding to drown herself. It's a curious sequence. When the cops fish her out of the drink and arrest her, she ends up in the same jail where Paul is being held. One thing leads to another. I looked down the aisle at Cleo and wondered if art was imitating life, or vice versa. Then I turned to Daisy and excused myself.

"Where are you going?"

"Stretch my legs," I said.

"Can we talk after this?"

"You mean about the things?"

"Exactly," she said.

"Sure, I won't be far. But I have to drive out to Chester after this."

"I could ride with," she said.

"Sure."

Out in the lobby, a janitor was cleaning the first-floor men's room. I took the stairs to the balcony and used the bathroom there. I came out and paused at the ellipse I'd noticed earlier. People came and went through the concession area with its burgundy rug and popcorn smell. I daydreamed about a dancing cigarette with a little top hat and cane.

The janitor emerged from the bathroom with his cart. He was a skinny, older Black man in a neat gray uniform. He was giving an earful about church and Jesus to a kid in street clothes with more attitude than brains. It turned out the kid was his nephew. I didn't think much of it until I got a closer look at the kid and saw the pink scar on his cheek. He looked like one of the bunch who'd jumped me in the alley the night before. I needed a better look to be sure, so when he left a minute later, I took the stairs down and followed him out through the theater's front doors.

He took a right and walked west on Broad. Two blocks later at Fifth, he paused to light a cigarette outside Adams Camera. I loitered near a shoeshine stand and watched him take a right up Fifth and cross the street in front of the Union Bus Depot. He took a left at a parking lot, heading west on Clay.

Sidewalks in the Ward were filled with the usual post-church crowd socializing on a warm fall Sunday, and I was starting to get that sore thumb feeling. There was no overt hostility, but a wariness. At least until half a block later when the kid stopped to talk to a man in a straw fedora leaning against a short wooden fence. The man motioned in my direction with a piece of paper that could have been a church program or a betting slip. The kid looked back at me and flicked the cigarette away. Looking at him now, I couldn't even be sure if it was the same kid. I shuffled my feet outside the entrance to Martha Ellen's Beauty Shop like a big, fat schmuck. I was made.

The kid took off in a dead sprint, crossing to the sidewalk and hauling ass up Clay. I yelled for him to stop, but of course he didn't. I looked down at my feet and apologized. They had already started to hurt in anticipation of running after anything. I gave chase across the street and onto the uneven brick sidewalk.

At Fourth, he bolted into the intersection against the light and into the path of an oncoming car. He drew the honk of a horn, a rarity in Richmond. Another horn blew at me as I ran in front of a Buick heading in the other direction. It screeched to a stop and was itself struck from behind by a third car. The Buick's driver cursed me, but I made it to the curb and kept going. The kid slowed near a line of row houses and grabbed a fence post to stop his momentum. He doubled back through a gate and up the front steps and into the open door of a narrow residence. I followed him inside and heard a woman's voice shrieking.

"Oh Lord! What is happening in this house right now?"

Inside I saw two round Black women in their Sunday best, sitting in a round room. They were enveloped in a cloud of gardenia perfume. One of them fanned herself with a program from that morning's service.

"Oh Lord, who is this evil white man?"

I was starting to wonder the same thing. I apologized and ran on like a man possessed. Down a hallway through the back of the house, I passed another room where an older Black man in an undershirt and boxer shorts waved his fork at a TV set showing the Redskins-Chicago Cardinals game. He hadn't noticed the kid or me.

"I told you to run the got damn ball!" he shouted.

The back screen door was swinging on its hinges as the kid made for the alley and veered right, his heels kicking up dust puffs in the muted sunlight. I followed another half block until the alley let out at Third Street. I was gassed but now there was less traffic to dodge. The kid hurdled a fence into the backyard of a residence. He reached its wooden back porch and climbed a staircase to the second floor.

I dragged ass over the fence and made for the house as a mutt in the next yard started barking. I took the stairs two at a time and heard a heavy thunk from the top porch. The kid had pushed open a small square trapdoor to the roof and pulled himself up. Even when I was young and stupid in the army, doing pull-ups was among my least favorite activities. Now, in a halfway-decent suit, I liked it even less. I looked at the opening and shook my head, then jumped as high as I could. With a grunt, I pulled myself up to the rooftop.

It had never occurred to me to tour the Ward in this way, nor did I particularly want to now. Some of these structures dated back to Reconstruction or just after. The footing along the flat tar paper rooftops was uneven and spongy as though on the verge of collapse. Brick partitions about a foot high separated the rooftops, a mocking reminder of my days as a hurdler on the Troy High School track team. Fourteen years later and too many cigarettes to count, my goose was cooked.

The kid was doing all right, though, almost a block ahead and gaining. Halfway across one of the rooftops, I stopped. Panting in the afternoon sun and in a full sweat, I placed my palms on my knees and caught my breath. I coughed and felt my jacket pocket for the pack of Marlboros, then patted my pockets for the Zippo.

At my feet, the roof creaked once. It was my one and only warning before it gave way beneath me in a jagged sea of splintered wood, cracked plaster, dust and chaos. I had a memory of landing hard on the linoleum floor of a kitchen where someone was boiling pigs feet. Then another creak under me as this floor gave way to the next, and when I landed there all my memories went away for a little while.

CHAPTER 17

Whitemail

Richmond, Virginia

Monday, October 29, 1956

I awoke gradually from a Man Ray dream, the images blurred and swirling. The droning noise of a small airplane engine came in through an open window to my right. At least I think that's where it was coming from. I sat up and found myself tucked into a bed inside a small white room. At some point I'd been stripped to my boxers and T-shirt. My vision was spotty, and my head throbbed like a hangover with a hangover. My muscles ached. As the room came into focus, black linen curtains billowed at the window and cool, muggy air flowed into the room. On the wall above my head, Jesus on the cross looked like he was having a hard time getting comfortable.

The last time I woke up feeling this bad was outside a battalion aid station on Saipan. I'd been surprised to wake up then too. A surgeon on a smoke break had just happened to see me, lying there in a neat row of stretchers that lined the entrance. When he saw one of the bodies convulse and start coughing blood onto the sheet that covered him, he approached and called out for help. Mind you I remember none of this, only heard about it later. At the time, I was only aware of his footsteps on the wooden gangplank as they got closer.

Back in the room, I coughed once and felt the old pain in my lung, that tightness I sometimes managed to forget. I realized for the first time I was unharmed, just some bruises and cuts, nothing serious. Nor was I restrained in any way. I thought I might be at MCV, but it didn't smell like a hospital. It was then that I noticed the portly Black man in a suit sitting in a wooden chair by the door. He stood up without a word and walked over to the bed.

He inspected my face and watched me blink a couple of times. Then he turned and opened the door and left the room.

I tried to lick my lips, but my mouth was dry. Chasing the kid through an alley was the last thing I could remember; everything after that was a blank. My breath was foul and acrid as though I'd been vomiting. Through the window, the droning engine came again as the plane circled back around. It was accompanied by a muffled voice through a loudspeaker. In my stupor, the message was garbled, but as the plane flew closer I could finally make it out.

RICHMOND . . . COME SEE . . . PRESIDENT EISENHOWER . . . AT BYRD FIELD . . . TODAY AT 4:30

It seemed to be playing on a loop. I shook my head but all I heard was the same thing over and over with occasional static. I wondered if they were throwing out leaflets warning about what would happen to white women and children if Stevenson got elected. But that was more of a Harlan Hawkins trick, or a Tricky Dick trick. Who knew? These days, every asshole with a TV set was suddenly an expert on world affairs.

I was starting to wonder where the rest of my clothes had gone when another Black man walked into the room and closed the door. He was dark-skinned and immaculately dressed in an expensive suit, crisp white shirt, and tie.

"You're awake, Mr. Bostic."

"Am I?"

He smiled. "Relax. You've landed in a house of God."

"For my funeral?"

"Not just yet. Rest assured, you are under His watchful eye."

"In that case, God sounds like a plane with a loudspeaker."

He craned his neck toward the window. "It's been circling for about a half hour," he said. "Mr. Eisenhower is giving a campaign speech at the airport later this afternoon. Do you vote, Mr. Bostic?"

"Not since the Fillmore administration. What church, and how do you know my name?"

"All in good time, Mr. Bostic," he said. "Though I should think it obvious that we've been through the contents of your pockets. Imagine our surprise to learn that you're a locksmith."

"What's so surprising about that?"

"Nothing, in and of itself. But it is odd that a locksmith would be chasing a young Black man through Jackson Ward at rooftop level, wouldn't you say?"

"I guess it all depends on the locksmith."

He gestured to a closed wooden door in the far corner.

"Your suit is in the closet. We got it as clean as we could, but I'm afraid it's a little worse for wear."

"Where is here?"

"You fell through the roof of an apartment house in Jackson Ward where an esteemed member of this very church happens to reside. Miss Hattie Jenkins occupies the top floor of the dwelling, and after you dropped in, unannounced, she called her church for help."

"Her church?"

"Who else would she call, the police? Luckily for you, Sixth Mt. Zion has some skilled carpenters in the congregation. Some of them are over there right now assessing the damage you caused and getting started on repairs."

There was a knock at the door, and another man in a suit stepped into the room carrying a black leather doctor's bag. He set it down on a dresser and opened it. He inspected my face, then held each eye open and flashed a penlight into it. He took out a stethoscope and listened to the sounds in my chest and back.

"Am I gonna live?" I asked.

"You got your bell rung yesterday and you've been vomiting, but you didn't sustain any serious damage that I can find. Any nausea now?"

"Plenty," I said.

He wrapped up the stethoscope and stuck it back in the bag, then got out a small brown vial and a hypodermic needle.

"Easy!" I said.

"Relax, tough guy," he said. "It's hyoscine for the nausea. Only fatal in large doses." He filled the hypodermic from the vial, then jabbed the needle into my shoulder. "You should feel better in fifteen to twenty minutes."

"I hope that's all I feel."

The doctor stood and motioned toward the scar he'd seen at the base of my ribcage. "Where'd you get that?"

"Pacific," I told him.

"I was in Europe," he said. "A medic. Black soldiers only of course. Because who would ever think I could treat a white one?"

He blinked at me for a few seconds, then turned and collected up his bag and left. When he opened the door, I got a snootful of breakfast cooking somewhere and my stomach growled.

The man in the chair had been watching patiently. "My name's Washington," he said. "George Washington. My friends call me Darnell, so you may call me Mr. Washington."

"Nice to meet you, Mr. Washington," I said. "I'm Thomas Jefferson, but you can call me Jethro."

Darnell cracked a smile and picked a piece of lint from the arm of his suit. "If the business cards we found in your possession are any indication, you are one R.E. Bostic, a locksmith with a shop on Main. Further inquiries found that you go by Eddie. What's the R stand for?"

"Rots of things," I said.

"Are you always so cavalier?"

"You can't be too careful with the truth," I said. "People always say they want it until they actually get it."

"As an attorney with the NAACP, I'm no stranger to hard truths, Mr. Bostic," he said. "And having recently saved your life and covered your sorry tracks, I don't think a few minutes of your time is asking much."

"So the room and board isn't free?"

"It is not. Oh, if you would care for one of your cigarettes, they're in the night table beside you."

"Good God, yes," I said.

I opened the drawer and found the pack beside my Zippo and a glass ashtray. I lit up and, with a cough, began to feel almost human again. It took me a second to remember to offer him one, but he refused with a shake of his head.

"Filthy habit," he said.

"So," I said. "What's the pitch?"

"As mentioned, we're inside historic Sixth Mt. Zion Baptist Church," he said. "Founded by the Reverend John Jasper, an ex-slave and author of the sermon 'De Sun Do Move.' It was quite famous back in its day; people came from miles around to hear it. Even white folks. Now, Reverend Jasper's church has been spared the wrecking ball, unlike so much of Jackson Ward."

"Divine intervention?"

"All too human, I'm afraid," he said. "Civic leaders waging a very real battle to keep the Turnpike at bay. I don't guess you've ever heard of a woman named Cerelia Johnson?"

I shook my head.

"She's a secretary here who also happens to work as an elevator operator at City Hall. She reports to Pastor Brown daily, keeping him abreast of the latest developments in the corridors of power. That the church will survive is a small victory compared to the roughly eighteen city blocks torn asunder, but a victory nonetheless."

I thought better of mentioning my own issues with the RPTA. "It's a big project," I said instead. "Everyone from south Petersburg to north Richmond is feeling the pinch."

"Perhaps," he said. "But none of those places are known as the Harlem of the South, the very soul of Black culture and commerce south of the Mason-Dixon. That historic designation is why, despite variations elsewhere, the route has consistently targeted Jackson Ward every single time over the last ten years."

"We both know the Ward hasn't been the Harlem of the South for some time. I've seen some of the areas slated for clearance with my own two eyes. Those sections of First Street, St. John, and St. James? Everything up to North Ninth? That's not the soul of anything except poverty."

"Property values are difficult to maintain on real estate that's constantly in the crosshairs."

"The papers all call it slum clearance."

"Crackers like to throw that phrase around when it comes to uprooting Black communities."

There was a knock at the door. It creaked open, and an older woman in a gray dress and white apron came into the room carrying a metal tray. On it was a plate of eggs over easy, bacon, beans, and a biscuit, along with orange juice and coffee. It was the best-smelling plate of food I'd seen in forever. She set it down in my lap and I thanked her. As soon as she left the room, I started in on the food like I was feral.

"Do you know who that is?" Darnell asked.

"Please stop quizzing me on churchgoers."

"That's Emma Simmons. When she's not here, she's a maid."

Between bites, I looked at him. "She's doing a fair impression of one here," I said.

"The first man who was in here when you woke up. His name is Lester. Did he look familiar to you?"

I shook my head.

"Strange," Darnell said. "Lester claims an RPD cop named Eddie Bostic arrested him some five years ago."

I paused, the memory rushing back to me. "I'm glad to see he's changed his ways," I said. "If memory serves, I busted him for running numbers in '48 or '49. All I can tell you is I've had a career change since then."

"Not much of one, apparently. You've simply gone from arresting Black men to chasing after them."

"The kid and his buddies jumped me outside the Eggleston the other night. All I wanted to do was ask him a few questions. I tailed him from the National . . . at least I think."

Darnell was quiet a moment, judging the merits of my story.

"Word has it you're a washed-up ex-cop and failed private eye who sometimes works side jobs as an investigator. When you're not picking locks and making keys for lonely housewives, that is."

"You missed some of the nuance," I said. "I don't know what to tell you, Darnell. I got blacklisted and had to make a living somehow. Life as a burned-out, alcoholic PI with no business prospects looks like fun in the movies, but it's not nearly as lucrative as you think."

Darnell smiled briefly. "The timing of your resignation from the RPD is curious. Wasn't that around the time of the Martinsville Seven?"

"It was."

"Seven Black men executed for the rape of one white woman."

"In one weekend, at the state pen down on Spring Street. I was the detective assigned to walk each man from his cell to the electric chair."

"And I don't suppose that had anything to do with your resignation."

"You're as sharp as you look, Darnell."

"The man who was in here earlier, Lester . . . when he's not here helping out at the church, he's working two jobs. During the day he's a porter at Central Hospital, and at night he works the dining room of Slaughter's Hotel on Second. I've never eaten there, but it's recommended in *The Green Book*."

He was quiet for a minute, and so was I, waiting to see if he was going to bring up the arrest. Then he continued.

"Cerelia, Lester, and Emma are all Ralph Ellison's invisible man. There but not there, because men like you choose not to see them. But invisibility,

Mr. Bostic, is a double-edged sword. Sometimes, being seen is the problem." He paused, then continued. "Despite the sorry state in which you were found, I may yet have a use for you. Would you agree that you look like the average whitey in this town?"

"Remind me to add you to my Christmas card list."

"Do you have plans for this coming Friday afternoon?"

"High tea at Miller & Rhoads."

"Good," Darnell said. "You know where the Belgian Building is on the VUU campus?"

"The one with the tower?"

"Correct. There's a teachers' conference in town this week. No, actually, that's not quite right. There are *two* teachers' conferences here this week. One for white teachers and a separate one for Black teachers."

"Skip it," I said. "Believe it or not, I've heard the spiel."

"Then you know that Dr. Martin Luther King, Jr. is scheduled to address the conference on Friday afternoon."

"I do," I said. "Heard it two or three days ago, depending on what day today is. I wasn't planning to attend if that's what you're hinting at."

"You are now," Darnell said. "Consider it your next side job."

By this time I had finished eating. I placed the tray on top of the dresser by the bed and had my feet on the floor. I was woozy, and for a moment I thought I might taste breakfast again. I stayed put and got my bearings.

"Dr. King is scheduled to give the keynote address this Friday afternoon at four. I'd like for you to work the event as a bit of, well, let's say extra security."

"So the RPD and King's own personal security can't keep him safe?"

"That's not what I'm saying. But as you can imagine, a Black man of Dr. King's stature is not a popular man in the South. He has even received some hate mail from someone who lives right here in the former capital of the Confederacy. Shocking, I realize."

I stood up. My pins were steady enough, but my head wasn't. I braced myself on the dresser and took a breath. The floor at my feet did not spin, and breakfast stayed down. I went to the closet door and opened it. He wasn't kidding about my suit; it was in a bad way. I put on what was left.

"I don't guess I had a hat when you found me?"

"Not even close."

"All right, Darnell," I said. "If you don't mind coming to the point."

"We need you to make sure Dr. King stays safe during the event."

"When you say *we*, who exactly are you talking about? Would I be working for Mt. Zion or the NAACP? Or just you?"

"You would be working privately for me, Mr. Bostic. In return for keeping you from getting dead all over the place."

"Do you have the letter? The hate mail?"

Darnell produced an envelope from the inside pocket of his jacket and held it out. I took it and checked the postmark, but it wasn't much to go on. The letter itself could have been crafted by any racist half-wit from anywhere—lettering cut from a magazine and misspelled threats in primitive handwriting.

"When did he receive this?"

"Last week in Birmingham. We feel this person has been tracking Dr. King's whereabouts and is just waiting for him to show up here."

"I'm sure the RPD is on it," I said.

"I'm less sure."

"Are there any other letters?"

"At least one that we know of, but I don't have it to give you. Trust me, the sender who sent it did not leave a helpful return address."

"Not much to go on," I said. "What happens if I find him?"

"Use your best judgment," Darnell said. He put his hands on his knees. "Unfortunately, you will be unable to reach me directly for the next several days, as I am leaving this afternoon on a plane for Florida. Have you ever heard of Wildwood, Florida, Mr. Bostic?"

"Can't say that I have."

"Until yesterday, neither had I. The only reason I've heard of it now is that the Klan there is up to one of its old tricks. See, the local sheriff takes a Black man into custody and tells him he's going to be charged with a crime. The sheriff keeps him in jail until it's good and dark outside and then says, 'Good news! The charges are dropped.' The Black man leaves the lockup, only to be followed in a car or two by some of the very fine people from the local Klan who offer him a ride. In this particular instance, the man is a farm laborer named Jesse Woods, who is still missing. So Wildwood is where I'm headed. I'm not looking forward to it."

"I don't generally work on the barter system," I said. "After this, we're even."

Outside, the plane with the loudspeaker had circled back and was now directly over northside.

"Depending on your results, we might negotiate a modest fee. But until then, I'm afraid that saving your sorry ass from certain death will have to suffice."

That was starting to sound like the story of my life.

CHAPTER 18
Little Bird #2

After I left Mt. Zion, I found that my legs were not up to a crosstown walk. Hell, they barely got me to the bus stop. I felt ridiculous standing there with my tattered suit and bare head, but the bus came soon enough. I took the #35 to Eighth and Broad. The ride was slow and bumpy, but it gave me some time to think. Between Casey Lloyd, the Turnpike Authority, and now the teachers' conference, I had more than enough to sort out. What I didn't have was a single clue about any of it. I found the van where I'd left it yesterday and arrived at my shop a little after one. As soon as I walked in, a ringing phone greeted me. I picked up.

"Eddie? It's Daisy. I've been trying to reach you all day. What happened to you?"

"Sorry," I said. "I ended up having to work."

"In the middle of the movie? Or did you forget we were there together?"

"I'm sorry," I said again.

"Did you drive out to Chester?"

"Not exactly," I said. "How did the premiere end up?"

"Oh, it was fine," Daisy said. "The Times-Disgrace gave it a good notice, at least. And we got our picture in the paper. You and me."

So there's a "you and me" now, I thought. "I'm sure you look wonderful," I said. "Say, is Mort around?"

She paused. "No, he's not here at the moment. Why do you ask?"

"No reason," I said. "I'll catch up with him later. How much longer are you in town?"

"Paul and Cleo are already gone. There's a screening in Atlanta next weekend. I'm on the Silver Comet tonight at 7:35. Care to see me off at the station?"

"I do," I said. "We can talk about the things some more."

"I'd like that," she said.

I promised I'd see her there and we said goodbye. When the phone rang again, I watched it for a moment and contemplated the nature of free will. I'd just gotten to the part where bills have to be paid and income is good when the ringing stopped. Probably someone locked out of their house or apartment. But at the moment I wanted to get on the road to Chester for a look around Dixie Trailer and Hauling. I was almost out the door when it rang a third time.

"Bostic," I said.

"A little bird told me to give you a call," a man's voice said. It was familiar.

"There's a lot of those flying around these days."

"About a certain stiff found down by the tracks the other morning."

"Who is this?"

"McGivern with RPD."

"Hey, Charlie," I said. "I'm guessing this particular little bird was in a cage downtown, and he sang a few songs in exchange for a favor. Reduced charges, perhaps?"

"Dropped altogether, unfortunately. Damn country's going to hell."

"What is it you need from me?"

"Nothing much, but I thought you might be interested in a shoplifter we just brought in."

"Why would I be interested in that?"

"Funny thing," he said. "You're looking into the death of Casey Lloyd, right?"

"So?"

"Well, according to the ID we pulled off the shoplifter, Casey Lloyd is sitting right here at the station and she's looking right sprightly."

* * *

The trip out to Chester could wait. I drove to my apartment for a change of clothes and circled back to RPD headquarters in the City Hall Annex. It was directly across Broad Street from City Hall itself, a four-story granite monster, gothic in design and incongruous with every building nearby. The annex, by contrast, was a nondescript four-story building of dingy white stone. As always, it paid more to make the laws than enforce them.

Broad Street Methodist stood at Tenth and Broad, the same block as the annex. As I looked for a place to park in front, a light mist began to fall. A minister in a black suit and white clerical collar emerged from the front of the church and closed the doors behind him. He reminded me briefly of my father as he descended the steps and crossed the sidewalk to a car waiting at the curb. I took the spot as they pulled away.

Police headquarters hadn't changed much; it still smelled like ulcers and hair tonic. Charlie's desk was in the detectives' room on the second floor. I thanked him for calling me and told him I was surprised he'd reached out. He looked at me.

"I always thought you got a raw deal, Eddie," he said.

"I appreciate that, Charlie."

"Truth be told, I was surprised to learn you're investigating much of anything these days," he said. "Last I heard, you'd found a new line of work."

"I did," I said. "Turns out there's a surprising amount of overlap."

"If you ever want to go private eye again, just let me know. I can put in a good word for you with the license."

"Thanks," I said. "You'd do that?"

"In a heartbeat," he said. "I don't blame you for doing what you did. As for the reason I called, it turns out our shoplifter has been assigned to another detective, a new man named John Clay."

I went over to Clay's desk, trying to remember where I'd heard the name. He seemed like a decent enough sort, good handshake and suit, who'd recently transferred to the RPD from the force in Jacksonville. He had served in the navy during the war and was still getting used to Richmond and the way things were done here. Fortunately, he hadn't been around long enough to know anything about me. I didn't feel like getting into it, so I introduced myself simply as a friend of Charlie's who was investigating some identity fraud. Clay didn't seem to think anything of it. I sat in a wooden chair next to his desk and noticed the photo of his wife and daughter in a silver frame on his desk.

"You a family man, Clay?" I asked.

"Yeah," he said. "Just got our Cynthia settled in school."

"Which one?"

"St. Patrick's," he said, "in Church Hill. How about you? Family?"

"Still working on it," I said. "So our shoplifter?"

"She doesn't know it," he said, "but the store isn't even going to press charges. If not for the fake ID, she'd be free to go."

"What'd she steal anyway?"

Clay produced a little blue and white tin of Phillips' Milk of Magnesia tablets from his pocket and threw it on the table. It was the saddest crime I'd ever seen.

"From the Peoples Drug at Broad and Boulevard," he said.

"Has she said anything?"

"Some crazy shit about men she says are after her. Claims she's been hiding from them."

"Anything to it?"

"Doubt it."

"Any luck on a real name?"

"Not yet," Clay said. "Running the prints now."

"Can I see the ID she had on her?"

He fished a small blue clasp wallet out of his jacket pocket and handed it to me. Made of Moroccan leather, it was dry but slightly swollen as though it had recently been in water. Inside was a Virginia operator's license issued about a year ago in the name of Casey Lloyd. The address was the same one I'd visited Friday evening on Jeff Davis. The height, weight, and eye color checked out with the autopsy report, the DOB was at least in the ballpark. No cash, just a handful of blurred receipts and a piece of paper with an illegible note in smudged blue cursive.

"When was she picked up?"

"Uniform brought her in this morning," Clay said.

We made our way to the interview room on the east side of the building. The shoplifter was seated at a table in the small room, smoking a cigarette, her fingertips smudged gray with ink. On the wall across from her was a large window with a fogged-up view of McCleary's Restaurant across the street. The window was cracked open, and the smell of cooking hamburgers wafted in with the breeze. It had been a few hours since breakfast and I realized I was hungry. Clay flipped the tin onto the table.

"So, Casey," he said. "What's your real name? We know it's not Casey."

"I never said it was," the woman said. She had a rough face and short dark hair, could have been anywhere from twenty-five to fifty. She was fidgety and couldn't maintain eye contact, a drinker for sure, but unlikely a murderer. She opened the tin and stuck one of the tablets in her mouth, then nodded up at me. "Who's this?"

"A friend," I said. "I think we can persuade the store to drop the charges if you tell us your real name and where you got the wallet."

"Some friend," she said. "You look just like every other bastard cop I've ever seen."

"Maybe," I said. "But I can get you out of here today if you just tell us the truth."

"What makes you think I want to get out of here? This is the safest I've felt in days."

"What is it you need to feel safe from?" I asked.

"Them men who kidnapped me," she said. "Same thing I've been telling this dunce all day." She jerked a thumb toward Clay, who gave me an I-told-you-so look.

"Did you kill Casey Lloyd?"

"Kill her?" she said. "Never even heard the name until I picked the wallet up. Only reason I kept it is cause it's fancy. I wish I hadn't."

"I'm sure it's all a misunderstanding," I said. "What's your real name?"

"Uh-uh," she said. "If I give you that, it's a whole other can of worms."

There was a knock at the door. Clay opened it and spoke quietly with a uniformed policewoman who handed him a folder. He stepped outside for a moment with the door ajar.

I was starting to get a headache but could feel the hyoscine working. "Are you hungry?" I asked her.

"Starving," she said, stubbing the cigarette out. "Haven't eaten since yesterday."

Clay came back into the room reading from a page in the folder. "Lila Cummins," he said. "No outstanding wants or warrants. Spent two weeks in Powhatan County jail in April for battery, petit larceny and suspicion of prostitution. Charges dropped."

"Oh bullshit," she said.

"Fingerprints don't lie," Clay said. He set the open file down on the table in front of me. The mug shot from Powhatan didn't do her any favors, but it was clearly the same woman sitting in front of us. Age thirty-one, no known address, small time rap sheet. Her shoulders dropped as she sank down in her chair.

"Can I have another smoke?" she asked.

"Sure," I said. "As soon as you tell us where you got the wallet."

She sighed and shook her head absently, looking at her hands on the table.

"Can I at least get some damn food?" she asked.

I looked over at Clay, who seemed bored. I motioned him into the hallway.

"She doesn't know anything," I said. "A small-time loser who belongs to the wrong wallet."

"Agreed," Clay said. "Nothing to hold her on. Have you already been out to the address on the permit?"

"Yup."

"Anything to it?"

"Nope. Somebody tossed the place before I got there."

Clay nodded, and I suddenly remembered where I'd heard the name. Herb Ivor had mentioned him at the morgue. I could tell Clay was starting to wonder who I was and what I was up to, but he said nothing. Back in the interview room, Clay said, "Good news, Lila. You're free to go."

"Thank God," Lila said. She stood and straightened her blouse. "I haven't shit in five days, and I have to go right now."

CHAPTER 19

Hot Shoppes

I smoked a cigarette outside and waited for Lila to emerge. Stuck between the station house and Broad Street Methodist was a three-story brownstone that housed the city's social services and welfare department. I took a brochure from a wire rack outside the front door. When Lila finally came out, I handed it to her and told her she could apply there for help. She didn't seem interested.

What she was interested in was food. She mentioned McCleary's but was less keen on it when I pointed out that every hungry cop in the city was probably there. The Peoples Drug lunch counter was nearby, but given her recent history with the chain it wasn't the brightest idea. I suggested Angelo's at Fifth and Marshall, best hot dogs in the city, but Lila sensed a meal ticket. She fixated on the Hot Shoppes Cafeteria across from Thalhimers, which she had passed in her travels around the city. She kept calling it the Hot Shoppeys. She stopped short when we got to my work van.

"What's this?" she asked. "It says locksmith on the side."

"I know," I said. "I'm disappointed too. But if you wanna eat, get in."

She climbed in beside me. I put the van in gear and drove us through the late afternoon drizzle to Seventh and Grace. There were no places to park on the street, so I pulled into the deck located above the Hot Shoppes and found a spot on the third level. The restaurant itself was your basic clean, well-lighted place of beige, brown, and yellow. We sat in a booth under a tall window that looked out on Grace Street. The sidewalk was crowded with workers from C&P Telephone and shoppers from Cokesbury Books and Thalhimers. Moviegoers rushed to and from the Loew's Theater where the WWII movie *Attack!* was playing. Lila and I got the dinner special: fried chicken with dressing, gravy, and cranberry sauce. It seemed like the closest either of us might get to Thanksgiving this year. Lila was not a dainty eater and went back for seconds halfway through. After we ate, I gave her a cigarette and lit it. Then I asked her to tell me what she'd told Detective Clay about the men.

"It was in Manchester about a week ago, I guess," she said. "I'd just spent my last nickel on a cup of coffee at the Sunlight Grill. You know that place?"

"That greasy spoon on Hull?"

"Yeah. They were nice to me though. Kept filling my cup, anyway. I'd just left and was standing out on the sidewalk when this big car pulls up."

"What kind?" I asked.

"Hell, mister," she said. "I don't know. It was a older car with a couple of men in it. They asked me if I wanted to make some money."

"What did they look like?"

"They were in suits and hats. I didn't get much of a look at the driver, but the man on the passenger side was a short little fella."

"What happened next?"

"I'm no dummy. I know when a man offers you money it's only ever for one thing. But I went along. They picked up one other girl and we drove south down Route 1 into Chesterfield. The little fella gave us a flask with some whiskey in it that I shared with the new girl. It was a long trip but almost fun in a way, like a little rolling party. I was pretty drunk by the time we got there."

"Got where?"

"Some abandoned, plantation-looking house out in the woods. Two stories, big white columns in front. No electricity to speak of, just kerosene lamps and candles. We got out and they told us to get cleaned up. There was a well out back and we used that to wash. When I looked up at the house, I saw some other women staring out at us from the upstairs windows. It gave me the creeps. But then the short fella saw me starting to backpedal and told us all to get inside."

"What then?"

"We each got a room. Mine was on the second floor with a door that locked from the outside. Before long I heard a big truck pull up. My room had a view of the front, and I saw a bunch of men piling out of it. They were just a bunch of loud, dirty roughnecks. Later on, one of 'em told me they were from the turnpike clearing crews. For whatever that's worth."

It was worth something all right. Lila shuddered and went quiet. The dining area was noisy with the early supper crowd. At the next table, an antsy, tow-headed brat regarded us like a couple of zoo animals.

"Anyway," Lila continued, "a little later I heard a girl down the hall kicking up a stink about when she was going to get paid. I was starting to wonder about that myself. But then they slapped her around some and that was that. I probably had six men in my room that night and nobody ever said a damn thing to me about money."

The mother of the brat at the next table gave us both a shocked look and put her hands over the kid's delicate little ears.

"Forget 'em," I told Lila. "My money's as green as hers, there's just less of it."

We ordered some coffee, but Lila was in no hurry to leave.

"How'd you escape?" I asked.

"The girls had to beg to use the bathroom. There was no indoor plumbing, just an outhouse. They had a guy who had to take you there and wait for you to finish to make sure you came back to the house. I told the guy guarding me there was no toilet paper and to go inside and get some more. He did and I made a break for it. I found the main road and hitched my way back to town."

"What brought you out to Sharp's Island?"

"I thought if those men came back looking for me, they wouldn't think to look there. The island looked safe. There's a big house on it."

"Don't take this the wrong way, but do you know why they picked you?"

"Random, I guess," she said, shaking her head. "Who knows how any of those girls ended up there? Most of 'em weren't talking English. I'm just glad I got out."

We collected up our things and made for the door. When we were back outside it was dusk. I asked Lila where she was headed.

"I don't know," she said. "I could use a roof over my head. I've slept out in the open on that stinking island all I can."

"Can't say I blame you," I said. "There's a YWCA on Fifth Street not far from here. Can I drop you there?"

"Okay by me," she said. "So long as I don't have to be no goddamn Christian."

CHAPTER 20

Blue Light, Red Light

Outside the Y, I gave Lila ten bucks along with my business card and told her to call me if she remembered anything. I was about to drive off when I remembered the tin of Milk of Magnesia in my pocket, so I called her back and gave it to her. She'd earned it. When she went up the brick steps and vanished inside, I sat for a moment by the curb with the motor running. Facing south down the hill on Fifth Street in the fading October light, the chimneys of Gamble's Hill and the smokestacks of Tredegar stood before me in hazy silhouette. A few blocks ahead, the C&O elevated line ran parallel to the river's north bank. Even at this distance and over the noise of rush hour, I could make out the rumble and churn of an eastbound locomotive hauling coal.

I checked my watch and remembered I'd promised to meet Daisy at the station by 6:30, which didn't leave me much time. I arrived as her Yellow Cab pulled away. We found a porter for the luggage and made our way up the steps to the front of the station. Outside the main door a bluesman had stationed himself, a guitar case open in front of him. He was playing Robert Johnson's "Love in Vain," which I'd first heard years ago in Kansas City on my way home from the war. I didn't much appreciate the message, but I left a dollar and some change in the case anyway. If nothing else, it was a nice version.

The station's dining room was noisy and packed, but Daisy and I secured a table for two by a window and ordered a couple of beers. By this time she was composed but not quite herself.

"Hungry?" I asked.

"No," she said. "Just ate."

"Me too," I said. "Everything all right?"

"Oh, yes," she said. "Fine."

"Fine, huh? That can't be good."

"No, it's not that. I just remembered this is the last place I saw Archie alive. Mom and Dad and I saw him off in the spring of '42. He was headed for training down in Alabama. I remember him leaning out the window waving goodbye to us as the train pulled out of the station."

"There was a lot of that going around back then."

"I try not to think about it, but it's hard not to when I'm here."

"Is that all that's bothering you?"

"No, I'm worried about Dad."

"What happened?"

"Nothing," she said. "I just hate that he's here all alone."

"He seemed chipper enough Friday night," I said.

"Sure," Daisy said. "In a house full of people with his hands busy and no time to think. But when he's all by himself in that big empty place, I think he gets lonely."

"Invite him out to L.A.," I said. "Some time with his grandson in the California sun might do him some good."

"I would," she said. "But I'm afraid of what he might see if he came out there."

"Is this what you wanted to talk about?"

"Tip of the iceberg." She looked away and worried the sleeve of her blouse for a moment, then glanced around the room.

I placed my hand on hers, and our eyes met once again. "Is your husband violent with you or your son?"

"No," she said. "Not yet anyway. But I'm terrified of him regardless. I would have left him by now, but he has control of the money."

"That's what lawyers and accountants are for. I can give you enough money to get you and your son back to the East Coast."

"Eddie, if only it was that easy. I have a career to think of."

"And a kid who loves you," I said. "Look, I can't tell you what to do. What do you want me to say?"

"I need guarantees, Eddie."

I smiled. "Such as?"

"If I moved back home, I could live with Dad for a while until I got back on my feet. But I need to know if you would be there for me."

Our beers arrived. I told the waiter we wouldn't be eating and paid the tab.

"Course I would," I said. "That's all I've wanted since you left."

She looked me straight in the eye. "Is that a guarantee?"

"Yes," I said. "I'll put the investigating aside and make my money as a locksmith. There's good money in it and a stable life for you and your son. For us."

Daisy looked at me as though trying to divine the future. With a tear in her eye, she lifted her glass. "To old times."

We clinked our glasses together and took a drink. "How old?" I asked.

Daisy didn't answer, then went quiet. She set the drink down and ran her fingertip along the lip of the glass. She smiled. "Do you ever wonder about how things might have been different?"

"Every day," I said. "It's too pretty not to."

She nodded. "It's funny. Every generation that comes along thinks they've got it all figured out. How they're not going to make the same mistakes as their parents, or they're going to make more money and be smarter and make all the right choices and none of the wrong ones and live perfect little lives."

"Sometimes the choices aren't ours to make," I said. "Sometimes they're made for us, and we just have to make the best of it."

"Yes," she said. "But even then, people still find a way to screw it up."

"Like I did. When do you get to Atlanta?"

"7:20 tomorrow morning. The studio arranged a sleeper. Wanna see it?"

"Sure," I said.

We gathered up our things and made our way through the crowded station to the main platform. Around us, men in suits and women in dresses milled around the concourse to the echo of station announcements over the PA. The Seaboard Air Line passenger cars were being cleaned by a legion of Black workers in neat black and gray uniforms. The Silver Comet had arrived from D.C. not long before, its green and yellow locomotive idling under the train shed. Now headed farther south, a coach marked "Colored" had been coupled behind the engine and was separated from the rest of the train by baggage cars. I couldn't tell when this boxcar ballet had taken place, but it was clearly more out of respect for Jim Crow than the law.

We stepped aboard and sidled past the cleaning crews on our way to the Pullman sleepers. Daisy had a double bedroom, slightly larger than the roomette and plenty cozy. It was heavy on the wood paneling with an olive-green ceiling. The heavy bench seat by the window converted into a bed, and the cabin had its own private bathroom. And as it turned out, its own locking door.

I closed it behind us and set her bag down on the luggage rack. We were together alone finally for the first time in three years. And yet seeing her now, on this night and in this moment, I wouldn't have guessed that so much as a day had passed. Daisy turned to me and stood on tiptoe and reached up to pull me closer. I took her in both arms and lifted her off the floor and kissed her. She leaned her weight back just enough, and I lost my balance as we fell into the chair mid-embrace. In the hallway outside, the decent and well-mannered travelers of the Silver Comet traipsed by, their carpeted footsteps occasionally punctuated with conversation. Daisy and I stopped and listened for a moment.

She put her index finger to her lips and made wide eyes at me as we both laughed. In seconds we resumed. I got her coat off and pulled the blouse free of her skirt and then started in on the buttons, while she made similar progress with my belt and trousers. I pulled her skirt up around her waist and freed her garters. As I pushed into her, she let out a gasp and wrapped both legs around me. Outside in the hallway, a porter bashed against the door with an errant cart.

"Oh, excuse me, ma'am!" he said.

I pushed deeper in her and buried my face in her neck. Despite the years between us, the scent behind her ear was instantly familiar, an echo of our past. I felt momentarily guilty at having not shaved that day and eased off, only to have her pull me in closer, a handful of my hair in her fist. She moved forward in the seat and took me all the way in. There were more voices out in the corridor, and someone tried rattling the door handle.

"Oh, is this the right cabin?" an older woman's voice asked.

Daisy shifted her weight forward and tackled me to the floor without missing a beat. We landed with a thump. I grabbed her hips as she grinded against me quietly and quickly and steadily until she suddenly tensed and stretched her legs against mine. Her mouth opened but didn't make a sound. She covered my mouth with her hand, and somewhere in that absurd, careening, silent symphony, I lost control and came.

Someone knocked at the door, and an older man's voice said, "Hello?"

"Just a minute," Daisy replied, then said quietly to me, "Get up!"

Her feet got tangled in my pants leg, and she fell to the floor beside me. The voice out in the hallway spoke again.

"You stay here, dear," it said. "I'll go see if I can find that porter."

Daisy and I got up and dressed hurriedly. I had no idea what to say to her or if I should say it, or where I would even start. When we were both dressed and vaguely presentable, Daisy took one last look at her reflection. When she turned away from the mirror, she looked at me in a way that was at once completely familiar but also utterly alien. Then she slapped me hard across my left cheek.

"God damn you, Eddie," she said.

I pulled her toward me and kissed her, but she pushed me away. Then she picked my hat up off the floor and jammed it into my chest. I'd never seen anyone go from happy to enraged quite that quickly.

There was a light knock at the door, then the jingle of a key fumbling for the lock. The door opened a crack. When the porter saw us, he touched the brim of his gray cap and turned his eyes to the ground.

"'Scuse me, folks," he said. "But I think y'all might be in the wrong cabin."

CHAPTER 21

The Sextant

As it turned out, that was exactly where we were. We found Daisy's ticket and sure enough, she was booked in cabin eight whereas we were in cabin six. An honest mistake we assured everyone, with repeated apologies. The older woman in the hallway seemed to understand. Further, she suggested that Daisy stay right where she was, and she would take Daisy's roomette instead. A sensible offer. The porter made a note of it in his book and that was that.

After they'd left for the cabin next door, the conductor appeared down the center aisle and announced in a crisp voice that Seaboard Air Line train #33, the Silver Comet, direct to Atlanta with stops in Petersburg, Raleigh, and Athens, was departing Main Street Station. I stood for a moment and looked at Daisy like an idiot. I knew what we both wanted to say, as much as I knew that neither of us would say it.

"You need to go," she said.

"Seeya in the funnies," I said.

I put on my hat and stepped into the corridor as the door slammed shut behind me. I made my way to the back and jumped onto the platform as the train lurched forward. Outside the station, the bluesman had decamped, but his mournful tune lingered. I smoked a cigarette in the shadow of the streetlight as the train's last cars cleared the overpass. When their noise and echo lifted, the street was quiet, and Daisy was gone from my life once again. I wondered how it was I kept losing this woman, over and over. Each time it hurt a little more than the last.

Across the street in my shop, I went to a desk in the back and just sat there in the dark. After a minute, I clicked on the light and took a half-full bottle of Old Stagg bourbon from the bottom right drawer. I downed one shot, then another. The label claimed it was aged six years, which certainly included time spent inside the stag. I was tired but forced myself to pack some boxes and take them home. It wasn't much, but it gave me something to do besides sit there and think.

* * *

I awoke the next morning with a headache behind my left eye. For a moment it seemed the stag had kicked me, but then I remembered the concussion I'd sustained over the weekend. I rooted around in the nightstand drawer for some aspirin, then got up and went to the dresser. In the bottom drawer was an old pair of work pants too snug at the waist. I found a denim shirt in the closet and a smelly blue ballcap inappropriate for any occasion save this one. A paint-spattered pair of work boots completed the look. On my way to the shop, I grabbed a quick breakfast at City Diner just a few doors down. They had a "Going out of business" sign in the window; Friday was its last day. All anyone there could do was gripe about the damn Turnpike.

The first of my errands was to Dixie Trailer and Hauling in Chester. I was greeted by a locked door and deserted storefront. I could have picked the lock pretty easily and would have, save for the slobbering mastiff inside. The back of the lot was full of trailers similar to the ones I'd seen at the RPT worksite. Thoughts of scaling the chain link for a closer look were discouraged by yet another mastiff. But the trip was not a complete waste. In the gravel parking lot, I found a chewed Mohawk Chief cigar stub with its bright red and yellow band. It matched the one I'd found along the tracks in Shockoe Bottom. I made my way back into town.

Halfway across the Fourteenth Street Bridge, I pulled the van into a dirt lot on Mayo Island, a tapered stretch of land in the middle of the James. Now home primarily to Overnite Transportation, a trucking company, and a couple of service stations, the island had once hosted the city's baseball park, Tate Field, now just a memory. A trestle for the Seaboard Air Line had run parallel to the right field fence. Legend had it that once during an exhibition, Babe Ruth had hit a ball so far over it that the ball landed inside a passing coal car and kept going, making it the longest homer in baseball history that didn't count for shit.

The Richmond Boat Club was another vestige of that era; fortunately, it was still in business. Housed in a three-story brick building on the banks of the James, the club was quiet in the middle of a gloomy fall Tuesday. I backed into a space near the entrance reserved for one of the club's muckety-mucks and sat for a minute, eyeing the steady stream of cars and trucks going to and from the island. I got out and lit a cigarette and followed a line of vehicles toward the eastern end of the island.

Lo and behold, I was among my fellow contract employees working to make the Richmond-Petersburg Turnpike a reality. Unlike me, these men brought actual skill to their labors and were employed by a different contractor, Bowers Construction. At the moment, they were putting the finishing touches on a temporary work pier that stretched from the south bank of the James to the eastern tip of the island. I squinted through the trees across the river. A series of cranes angled into the sky above the white concrete stumps of the interstate support columns sprouting up from the water. I was reminded of nothing so much as the first fish in prehistory flopping to shore and deciding it would rather be an amphibian.

I stepped toward the bridge. The sound of hammer to nail filled the air, accompanied by the sound of a crosscut saw as two men worked to fell a large tree. I kept going past them, then dodged a cement mixer on its way off the island. I found a white hard hat resting on a table and put it on. The pier was constructed of rough, unprocessed timber, much of which appeared to have been live trees only the day before. Bits of scrap wood littered the area along with the musk of fresh sawdust.

Workers came and went from the pier, and with my hard hat I fit right in. There was, however, one Black man in a suit, raincoat, and hat standing at the middle of the pier. He was tall and lanky and sketching carefully in a notebook. Resting on the pier in front of him was a metal bucket that held a large, rusted anchor that appeared to be quite old.

"Evening, professor," I said.

The man put the finishing touches on his sketch, then closed the notebook and tucked the pencil behind his ear. He had long, delicate fingers and was quite young, with expensive glasses and angular chin hair. He looked at me like I'd escaped from Tucker's Sanatorium.

"Can I help you?" he asked.

"I expect so," I said, motioning toward the bucket. "What are we looking at?"

"A ship's anchor," he said. "From the late Eighteenth Century or early Nineteenth."

"You can tell that much just from looking at it?"

"Yes," he said. "They're not common, but in all likelihood it's from a slave ship of that era named the *Sextant* that was lost near here. But I won't know for sure until we get it back to the lab for study."

We both regarded it for a moment. It was a piece of dark, heavy, corroded steel in the familiar anchor shape with a loop at the top. A bent metal bar passed through the loop and was attached to a short length of rusted chain.

"Which is why you're here."

He adjusted the glasses on his face. "How perceptive."

"Where's the lab?" I asked.

"Virginia Union, where I am an adjunct professor. Which is why I was taken aback just now when you addressed me as professor."

The platform creaked and swayed as the river raged at its pilings, a cold wind rising off the water. The hollow echo of heavy boots filled the air as men passed around us in conversation. A few feet away, a team of concrete workers caught my eye. They were standing atop the rebar floor inside a cofferdam that had been driven into the riverbed maybe a week ago. When the mixer arrived, it would pour the concrete for what would eventually be a T-shaped interstate support column. Further south down the pier, a handful of them were in various stages of completion.

My curiosity satisfied, I thanked the professor for his information and went back to the boathouse.

CHAPTER 22

Blue Heron

A neatly terraced sloping path led to the back of the clubhouse. There I found a series of four wooden garage doors, three of which were closed and padlocked. The fourth was open, and I could hear the sound of someone working inside. I approached and knocked.

"Yeah?" a voice growled.

I peered into the darkness and could see a man about twice my age sanding the bottom of a small boat balanced across two sawhorses. He had short gray hair and was dressed in shorts, a black turtleneck, and deck shoes. He was muscular and had a sort of permanent tan that leathered his skin. It seemed entirely possible the old salt had paddled his way out of the womb.

"I need a boat," I said.

"You don't say."

"Is now a bad time?"

"No," he said. "Just not expecting company. Hold on."

He put the sandpaper down and went over to a small desk against the wall. He picked up a notebook, licked a finger, and flipped to a page toward the end. He asked for my name. I gave him an alias, since that was who I seemed to be at the moment, and offered to show him an ID. He scribbled it all down in a ledger.

"Destination?" he asked.

"Bailey's Island."

He looked up from his notebook. "That's upstream," he said. "Water's high. Purpose of trip?"

"Blue heron."

He raised an eyebrow. "You don't look like much of a birder," he said. "That's two-fifty."

I dug into my pockets and paid up. He gave me a receipt that I tucked into my shirt pocket.

"This way," he said.

I followed him over to a rack of boats standing against the back wall. He picked out a wooden dinghy and reached up with both arms to tip it forward. I grabbed the bow, and we lugged it outside to a large ramp that led to a short wooden landing.

"Set 'er down," he said.

We plunked the boat down in the water, then he vanished back inside. A breeze off the water made me zip my jacket. When the man came back out, he was carrying two wooden oars in one hand and a round white life preserver in the other. He tossed everything in the boat, and I climbed in.

"Have 'er back by four," he said.

I secured the oars and started rowing. Soon I was moving under the concrete arches of the Mayo Bridge and thinking this wasn't such a bad thing after all—cool wind in your face, a little exercise, some fresh air in the lungs. Two minutes later, I was cursing the boat, the water, and every last Phoenician who ever thought this was a needful way to get around. I unzipped my jacket and threw it across the bench opposite me, then wiped the sweat off my brow and started rowing again.

I wasn't going to Bailey's Island. My destination instead was Sharp's Island, a wooded, one-acre scrap of land in the James south of the Mayo Bridge. Like everything else in and along the river, Sharp's was prone to flooding. As real estate locations go, it left something to be desired, but that didn't stop somebody from sticking a house right on top of it. The house had a brick foundation and basement, then another two stories on top of that, with a wraparound porch. A brick chimney ran up one side to a pitched metal roof. On a gray and misty day like this one, the place would give Edgar Poe himself the creeps.

I brought the boat up to the shore at the nearest point, then got out and tied it to a tree. I put my jacket back on and pulled the bill of my cap down as drizzle fell. It was a longshot, but I was looking for anything Lila Cummins might have discarded from Casey Lloyd's wallet. I was assuming there was something else in the wallet besides cash and identification, and that it might still be here. The river level had risen since Lila had been here, so anything left by the shore would have washed away by now.

With one eye on the house, I worked my way east along the water's edge. I grew clammy as the sweat on my T-shirt cooled. I found a child's red wagon rusted through, a torn blanket covered with mold, a wet mitten on the branch of a tree, some broken beer bottles and rusted cans, and an old wool sweater stuck between two rocks. What I did not find was evidence that anyone had recently stowed away here for several days. By the end of my second circuit of the island, I'd learned exactly nothing.

I walked up to the front of the house and stood in wet sand at the base of the wooden staircase. The porches on the upper and lower levels made the place look bigger than it actually was. The lower one was cluttered with cardboard boxes, bottle crates, wood scraps, and discarded building materials. It had a tall door and two large windows covered with curtains. I climbed the rickety steps and gave the door a knock, but no one answered.

Around the side of the house was a door to the basement, but it was locked up tight and wedged shut with river stones. In the back was a woodpile not far from the house, and near that the remnants of a recent campfire. I ran a stick through the damp debris and turned up a few pieces of singed paper. I knelt down and picked one up, turned it over, and blew the dirt off. It was a business card, slightly mottled and burned on its right edge. The embossed blue and yellow logo was faded, but instantly familiar in a way I didn't want it to be. There was also a handwritten name on the back along with a phone number whose last digits were lost to the fire. I was turning this information over in my head when the cold end of a gun barrel nudged the back of my neck.

"You might want to not move, friend," a man's voice drawled behind me.

"Not moving," I said.

"Hands in the air," he said. I sensed him taking a step back. "Stand up and turn around slowly."

I did as he said and found myself facing a wiry young man with a lazy eye. He was holding a Remington pump-action shotgun on me and looked more than ready to use it.

"You the owner?" I asked.

"Shut up," he said. He spat a stream of tobacco juice. "You armed?"

"No."

"Show me."

Slowly, I unzipped my jacket and lifted the right side and then the left.

"Awright," he said. "What are you doing out here?"

"Having a look around."

"What for?"

"A woman," I said. "She spent a couple of days here. From the looks of it she made this here fire." I gestured toward the ground with my head but kept my hands in the air.

"I weren't here last week."

"Well, she was. And that's why I'm here now."

He lowered the shotgun. "Awright," he said. He motioned with the barrel toward the other end of the island. "Go get in your boat and get the hell off this island."

He didn't have to tell me twice. He walked about five yards behind me across the island until I reached the boat. I untied it from the tree, shoved off, and started rowing. When I looked back at the shore, he had vanished among the trees as though he'd never been there. Maybe he never had.

CHAPTER 23

Businessmen

Thankfully, the return trip was downstream. The man at the boat club was surprised to see me, as if he'd fully expected me to drown. We guided the dinghy up the ramp and back into the clubhouse. By this time, he was drinking out in the open. The glass in his hand and open bottle of rum on the desk were a dead giveaway. I managed to get away before he started in with a sea shanty. As I walked back to the van, the muscles in my upper back were none too happy with the waterborne exertion.

Back at the shop, I checked with my messaging service. I'd missed calls from JW Coulson, Darnell Washington, and Randy Daigle. It was good to know I was missed. Randy was the only one I wanted to talk to, so I rang him up.

"Randy," I said. "What do you have to say for yourself?"

"I'm not going to apologize, if that's what you're getting at," he said. "I did what I had to do to get out of lockup."

"Understood. But now, thanks to you, I have to worry about tripping over the RPD while I work."

"Not my problem," he said. "Besides, something tells me they're not exactly going out of their way to solve the murder of some homo."

"Maybe not," I said. "But they might if they figure out who his family is."

"Speaking of which," Randy said. "I have news that may be of interest to you."

"Such as?"

"Uh-uh," Randy said. "In person, mister. Information is worth something."

"Funny," I said. "You got it free the last time we spoke."

"Fine," he said. "Maybe I'll see if that nice Detective Clay is interested. He's handsome in a hangdog sorta way."

"He'd just as soon bust you as talk to you. Can't you spill it over the phone?"

"Sure," Randy said. "Way back when, Casey Lloyd was part of the scene. The poor thing, his dick was pitiful. Everybody called him Princess Tiny Meat."

"Helpful," I said. "Is that the quality of information I can expect in person?"

"Only one way to find out."

I sighed and closed my eyes, massaged my left temple. "All right," I said. "When and where?"

"The back room at Benny Sepul's, tonight at seven-thirty."

"Back room, huh?" I said. "I guess that's why you like it there so much."

"Eddie Bostic, have I ever told you how hilarious you are?"

"No."

"There's a reason for that," Randy said. Then he hung up on me.

I made another call to a contact in Jacksonville who worked for the *Florida Times-Union*. I asked him if he'd ever heard of a cop named John Clay. As it turned out, he had.

* * *

I went back by my apartment and got cleaned up. The last thing left to eat in the icebox was a half sandwich of unknown provenance and a sad pickle. A good title for my memoir, should I live that long. If the mold on that sandwich was the kind that cured polio, I was set for life. I left it where it was and drove to the Admiral Security offices at the Hotel King Carter. I had information to use for bait, and this was the only way to make them take it.

In the lobby, the coffee shop was closing for the day, but the cigar stand and news kiosk were still open. I went up the stairs and past the elevator through a door with a logo labeled Admiral Security. It was the same logo on the business card I'd found in the ashes at Sharp's Island.

The lobby was as cozy as the interior of a bank but less cheerful. It had high windows and bright fluorescent light, all new furniture, carpet, and paint. It had a row of square offices with hardwood doors, each accompanied by a secretary's desk. The nameplates were black with white lettering. I walked past the receptionist without a word over to the row of desks until I found Mort's office. The door was closed.

"Is he in?"

"Mr. Williams asked not to be disturbed."

"How long am I not supposed to disturb him?"

"He didn't say."

She gave me a look. The clack of typewriters filled the air around us. I stood for a few seconds and looked around. Then I heard a thump inside Mort's office, then someone crying out in pain. I looked down at her as she stared at her keyboard.

"Your concern for your fellow man is touching," I told her.

"Mr. Williams is not my fellow man," she said. "He is my boss."

The typing carried on in the background. I went past her, opened the door, and stepped into the office. Mort was leaning against the front of his desk holding his forehead in his palm. He lowered his hand to reveal a red blotch and a trickle of blood from a cut. I closed the door and went over to him, gave him a clean hankie, and told him to hold it against the cut.

"Jesus, Mort," I said. "What the hell?"

"Looks like I can't hold my liquor anymore," he said. "I tripped."

"I don't suppose you have an ice pack," I said.

"Actually, I do," he said. "Lower drawer."

I dug it out and filled it with some cubes of ice from a bowl on the drink tray, where a bottle of whiskey sat empty on its side.

"Stupid me," he said. "What brings you here?"

I went over to him and gently pressed the pack to his head. He looked like a different person from the one I'd seen Friday night. His eyes were moist and bloodshot, circled by rings deep as trenches.

"Work," I said. "I have an assignment with one of the RPT work crews tomorrow north of Petersburg. Look, I know what's going on, Mort. You don't have to hide it from me." I took out the business card I'd found on Sharp's Island, the one with the Admiral Security logo and Mort's name and title just below it. "Your home number is on the back of this, in your handwriting."

He shook his head and wiped away a tear.

"Is it all worth it?" he said. He bowed his head and broke into silent sobbing.

"Mort," I said. "I can help you. That's why I'm here."

He sniffled. He was holding my hankie in one hand, the ice pack in the other. "All this trouble in life," he said. "We do it all thinking there's going to be some reward in the end, but there never is. It's just more trouble. Why do we do we put ourselves through it all?"

"I dunno," I said. "Maybe the cheeseburgers."

It wasn't my best work, but he laughed to break the tension. "What would I do without you, Eddie?" He clapped his hand across my shoulder and squeezed.

I leaned in and looked at him. "I know about Casey Lloyd," I said. "I just don't know how or why."

His face straightened up. "I just got the news about him," he said. "Maybe fifteen or twenty minutes ago. I can't say I care much for hearing news anymore. It almost always seems to be bad."

He blew his nose into my hankie. I got up and made us both a drink and handed him his. He tossed the ice pack aside, then brought the glass up to eye level and finished it in one gulp.

"I wanted it to be something good, y'know. That something decent would come out of all this."

"Mort," I said. "Just tell me how you know Casey Lloyd."

"It's not just that," he said. "What this company does is monstrous. What I do for them makes me complicit."

There was an assertive knock at the door. They tried the knob but found it locked.

"Mr. Williams," a man's voice said. "Is everything okay?"

"Yes," Mort said.

Whoever it was wasn't convinced. I heard a set of keys jingling.

"Friends of yours?" I asked.

"Co-workers, I'm afraid," he said. He lowered his voice to a whisper. "There's proof in the cabinet, I assembled it myself. Documents and pictures, it's all there. The missing Wynant girl is mixed up in it."

A couple of heavies came in, real friendly like. The first one was my old buddy Buford, whose shoulder I had dislocated a few days before. He looked at me and drew his gun.

"Howdy, Buford," I said.

"Well, looky here." He gestured with the gun for me to raise my arms. "Up."

The second man came over and frisked me; he was a short little guy with a mean face. He grabbed my wallet and looked inside. "Bostic Lock and Key," he announced, reading one of my cards.

"You got a name?" I asked the short man.

"Miller," he said. "Mick Miller."

"Let's take a little trip downstairs," Buford said, waving the gun toward the door. "After you, locksmith."

"Put it away, old man," I said. "It makes you look small."

He holstered the weapon as we went through the door into the hallway. Mort followed us out. We made our way past the sour-faced secretary and the small, mean-looking man stopped. Mort stopped and spoke to him.

"I'm sorry, Mr. Miller," he said. "There's really nothing to it. Eddie's a friend."

They stayed behind as I was frog-marched out of the office and into the open corridor toward the mezzanine. We came to the stairs that led down into the busy lobby.

"Did Shemp take the day off?" I asked.

We reached the bottom of the stairs and were headed for the side entrance when we took a left down a wood-paneled hallway. We came to a door that said Billiards Room and went inside to a large open room with four pool tables. Sure enough, a friendly game was in progress at the very first table between a couple of hoods in cheap-looking expensive suits. One of them leaned over the table in mid-shot. He arched an eyebrow under his fedora and paused with his cue, then took his shot and missed. The balls skittered across the table toward me with a sharp clack as the two men behind me closed the door.

"We don't take kindly to having our employees harassed," said the man with the gun behind me.

The second man went over to a rack and grabbed a cue. For some reason he didn't bother to chalk up. He just stood there wielding the cue with both hands.

"You guys are not cut out for the hospitality business," I said.

I grabbed the 8-ball off the table and spun around toward Buford behind me. I slammed the ball into the side of his head; he fell screaming with his scalp split. I turned and stepped into the throw as the other man holding the pool cue braced for impact. He went down quick when my low throw caught him in the nuts.

The other two men looked at each other. I grabbed the 3-ball and gave one of them some chin music that shattered his front teeth. The impact made a wet and sickening sound as he fell to the floor in a screaming heap. The fourth man took a swing at me with the cue, splintering it across my back. He jabbed the broken end at me twice. I grabbed it and yanked him forward, then put my knee to his stomach. I finished with an uppercut that put his lights out.

As they lay there groaning, I went back to Buford who was reaching across the floor for his gun. Blood dripped into his eyes and onto the carpet. I stepped on his hand with my heel and leaned down and picked up the gun. Then I straightened my coat and tie, found my hat.

"Tell your boss he knows where to find me."

CHAPTER 24

Benny Sepul's

On my way out, I cracked the revolver in two and dropped it into separate trash cans. It was a shit weapon, a cheap .32. My shoulders and arm were sore, and the cue stick had left a welt on my back, but otherwise I was intact. It was nice to know my arm was up to throwing a few fastballs. I had seen that trick in Honolulu once when some MPs tried to subdue a mean drunk in a pool hall. They caught the worst of it—the rest of us just kept our heads down and waited for the dust to settle.

It was dusk, the store-lit sidewalk crowded with office workers heading home and shoppers hunting bargains. I smoked a cigarette at the side entrance of the King Carter and waited to see if anybody followed. Nobody did. I retreated down Eighth Street and found my van where I'd left it, in front of St. Peter's Church. I retrieved the pictures from the glove box.

Benny Sepul's was on Grace next to the Capitol Hotel. Up front it was a quiet little mom-and-pop joint that catered to the usual crowd, nothing to see here. But behind a door in the rear of the dining area was a back room that catered to queers. It wasn't the best kept secret in town, but it was secret enough, and the cops left them alone for the most part. I checked my watch and saw I was a little early. There wasn't much point in going back there without Randy, so I took a seat at the end of the bar and ordered a Richbrau.

In the mirror behind the bar, I found the usual assortment of straight couples having dinner. At the other end of the bar was a businessman with a drink who looked over at me when I walked in. He raised his glass to me in the mirror and took a drink. I was still agitated from the brawl and just looked away. He mumbled something into his mug and downed the rest of it in one gulp. I wasn't hungry, but I asked the bartender for a menu and looked it over absently. A cigarette machine stood by the door to my right. The man at the bar got up and walked behind me over to it and started digging in his pants pockets for change. He found a couple of coins and made a bit of a show of pulling out the lining of his empty pants pocket.

"Brother," he said, "can you spare a dime?"

I fished one out of my pocket and placed it on the bar.

"Thanks," he said. "That's one I owe you."

"Forget it," I said.

He gave me a sour look and pulled the lever that released a pack of L&M's into the tray, which he stuck in the breast pocket of his jacket. On the way back to his seat, he stopped and looked at me.

"You know, friend," he said. "If you don't like what's on the menu, maybe you should find someplace else to eat."

"Drift," I told him.

At that moment, Randy walked in the front door. He immediately recognized my friend at the bar.

"Harassing the straights again, Charlie?" he said.

"Fuck you, Randy," he said.

"Not on your best day."

The bartender came over and told them to can it. Randy looked at me and jerked his head toward the back.

"Shall we?" he said.

I finished my beer and followed him through the door to the back. There wasn't much to it, just a dimly lit burgundy room with three booths on one side and two on the other. In the corner was a small stage, empty at the moment, with a mic stand and wooden stool. Only one of the booths was occupied. The two men sitting in it looked over at us as we took our seats on the opposite side.

"Is it always this busy?" I asked Randy.

"Idiot. It's early on a Tuesday night," he said. "If you stick around, you might see something that tickles your fancy."

"Pass," I said. "So, what's the skinny?"

"Easy tiger," Randy said. "You can at least buy me a beer first."

A waiter appeared from a dark hallway that led to the kitchen. He and Randy seemed to know each other. Thankfully, there were no introductions. We ordered some beers, and the waiter left to get them.

"Friend of yours?" I asked.

"More of an acquaintance," Randy said.

"So. What's the word?"

"Casey Lloyd found his way to the scene about four years ago. He just appeared one day, fresh-faced and skinny as a rail, which does appeal to a certain . . . type, I guess. Not me, of course, but some men like their little boys skinny and rough. That was Casey to a tee."

"I'm underwhelmed so far."

"Well, Casey liked being the new kid in town, so he did that for about a year, by which time he was no longer new, and people lost interest. But apparently it was mutual, so he up and left the scene one day. Word has it he got kicked out of his place on Hanover by whoever was paying for him to live there."

"Any idea who that might've been?"

"Some sugar daddy named Sam. I'd guess that wasn't all he was paying for. But they had a falling out, and Casey ended up in some dirt-cheap place off Jeff Davis. Nobody knew what he was up to, but there were some guesses."

"Did you catch Sam's last name?"

Randy shook his head.

"What were some of the guesses?" I asked.

"Rough trade, tricks, the occasional grift. I mean, Casey had his trust fund, but it looked to others like maybe he was saving up for something he didn't want anybody to know about."

"There are other places in town he could have lived and still saved money."

Randy shrugged. "I don't know why he chose there. Why does anyone live in Southside?"

I shook my head. Randy ducked in and whispered, "Word is he was not above the occasional honey trap."

"No kidding."

The beers arrived and I paid for them.

"He would find some unsuspecting closeted sap looking for love along Jeff Davis. No shortage of 'em—most are married men with families. Casey gets a room and gets the mark into a compromising position, then an accomplice with a camera pops out to capture it all for posterity. By this time, of course, they've gone through the poor jerk's wallet and gotten his address. He'd better pay up unless he wants his family to see the candids."

"Speaking of which," I said. I took out the envelope with the pictures and slid it across the table. "Anyone in here look familiar?"

Randy smoked a cigarette as he shuffled through the pictures one at a time. His expression didn't change the whole time. He looked at me and shook his head no. I asked him to take a closer look at the picture of Lamar Clemons, but Randy was certain he had never seen him before. I collected the photographs and put them back in my pocket.

"Did the name Mort Williams come up during your research?"

"Williams? Yeah, he was a mark. The old guy fancied himself some sort of father figure and Casey was playing it up. Spending time at his house and taking money when he needed it."

"Did you hear how they met?"

"A random encounter on Jeff Davis, I think it involved a broke down car. Casey was in the right place at the right time, or the wrong place at the wrong time depending on how you look at it."

"Did the name Admiral Security come up?"

"No. Say, did you know it was written into the trust fund language that if Casey Coulson wanted to keep his stipend, he had to live inside the city limits? He could travel but not relocate. Isn't that shitty?"

"That's old Virginia money for you," I said. "Nobody ever made it by being nice."

* * *

I'd hoped for more, but the information was not useless. I gave Randy a ten and told him to keep his ears open. Along with the beer, ten bucks was more than the information was worth, but I was tired and sore and ready to get out of there. I left through the front, passing Charlie still at the bar. I stepped outside and lit a cigarette in the cool drizzle, then got in the van and drove home.

CHAPTER 25

The Sticks

I arrived the next morning at the Bellwood parking lot. In the dim gray light, a number of white school buses were lined up and idling, the damp air heavy with diesel exhaust. The faces I saw looked a lot like mine: white, unshaven, and tired. Some of the men clustered together, their noise and laughter punctuating the quiet. Others milled around alone on the periphery or gathered in quiet groups of two or three, seemingly unsure if they wanted to work. In another part of the lot roped off from ours, Black workers congregated near their own buses. Between the two groups was a short line in which both Black and white workers stood. At the head of the line was a wooden table where two men were seated. I got in it and lit a cigarette. When it was my turn, the man on the right took a sip of coffee from a Styrofoam cup and asked me my name.

"Valentine," I said.

The other man at the table found my name on a piece of paper on a clipboard and placed a check mark beside it. The first man asked to see my hands, which I showed him. He inspected both sides a moment and looked up at me again.

"Crosscut," he said to the other man at the table.

The other man wrote the word "Forman" onto a slip of paper and handed it to me.

"What's this?" I asked.

"You're on the crosscut saw team. Your foreman is Forman."

"The foreman's name is Forman?"

The first man looked at the other one. "Hey, we got Bob Hope over here," he said. He jerked his thumb and barked, "Next!"

I wandered off to the right. Before long there was a shrill whistle, and both groups of workers began lining up slowly near the buses. A voice through a megaphone announced, "Five minutes!" Watching a reluctant group of men follow orders made me feel like I'd rejoined the army. I found the largest one and asked if they were Forman's crew.

"Fuck you, bwah," an older man said. His grizzled chin was slick with tobacco juice.

Everyone in his group laughed. I didn't. Almost before I knew it, my right hand was around his throat and squeezing. His eyes bulged and he made a gurgling noise. The laughter around us was replaced by surprise. I stared him down as he grabbed my wrist, his face crimson.

"You got anything else to say?"

I released him as some men pulled us apart. I couldn't say what had come over me, other than I was tired of taking shit from rednecks. But that wasn't what I was here for, and worse, I'd drawn attention to myself when I was supposed to be blending in. I watched him gasp for air across from me. He glared at me without another word.

"Over there," somebody else said. I looked over and saw a kid in chinos, a denim jacket, and blue baseball cap. He popped his bubble gum and pointed at the next group over. "Have fun."

I found the foreman Forman and helped load the long saws onto the bus through the open rear door. Then I took a seat on the bus toward the back. Minutes later we were loaded up and pulling out of the lot, heading south on Jeff Davis. Before long, our convoy had passed Old Mill Road and moved outside the city limits.

During the long and bumpy ride, I noticed most of the men were accomplished bus sleepers. I myself nodded off a time or two, but was jostled awake each time by a pothole or backfire. When I glanced at the men around me, few had felt the turbulence. I kept my ears open for idle talk but heard nothing. As we passed the parking lot at Dixie Trailer and Hauling in Chester, I noticed two men standing beside a pickup. One of them was the short white man I'd seen the night before outside Mort's office. The other was Lamar Clemons.

My seatmate was a stocky guy in a black knit cap whose primary contribution to the world was BO. With his humped back, wiry orange hair, and matching beard, he looked like some species of troll native to Richmond. I tried the friendly approach.

"Valentine," I said to him, extending my hand.

He stared at my hand, then at me. "Don't make friends, mister," he drawled. "If you last one day out here, I'll eat my hat."

I didn't blame him. In the army, nobody got chummy with the new guy. Having once been a replacement myself, I'd seen it firsthand. But if my luck was in, my work out here would be done quickly, and this guy would never have to know me. At Route 10, some of the buses turned east toward the first work site, then a few more toward the second one at State Route 618. A few minutes later, our bus turned left toward Walthall and eventually came to a stop on a dirt road in the middle of a heavily forested stretch of land near Swift Creek.

"Up and at 'em, ladies!" said the megaphone voice.

The driver killed the engine, and I heard the familiar groan of men stirring for a day's work. We filed off the bus and began unloading equipment. In addition to the long saws, there were axes, hatchets, and machetes—all recently sharpened. Above us towered all manner of birch, oak, elm, maple, and sycamore ablaze in red, orange, and gold as their leaves changed one final time.

"Valentine!" a voice said. "This way."

I turned just in time to catch a shovel flying at me. It was Forman. He was deeply tanned and lean, in a plaid shirt, twill pants, and straw fedora. He smoked a pipe and had a habit of speaking out of the side of his mouth. He led me to a gathering of four workers by the side of the road and addressed the group.

"Breaking in two new men today," he said. He paused briefly and motioned with his pipe at me and at the freckle-faced kid standing nearby. "Valentine and Boyce. You two are working shovels. That's Powell and Burnett on the crosscut, Inge and Rideout on axes. Water break in two hours, lunch at noon. Do what these men say, and you won't have any trouble. Watch for snakes."

With that, Forman bounded off to the next group. The two beefy country boys in charge of working the crosscut nodded.

"Y'all heard the man," Inge said.

They each picked up an end of the saw, then turned and started walking into the woods. Inge and Rideout followed alongside, axes over their shoulders. The forest floor was choked with brambles, saplings, fallen limbs, and standing deadwood. The more experienced men strode through it like Paul Bunyan. I did all right, but Boyce struggled to keep pace, mumbling to himself. He reminded me of a kid named O'Hara from the twenty-seventh. He was Irish-Catholic, and one day we were advancing through a sugar cane field on Saipan when I heard him saying his Hail Marys. He believed that the last words we say in this life are the ones that carry over with us into the next, and he wanted his to be Christian just in case. O'Hara's actual last words were, "It's shiny," whispered as he bled out in front of us under a jungle canopy, the medic still working.

After a few minutes, we came to a rectangular strip of cleared land that stretched south to the horizon. To our left was a neat pile of recently felled timber stacked ten feet high. In the middle of the clearing, a team of Black laborers was using a tractor and rope to pry a boulder loose from the ground. The engine growled and belched thick fumes into the air. We stopped and watched for a minute while waiting for Boyce to catch up.

"Awright, y'all," Powell said. "This is where we left off last evening. You shovel boys get to work on those stumps there. Use a axe if you need it."

What followed was four hours of the hardest physical labor I'd done since leaving the army. After twenty minutes, I was in a full sweat and had cleared just one stump. I leaned on the shovel and smoked a cigarette, wondering how I'd survive until lunch. The idea of an open-ended investigation out here was not appealing. The guys who'd turned down this gig before me must have felt pretty smug about it by now.

"You there!" Inge called out. "No loafing!"

Attempts to pry information out of my co-workers about much of anything were fruitless. As it turns out, approaching someone you've only just met and asking them about their involvement with prostitution can get a little awkward. The simplest and most innocent remark can be easily misconstrued. Toward the end of the water break, I made the mistake of approaching a man dressed in neat work clothes who was standing off to one side.

"Boy," I said, "I sure could use some pussy about now."

He sniffed the air and walked away without a word. A few yards away within earshot, another man with a slight Southern accent spoke up.

"You ain't gonna get anywhere with him, Bo. He's a fine man, a Christian man."

I walked over to where he was standing in the shade. "What about you?" I asked.

"What about me what?"

"Are you a fine, Christian man?" I asked.

"Only on Sundays."

"So how 'bout it then?" I said. "I heard we get women."

"Bo," he said, grinning, "what on earth makes you think there are any women out here?"

I was starting to wonder the same thing. I took out a crumpled pack of Luckys and offered him one, which he took. When I offered him a light, he noticed the Zippo.

"Can I see that?" he asked.

I flipped it to him. He studied the scuffed finish with the red and black logo of the twenty-seventh Division on one side.

"You in the service?" he asked.

Since I was supposed to be someone else at the moment, I just gave him a nod.

"Me too," he said. "But I never saw any action. I was in the navy but didn't get to Japan until the occupation."

I gave him another nod and exhaled some smoke.

"I tell you what, Bo," he said. "I like you. If it's women you're after, just wait 'til Friday. They got us a whole setup at a house close by."

"Is that so?"

"Yeah, every Friday since I started. A big ol' place out in the woods. They got beer and some of the prettiest little Mexican girls you ever did see. And if you don't like those you can always get yourself a white girl."

"How do we get there?"

"Taken care of, Bo. They drive us out and back."

"Okay," I said. "Count me in. What do I do Friday?"

"Just work your shift like usual. I'll look for you around quittin' time," the man said. Then a whistle blew and break time was over.

CHAPTER 26
Dirty Work

We joined the group gathered around the water buffalo. On the edge of the group, I noticed the small man I'd seen the day before outside Mort's office at Admiral Security, the same one I'd seen earlier this morning talking with Clemons. He was dressed in outdoor work clothes and didn't look at all out of place. He stood on the group's outskirts talking to Forman, who then pointed in my direction. The small man squinted at me for a moment, then turned and vanished into the crowd.

By lunchtime, I had uprooted three more stumps. The last one was a real bastard. My hands were blistered, and I was covered in sweat and grime. I sat down on the ground to eat a sandwich and kept my ears open for scuttlebutt. One man nearby kept referring to his food as his *lunchcake*. I'd never heard the term before, but some parts of the Commonwealth had their own strange lexicon. Maybe someone would teach me one day.

In the Pacific, a kid from the Bronx named Manny Flores had taught me some Spanish. He was first-generation Puerto Rican American, had a mustache, dark hair, and a deep tan from too many days in the field. Nowadays my Spanish was pretty rusty, but I still remembered some of what I'd learned. It was handy on occasion. I noticed a small group of Hispanic workers taking their break away from the main group. When they spoke at all, it was in hushed tones, so I couldn't make out what they were saying. But I made a note to talk to them before the day was out.

After I finished lunch, a form of rigor mortis set in. I was lying on my back with my arm over my eyes about to doze off when Forman came back around to the group and found me.

"Valentine," he said.

"Yeah?"

"Having fun yet?"

I sat up. "Not exactly."

"That's fine," he said. "How about something a little lighter?"

I looked around at the rest of the crew beginning to stir and knew they were a dead end as far as my investigation went.

"Swell," I said.

"Follow me."

* * *

I was paired up with two heavyset men working a field of knee-high grass. I didn't catch their names, but they looked none too smart. One of them was my buddy from the Bellwood parking lot. He turned and looked at me, a fresh wad of tobacco in his jaw. He spat.

"Sup, bwah?" he said.

I could see the marks my hands had left on his neck. He hefted a machete, the other man an axe. I myself was given a set of dull loppers and was told to use them on every bush and shrub I could find. As we walked, the man with the machete stayed several paces ahead and swiped lazily at the grass, while the man with the axe stayed several paces back with it slung casually over his shoulder. Neither appeared interested in working.

We crossed the field and approached the tree line. I stopped walking as the first man advanced into the forest and disappeared from sight. I thought back to my time in Hawaii, where our training involved defending yourself against whatever weapon the Japanese might use on us. One of those weapons was a bolo knife, similar to the machete. The only trouble was I'd forgotten most of it.

"Hey, Valentine," he said, laughing. "You gotta see this."

The second man came up behind me and gave me a nudge with his elbow. "C'mon," he said. "It's fuckin' hilarious."

I followed him into the woods. He joined the first man who stood at a small campfire clearing near a rotted tree trunk. I walked over to see what they were looking at.

"Payback's hell," he said.

He lunged and swung the machete at me with a crossbody slash that ripped the front of my shirt. He followed that with another hard slash which I ducked, then a flat horizontal slash aimed at slicing open my midsection. I jerked back and tried to block it with the loppers. They shattered on impact, leaving me with two broken sticks for self-defense. I tossed them away and kept my hands low, moving from side to side.

The second man took his turn at my head with the axe, but the weapon was too heavy for him. I dodged and his momentum took him directly into the path of my fist, which caught him once in the stomach and once on the jaw with an uppercut. He dropped the axe and fell to the ground. The machete man brought the blade back around for another swipe at my innards, then jabbed at me. I sidestepped it as the man with the axe got to his feet.

The man with the machete raised it over his head but brought the strike down in a wild arc that missed. Before he could set his feet, I pivoted to his right, grabbed his wrist with my right hand, and straightened his arm. I elbowed him twice in the cheek, snapping his head back, then popped his elbow with my left hand and felt his sweaty grip loosen. Then I palmed the flat base of the blade above the handle and wrestled it away.

The axe man held it in front of him with both hands like a baseball bat. He took a swing at me like a batter letting loose on a pitch, but missed and lost his balance. I brought the machete down across the side of his neck, and at first I thought I'd missed because I hadn't felt the contact. Then he screamed and put his hand over the deep gash as blood spurted through his fingers. He stumbled and dropped the axe and fell to one knee, the wound gushing blood. He screamed again, got to his feet, and took off running for about ten yards into the woods. The screaming continued for a few more seconds before he spun in a circle and collapsed.

The first man approached me, his eye on the axe behind me. Crouching, we moved in semicircles while I caught my breath.

"We don't have to do this," I said.

He spat, then charged and tackled me with both arms around my torso. We landed in a heap on the forest floor, his hand on my wrist. I shoved my palm under his chin as he pounded my wrist into the dirt. The machete fell free again. He dove for it and found the handle. Before he could right himself, I flipped him onto his stomach and drove my knee into his back and saw that he had landed near the shattered wooden handle of the loppers. It was about a foot long, one end smooth, the other a mass of splinters. I took an end in each hand and worked it under his chin, then pulled up against his windpipe. He began thrashing violently, still gripping the machete. I gave the stick a sharp tug and heard a crack as his windpipe gave way. He made a gurgling sound and stopped moving.

I threw myself off and landed face-up on the dirt, breathing hard, my heart pounding. Hazy sunlight filtered down through a canopy of blazing leaves, and I heard the shrill cry of a mockingbird. The nausea was on me quickly; I flipped onto all fours and vomited. After a moment I was still dizzy, so I stayed in place another minute with the two dead men. I pictured their spirits hovering above the scene, trying to figure out what had just happened. *Better them than me*, I thought. I felt a burning sensation on the skin of my chest and when I felt through the torn fabric of my shirt, my fingers came back slick with blood.

I went to the nearest man and rolled him over. His bearded face was a bluish gray, his tongue speckled with dirt and debris. I checked his pockets but found only a few damp dollar bills and a set of keys. I took it all and dragged him by the collar down to the riverbank, then did the same with the second man. Somebody would come looking for them soon but setting both afloat down the Appomattox might buy me a little time. I didn't think they'd mind.

CHAPTER 27

TNT

I walked west along the wooded riverbank, following the sun on its dappled arc toward the horizon. It was warm, so I stopped and tied my denim shirt around my waist. The cut on my chest had coagulated, but my T-shirt was torn diagonally and clammy with blood and sweat. I peeled it off and tossed it in the river, then kept walking. After a few minutes, I came to an area where the trees thinned. I made my way to the edge of a lumpy, rectangular strip of ground that had been clearcut some weeks earlier. About two hundred yards away was an overgrown and abandoned plantation house, similar to the one Lila Cummins had described. I crept in for a closer look and crouched down behind a bush.

Parked in the front yard next to an idled bulldozer sat a '52 DeSoto. I made a mental note of the license plate as two men in work clothes came out the front door, toting together a large wooden crate by its handles. The first man was Mick Miller and the second one was John Clay. They brought the crate to the DeSoto and placed it gently in the trunk. Both were smoking cigarettes, which looked like a risk given that the letters stenciled on the side of the crate were TNT. Then they got inside and drove off down a narrow driveway that vanished into the forest.

I sat still for another minute or two, watching the house and listening for signs of life. There were none, so I decided to have a look around.

Despite the muddied tracks of several heavy vehicles, I saw no other cars around. Though the property looked deserted now, it had been used for something recently. There was trash in the muddy front yard, broken bottles, and abandoned tires. It seemed like someone had tended the property until a decade or so ago, but now the structure was in poor condition. There were some outbuildings in back, just as dilapidated and ramshackle as the main house. Unless I missed my guess, those had been slave quarters.

The front left columns of the house were engulfed in ivy. I eased up the steps to the porch. It was late afternoon, the temperature dropping. I put my shirt back on and read the condemnation notice nailed to the door, a Dear John from the RPTA. Through a broken pane in the front window, I could see the living room was deserted. The door creaked open at my touch and I stepped inside. The reek of cigarettes and cheap aftershave lingered in the air. The only furniture was a mattress in one corner next to a short table with a kerosene lamp on top. I went through a few of the rooms and found an old mattress in each. The floors were cluttered with papers, old books, empty beer bottles, and a few records.

In one of the rooms, I found a thin black belt. I reached down and picked it up, and even in the dusk the design on the buckle was immediately familiar. It was part of the uniform worn by schoolgirls at St. Patrick's, silver embossed with the school's logo. I rolled the belt up and stuck it in my back pocket.

That was when I heard a noise from upstairs, the groan of a floorboard in the room directly above. I froze, knowing the men who wanted me dead were unlikely to stop now that they had me on the run. Whoever was here in the house with me was either part of that effort or an innocent person about to get caught up in it. Either way, I needed to find out who it was and fast. I found the staircase and crept up to the landing on the second floor.

Each door down the long hallway was closed. A window at the end cast a gloomy half-light on the proceedings. I went to the door where I'd heard the noise and tried the knob, but it was locked from the outside. I undid the lock and flattened myself against the wall and gave the door a firm push. It opened to reveal a large room strewn with trash and a mattress on the floor between two large windows. I stepped inside and felt the floorboard soft underfoot, making the exact noise I'd heard earlier. I checked the windows and found them both painted shut, one missing a pane. Across the room was a closet with the door shut.

"Whoever you are, you should come out," I said.

To my surprise, the handle began to turn. I tensed myself for an Admiral Security thug, but was greeted instead by a young Black woman with very dark skin. She was wearing a tattered, knee-length yellow dress smudged with dirt. In her hand was a metal fork which she pointed at me, right arm extended. She had wide eyes that darted from me to the room's open door behind me.

"Don't you even fuckin' think it," she said.

I raised my hands palms out. "I'm not here to hurt you. My name's Eddie."

"I don't give a damn what your name is, mister," she said.

She jabbed the fork at me and angled for the door as I backed away.

A man's voice shouted from the front yard. I looked out a window, and in the last of the light, it was just possible to see three men with long guns and torches approaching the house.

"Shit," I said.

"Who's that?" the young woman asked, still pointing the fork at me. "Friends of yours?"

"Not exactly," I said. "Look, I don't know who you are or what you're doing here, but these men are here to kill me. And if they kill me, they are certainly going to kill you. Do you understand?"

"Not really," she said. "But it makes as much sense as anything else that's happened to me in the last day."

"We can get into that later, but right now I need you to trust me. You can lose the fork. What's your name?"

She eyed me suspiciously for a moment, then lowered the fork the tiniest bit. "Millie," she said quietly. "Millie Staples."

"Stay here, Millie. I'll be right back."

I ran to a window at the rear of the house and found a fourth man holding a shotgun and a torch standing on the lawn. I returned to the front room and saw the three men getting into position across the front.

"Valentine!" the first one shouted. "Or Bostic, whatever the hell your name is. We know you're in there! You may as well come on out!"

I looked at Millie. "How well do you know this house?" I whispered. "Any secret passages or a side entrance?"

"Hell, mister, I don't know. I saw it for the first time yesterday."

The man on the front lawn called out again, "Easy way or the hard way!"

"All right," I said to Millie. "Come with me."

I took her hand, and we retreated into the hallway together.

We went through the house looking for anything that might be of use. The rooms were sparsely furnished and cluttered with refuse. In the near dark it was hard to see anything for sure. Millie found a crowbar inside a hall closet; it wouldn't do us much good in a gunfight, but it was better than nothing.

The man on the front lawn called out again. "Valentine!"

We were on our way to the kitchen and headed for the basement door when I tripped over a heavy wooden crate on the floor outside the pantry. Although I could guess what was in it, it wasn't until I found my Zippo that I could make out the stenciled black letters: "TNT 24 count."

"This should help," I said.

I took the box with us back up the stairs to the second-floor room facing the front lawn. I checked the window again and saw the two men still standing out there holding torches.

"Light him up!" shouted the man outside.

The men stepped forward, and I lost sight of them as they disappeared under the front porch roof. I could smell smoke through the broken window as the dead shrubs in front caught fire.

Millie handed me the crowbar. I had handled TNT once on Saipan when I helped unload some cargo for the Seabees. Which is not to say I was an expert, but it hardly mattered. These days, TNT even came with instructions that said it was meant only for construction purposes, and that unauthorized use could result in serious personal harm, even death. I took a stick in hand and lit it, then went to the window. I broke the glass with my boot.

"Be right out," I said.

I coughed at the rising smoke, then checked the fuse. It was ready. One of the men took a shot at me and missed, so I chucked the stick out the window in his direction. I heard him shout before the explosion tore through the air. More gunshots rang through the room, shattering what was left of the window. Millie helped me lug the crate into the hallway where we set it down at the top of the stairs. Downstairs the room glowed orange as the smoke rose. I told Millie to stay with the crate.

I took another stick to a back bedroom where the windows were broken out. Still holding his torch, the man stationed out back had his shotgun pointed at the door waiting for me to come storming out. He looked a little jumpy. I lit the fuse and paused, then tossed it at his feet. With both hands full, he kicked at it spastically, but his boot caught mostly dirt. He screamed as it exploded in a flash of orange heat, flipping his body into the air like a rag doll.

I found Millie in the hallway and grabbed her hand. We raced down the stairs to the back of the house amid thick, choking smoke and raced past the outbuildings to the tree line. When we were some distance away, we stopped to catch our breath and watch the old place burn. With all the gunfire, explosions, and screaming, I nearly forgot where I was and who I was fighting. I looked back and thought I might see the Japanese in pursuit.

When the house fire found the crate of dynamite at the top of the steps, the explosion blew the house to bits in a conflagration that would have made Alfred Nobel proud. We turned and started making our way south toward the Appomattox River.

CHAPTER 28

Emma

Living in a city makes you forget what real darkness is—desolate, deserted backwoods darkness. In the Pacific at night, it was possible to look up and see the arm of the Milky Way extending through space. It was almost that clear tonight, just a thumbnail moon lighting our way. I was tired and hungry; I knew Millie was too. We'd been walking for a while before she finally spoke up.

"You know where you're going, mister?"

"Not exactly," I said. "I figure if we head south long enough, we'll find Petersburg."

"We'll hit my house before that," she said.

"Is that so?"

"Yeah. It's a little cabin on the south bank of the river. I was staying there with my grandmother and brother when I decided to take a walk."

"When was that?"

"Yesterday morning. Won't make that mistake again."

"What happened?"

"I took our boat and rowed across the river, then got out and started walking. It was a pretty day. I packed a lunch and ate it. I guess I lost track of time. It was getting dark, and I was about to turn around when I saw that big house. There were some people hanging around, so I went up for a closer look. And then I got too close."

"Someone saw you?"

"A man with a rifle. He must have been guarding the place or something. Told me to get back inside, like I was trying to get away. If I'd known what was going on inside, believe me I would have. He walked me to the back of the house and kept his gun on me until I went inside."

Millie was quiet for a minute or two. I knew better than to press the point, so we walked in silence until we reached the riverbank. The land clearance continued across the other side. If everything went according to schedule for the RPTA, the spot where we were standing would be an interstate bridge in two years' time. Now, though, it was just a quiet and muddy strip of land along the Appomattox. The only sounds were the animals and insects that lived there and the heavy slog of our footsteps in the muck.

Across the river, I saw a lantern glowing yellow on the other side. I wiped my eyes with the sleeve of my shirt, but the light stayed there, as though looking out across the water.

"Is that your place?" I asked.

"I think so," Millie said. "The rowboat should be around here somewhere." After another minute of walking, we came to a series of abandoned cabins nestled among some trees. One of them had a small wooden dock with a johnboat tied to it. We went over and untied it, then jumped in and shoved off with the oar. Before I started rowing, I looked at Millie sitting across from me.

"Before we get there, can I ask you one last question?"

"If it's about that house, I'd rather not."

"I just need to know how you came to be locked in that room."

"It happened this morning. A bus pulled up, and they started loading all the women on it. When they came for me, I hid in the closet. Nobody besides that one guard knew I was even there in the first place, so they didn't look for me. After everybody was gone, I wanted to leave, but a couple of men downstairs stayed behind and didn't leave until just before you showed up. A few minutes before that, they came through and locked all the rooms on the upper floor."

I checked to see where the light was burning and rowed in that direction. The current was strong, and I could feel my back muscles still sore from the day before. There was a crosswind on the water, and about halfway across, the light blinked out and the shore was dark as ink. I stopped for a minute to see if it would come back on, then started rowing again through the blackness as straight as I could. After about two more minutes, we ran aground on the south shore. The boat had drifted east slightly, but we still landed near the shack.

I lashed the boat to a tree and we made for the shack. As we approached, I could smell smoke from lamp oil mingled with burning pipe tobacco. I took Millie's hand.

A gunshot tore through the night and kicked up the ground maybe six feet in front of us. We hit the dirt, and I covered Millie with my body as a second shot rang out and landed closer, spraying us with dirt and decomposing leaf matter.

"Jesus Christ!" I said.

"That's close enough, river man," said an old woman's voice.

Millie stuck her head up. "Grandma, quit shooting! It's me!"

"Show yourself, child!"

I stood slowly and helped Millie to her feet. We began to make our way to the cabin. Halfway there, I tripped and fell, landing face first in what appeared to be a shallow trench. I righted myself and sat up against the side. As my eyes adjusted, I could make out the silhouette of an idled backhoe at the other end. The earth was freshly dug and cool to the touch.

I could hear what sounded like Millie and her grandma reuniting, the words unclear but the sounds of their voices loud and high and relieved. I thought about standing up and climbing out, but who was I to disrupt that moment? Plus, the hole I was in felt safe, which I hadn't felt in a while, and I was reluctant to come out. I sat, enjoying the cool and the quiet. That is until I smelled fish frying, and my stomach growled in response.

As I stood, a sound came from the edge of the trench above me. I looked up and saw Millie's silhouette peering over.

"What's cooking?" I asked.

Millie turned her head and looked toward the house. "He says he wants to know what's cooking."

"Crappie," the old woman answered. "With some collard greens, bacon, and black-eyed peas."

"All right," I said. I raised my hands to the lip of the trench and lifted myself up. Once out, I brushed myself off and took a step toward the house. Millie and her grandma were halfway up the front porch stairs, the lantern lit on the porch once again.

The old woman stopped at the top of the stairs and turned to Millie. "Lord, child," she said, the stem of a pipe in her mouth. "You sure gave us a fright." She took Millie's hand with her unarmed one, then Millie kissed her grandmother on the forehead.

"I'm okay, Grandma," Millie said. "This is Eddie, he helped me."

I waved from the bottom of the stairs. "That's a lovely hand cannon you have there."

"This here peacemaker was my daddy's, and he served in the Rough Riders with Teddy Roosevelt."

Maybe guns weren't such weird gifts after all.

* * *

The old woman invited me to take a seat on the top step of the porch, which I did. Then she sat in a chair on the porch, no longer aiming the gun at my head but not putting it down either. In the halo of amber light, I could see she wore round sunglasses, an ankle-length flannel dress, and a green wool cardigan. She felt for the cardboard box of shells at her feet, took out two, and reloaded the ancient pistol, all while facing me. Millie had vanished inside the house.

"You lucky, river man," she said. "I'm a damn good shot. You get lost too?"

"More or less. Now I'm just trying to get back to Richmond."

"There's a road not far from here," she said. "They're doing a bunch of work for the interstate though."

"Looks like they're doing some in your yard too," I said, gesturing to the trench I'd fallen into.

The old woman was quiet. She took the pipe out of her mouth and spit into the night.

"Do you still live here while they're doing all this?" I asked.

"No," she said. She gestured toward a young man inside the shack. He was enormous and could see me well enough through the window. I gave him a nod which he did not return. "I live in Petersburg with him. Moved in last month."

Her name was Emma Staples, she told me. She'd been born in Petersburg eighty-five years ago and had been blind since birth.

"That's my grandson, Ronald, frying fish inside," Emma said.

She cleared the pipe's bowl with a whack against the arm of the rocking chair, then reached into the pocket of her sweater and took out a small leather pouch. She pinched some tobacco into the bowl and then set the pipe down inside a brown ceramic ashtray that sat atop a short side table.

Ronald appeared on the porch with two pie tins of food. "Here you go, Grandma," he said.

She reached for the tin and set it on her lap, then picked up the knife and fork and started eating. Ronald handed me the second tin and I started greedily. He disappeared back into the kitchen then reappeared with his own tin. He sat down in a chair beside Emma.

"You is a good boy, Ronald," Emma said. "Where's your sister?"

"She's gonna eat inside after she's done cleaning up."

I took a breath from eating and thanked them for the food. Ronald nodded, and Emma told me I was welcome. Watching them eat, I realized they both had better manners than I did. The hulking Ronald even ate with his pinkies out. I finished before either of them and could have eaten another tin right then and there. Instead, I just held it in my lap.

When we'd all finished, Ronald collected up the tins and brought them back inside. I tried to remember the last time I'd been this grateful for a meal.

"Will you be our guest for the night, river man?"

I had no watch but knew it was plenty late. I should have been exhausted, but as I sat there listening to the darkness surrounding the cabin, my heart was about to pound through my chest. I felt like I was hearing things that weren't there. If something were to happen, I didn't want to be inside an unfamiliar house surrounded by strangers.

"I might trouble you for a blanket."

"A blanket?" Emma said. "What on earth?"

"Nothing personal," I said. "I'd just feel better sleeping outside."

"Too good to sleep in here with us, is that right?"

"No ma'am," I said, "but after the day I just had, I can only sleep in a foxhole."

Emma was quiet for a few seconds as she considered the request. "Suit yourself," she said. "Ronald, get this man a blanket. Not one of the good ones."

Ronald gave me a look, then got up with the lantern and went inside. I heard him open a door and drag a box across the floor. A few seconds later, he returned to the porch and tossed a light-colored wool blanket at me.

"Thanks," I said.

"If you trying to get to Richmond, I'm headed that way in the morning," he said.

"I'd appreciate that."

"You know where your foxhole is, river man?" Emma asked.

"I think I can find it," I said.

I stepped off the porch and made my way to the trench, surrounded by the noise of frogs and crickets and the sort of darkness I hadn't known in a dozen years.

***

My experience out in the woods this afternoon had dredged up all sorts of pleasant memories, most of which featured explosions and tracer fire from the night of the Japanese Banzai charge. My hole in the ground felt just fine. It may come as no surprise to learn that on Saipan I fought a Japanese officer. In the years since, I've thought of him often, envisioned him as the purebred heir to a distinguished line of ancient warriors. I don't know if he was, of course, but I do know that in his hand was a samurai sword, a beautifully crafted weapon with blood on the blade. There he stood along some train tracks on an island far from home, facing off against me, an American mongrel armed only with a fixed bayonet. I bet his ancestors are still giving him grief for coming out on the short end.

That was also the night Archie Williams was killed, and the two events were nearly simultaneous. He was crawling back to the line with his feet blown off when I saw him. Amid that orgy of killing and madness, I lifted him in a fireman's carry and started back for the command post for a medic. The bloody sights I encountered along the way are the ones I try to keep buried—our wounded being hacked to death, in some cases beheaded. So many dead Japanese. When that officer with the samurai sword materialized in front of me out of the haze, he actually let me place Archie down on the ground, like it was part of some ceremony. As I did, I said, "So long, Archie." I don't know if he heard.

The fight itself didn't take long. Thanks to my M1, I had a reach advantage and was well-trained in bayonet fighting. I also knew that if I failed, Archie was next. So I did what I had to do to give us a chance. There were no heroes that night; they were all killed. All that was left on that dark beach were the living and the dead. I don't know how many other men I killed that night, but sometimes I'm afraid I'll see them all again one day. It was the last time I'd murdered someone in hand-to-hand fighting before today. I hadn't missed it one bit.

CHAPTER 29

White Man's Road

Early the next morning, Ronald honked the horn of his pickup and started the engine. He came over to the trench and told me he wasn't going all the way to Richmond but offered to take me as far as Colonial Heights. I gathered up my bedding and left it on the porch. I thanked Emma for her hospitality and climbed into the truck.

The drive north was quiet until Ronald spoke up. "You was hollerin' out there last night."

"I was?"

"Like a wild animal."

After a moment, I apologized. I wasn't sure what else to say so I said nothing. It wasn't exactly news that I sometimes had screaming nightmares that woke others. In my defense, it had been a while. I stared straight ahead at the line of cars in front of us.

We came to some construction traffic on Jeff Davis. An RPTA work bus had been in a minor accident. The workers milled around outside it smoking cigarettes. A few dump trucks and bulldozers sat idle nearby. We came to a halt and Ronald spoke up.

"It been like this since summer. Getting worse all the time."

"Get used to it," I said. "You might not recognize the place after it's all said and done."

"All this," Ronald said, "just for some damn highway."

I felt a little guilty for my own part in it, working for the Turnpike Authority. I looked at my hands, dirty and calloused from digging. Hands that had also murdered two men the day before, a third at the house with TNT. Self-preservation for sure, but I was still queasy from it.

Ronald and I were quiet for another minute until we came up to the accident. One of the work buses had hit a deer; it lay half-pinned under the busted front grille.

"Seeing more of that too," Ronald said. "Wildlife coming through town to get away from the clearing crews. I almost hit one the other night, no lie."

We got clear of the scene and picked up speed.

"I did a lot of living in that old house by the river," Ronald said. "Grew up there for the most part. My granddaddy owned it. Good neighbors, peaceful. Lots of wildlife."

Traffic slowed again as a bulldozer crossed the road a few cars ahead.

"You know what I see when I look at all this?" Ronald asked.

"What's that?"

"A white man's road," he said. "Going through a Black man's home."

* * *

Ronald let me out at a strip mall in Colonial Heights. After failing several times, I finally hitched a ride north on Route 10 from a man in a '53 Chevy. He was a salesman from Short Pump wearing a cheap suit and straw hat. He was a big fan of Harlan Hawkins, a Richmonder who'd inserted himself into the presidential race as a candidate for the States' Rights Party. Hawkins's platform called for a return to isolationism and an abolition of the income tax, ironic given that he had once served as the Virginia Commissioner of Revenue. But mostly Hawkins was an old-fashioned segregationist who didn't want the Feds getting in the way when it came to keeping Black folks down south of the Mason-Dixon. He may have had the Klan vote sewn up, but I doubt he scared Ike.

The salesman was too busy talking to ask me who I was or what I did, but I would have lied about it anyway. He dropped me off a couple of blocks from my van near the Bellwood. From there I drove home and got cleaned up. I called and checked my messages. No word from Vince, of course. I wondered if he'd taken the mechanic's version of the Hippocratic oath: First, Do No Work. My only call was from Darnell Washington, and I didn't call him back. I checked in with Malone and Gettle at the Turnpike Authority. Or at least I tried—neither one was available. I left a message to expect my report soon. The belt from St. Patrick's I'd found at the abandoned house wasn't their concern, but they had a right to everything else.

* * *

Inside the RPD detectives' room, John Clay sat at his typewriter, filling out a report hunt-and-peck style. He seemed surprised to see me—can't imagine why. When he asked if I had made any progress, I lied and said no. I noticed the picture of his wife and daughter on his desk was gone.

"How's the family?" I asked.

He stopped what he was doing and looked at me. "What's it to you?"

"Nothing, it's just a little odd that your daughter attends St. Patrick's, just like the missing girl, Jane Wynant."

"What's odd about that? It's a big school."

"I interviewed some of the students there, but there were no Clays on the list."

"I already talked to her about it. Cynthia is an underclassman. Jane is a senior."

I doubted it was just coincidence but changed the subject. "Who's heading up security at the teachers' conference at Union?"

He gave me a sore look. "McGivern," he said. "Say, where have you been keeping yourself, Bostic?"

It was none of his business, but just then McGivern walked into the room. I went over to him.

"Got a minute, Charlie?" I asked.

He gave me a quick smile and raised his eyebrows. "Just barely," he said, shaking my hand. "I swear, these damn colored teachers."

"You know about the threat letter sent to King?" I asked.

"Yeah," he said. "What's it to you?"

"I know an interested party," I said.

Charlie sighed. "Don't you always?" he said. "Well, your luck is in. We caught a break on it this morning."

"How's that?"

"Got an address on the sender. Some crackpot on Grove."

"Where'd you get that?"

"Anonymous tip," he said. "Clay took it this morning. There's a uniform there now; I was about to head over."

"Mind if I ride along?"

"I guess," he said. "Maybe we'll need a lockpick."

CHAPTER 30
Models

We pulled in behind a squad car across the street from 3555 Grove. As we did, two young men emerged from the building carrying something wide and flat to a green Ford pickup parked in front. They eased it into the truck bed and covered it with a canvas tarp, then shook hands. One of them walked away and took a left on Thompson. The other one got into the pickup and started the engine.

"Which one's ours?" I asked.

"The one in the pickup," Charlie said. "One Joe Curtis. I'll see where he goes. You and the uniform stay here and have a look-see."

I got out and shut door, then leaned down into the window.

"Say Charlie, did Clay work security at the Tobacco Festival Parade?"

"I think so, yeah," Charlie said. "Why?"

"No reason," I said.

I went to the cruiser and knocked on the passenger window. The uniform rolled it down. He was an earnest freckle-faced kid in his early twenties named Evans. He was a little wary at first, but when I explained what was going on, he was all too eager to help. We crossed the street and went to the super's office. Evans knocked on the super's door, and an elderly woman named Miss Hughes appeared and invited us inside. I never identified myself, but she seemed to think I was a plainclothes detective. I didn't disabuse her of the notion. I told Evans to check around back.

Miss Hughes was boiling cabbage on her stovetop and her humid little apartment reeked of it. There was a radio on a bookcase by the window tuned to *Backstage Wife* on WRVA. She went over and turned it down.

"What's all this about?" she asked.

"One of your tenants, Joe Curtis."

"Oh, he's such a nice boy," she said. "Quiet. Pays the rent on time, never an ounce of trouble out of him."

"Does Mr. Curtis have many visitors?" I asked.

"None that I know of."

"He had one just now, they put something in a pickup," I said.

"Mr. Curtis is a modeler," she said. "He does most of his work in the basement. Every so often he gets someone to help him move one, but if he has any close friends, I've never seen them."

"Does he seem violent to you?"

"Oh, heavens no," Miss Hughes said.

"Can you show me his workspace?"

She led me down the hallway toward the back, then took a skeleton key from her apron and unlocked the basement door. I flicked a switch that lit a pale light at the bottom. Miss Hughes retreated to her apartment as I went down the stairs.

There was a large, empty table in the middle of the room, and the air smelled faintly of glue and paint thinner. Evans came down the staircase and joined me.

"Don't light a match," he said.

The shelves were crammed with boxes and model kits, but only one completed model, a dusty clipper ship suspended from the rafters with twine. I turned to Evans.

"You keep checking down here," I said. "I'm gonna take a look at his place."

I went back up the stairs and found Miss Hughes standing in the doorway of her apartment. She seemed concerned.

"Something wrong?" I asked.

"No, not wrong," she said. "But I just remembered Mr. Curtis's brother-in-law visited him the other night."

"Can you describe him?"

"I didn't get much of a look, but he was a short little fella."

"What makes you say it was his brother-in-law?"

"He told me so. After the man left, I asked Mr. Curtis who his visitor was."

"I'd like a look at his place if it's not too much trouble."

"Not at all," she said.

She led the way to an apartment at the end of the first-floor hallway. The inside was clean and orderly. Atop a coffee table in the living room was a copy of *Time* magazine with Tricky Dick's floating head on the cover. Stacked neatly beneath were recent issues of *Popular Mechanics* and *Model Airplane News*. I leafed through them; none of them were cut up or missing any pages.

The walls of his bedroom were largely bare. Strung from the ceiling were detailed models of Spads, Fokkers, Zeros, Corsairs, and Messerschmitts—diving, climbing, and banking in perpetuity. The window looked out on Thompson Street, and beside it was a small desk. I went through it but saw only some past due bills and neatly arranged pens, pencils, clips, and erasers.

I found some wadded up paper in the wastebasket. Even his trash was orderly. I dumped the contents onto the floor, picked out the wads of paper, and flattened them out on the desk. The first was a Klan leaflet on cheap paper advertising a rally and cross burning last month in Bedford hosted by the UKA, the United Klans of America. It promised "Barbecue, Good Preaching, and Country Music," and for some reason felt the need to add it was for whites only. The speakers would be the grand dragons of Alabama and Florida. I flipped it over to the other side and saw the initials J.C. written in pencil in the bottom left corner. Joe Curtis, maybe. Or John Clay.

The other papers were aborted letters to someone named Kathy. Most of them got no further than "Dear Kathy," "My Dearest Kathy," "Hi Kathy," or "Katherine." Some got a sentence or two in before he gave up again, and a few of those bore violent scrawls across the page with a pencil. *Don't sweat it, kid*, I thought. *She'll only break your heart.*

Evans walked into the apartment and called out. I told him where I was and asked him to search the coat closet. He hadn't been at it long when he called me over.

"Sir, you're gonna want to see this."

I pocketed the leaflet and walked into the hallway. Evans was standing at the other end with his hand extended toward the closet. Inside it leaning against the wall was a rifle, an M1 Garand. It was nearly identical to the one that I and countless others had used during the war, except this one had a sniper's scope. I took out a handkerchief and hefted the weapon. As I did, a small stack of girlie mags tumbled onto the floor. I handed the rifle to Evans and told him to take it into the living room. When he was gone, I bent down and leafed through the issues on top and found that a number of them had been cut up and were missing letters. I collected them up and brought them into the living room.

"Must be our man," Evans said.

"It sure looks that way," I said.

CHAPTER 31

Dixie

We gathered everything up and put it in the trunk of the squad car. Evans and I had been waiting there about a minute when the kid in the pickup pulled up and went inside. Not long after, McGivern rolled up behind us and got out.

"Anything?" he asked.

"Enough for an arrest, but not much else," I said. "How about you?"

"Nothing," he said. "He dropped off some sort of model at the King Carter."

"Lots of model making stuff inside," I said. "Where'd he leave it?"

"Someplace called Admiral Security."

McGivern took a look at the contents of the open trunk. "Nice M1," he said. "What's with the girlie mags?"

"If I had to guess, I'd say they were cut up and used to make the threat letter," I said.

McGivern picked one of them up and flipped through it. "All right," he said. "Bostic, wait here. Officer Evans, just you and me on this one."

I didn't mind. I didn't have to; it was one of the nice things about not being a cop. As they re-entered the apartment building, I lit a cigarette, pushed my hat back, and leaned against the squad car. The afternoon was warm and overcast, its gray light closing in. Cars passed. The bad part of me wanted the building to erupt in a hail of gunfire so I could jump in, but no such luck. The front door opened, and McGivern and Evans appeared, leading the suspect through in handcuffs. Miss Hughes trailed them, worrying the hem of her apron. The two policemen crossed the street and approached the car, their prisoner in between. I opened the door and got a look at the kid's confused face as he was crammed into the back seat.

"I need a lift back," I told McGivern.

"Good," he said, with a smile. He tossed me the keys to his car. "Take mine."

***

It looked like a frame-up to me. I doubted that kid could even heft the Garand, much less fire it and hit something. The Klan leaflet wasn't great, but I suspected it had been planted along with the rifle and magazines. Nothing else in his apartment indicated violence or racial hatred of any kind. But if Miller really was his brother-in-law, that might explain it. A useful distraction, make everyone think the threat had been neutralized when it hadn't. I followed the squad car back to the station and went in through the lobby.

I made my way up to the second floor and found Officer Evans processing paperwork. Joe Curtis sat numb on a wooden bench staring down at his fingertips smeared with ink. The girlie mags and rifle sat out on top of a desk for everyone to see. McGivern stood near the interview room talking quietly with Clay. I walked over.

"Can we help you, Bostic?" Clay asked.

"I was hoping to sit in."

"Three's a crowd," Clay said. "It's our bust."

"Looks like Charlie's," I said. "Any priors on this kid?"

"No offense, Bostic," McGivern said. "RPD business."

"Your call," I said. "But if he's your guy, I'm Hut-Sut Rawlson."

I doubt Darnell Washington would have cared for the lax attitude. But in this life, you get what you pay for, and all he was paying me for was to be white. I had a few minutes to kill so I drove back to the King Carter for a look at that model the kid had dropped off earlier. The lobby teemed with guests, bellhops, and the noise of shopkeepers closing up for the day. I didn't see any of my friends from the billiards room, so I found a pay phone and dialed Mort's number at Admiral Security. I wasn't surprised when he didn't answer.

I went to the mezzanine where their offices were located and stationed myself at a water fountain outside the main door. From there it would be easy to sneak inside past someone leaving for the day. I leaned over for a fake drink of water as two tired executives walked out, but they were slow to clear out and I missed the door. A few minutes later, a short man in a suit stepped out and checked his watch as the door closed behind him. It was Miller, your basic bad penny. He didn't look tired. In fact, he looked like his day was just getting started. Having a look at the model could wait.

I followed him down the stairs and through the lobby to the hotel's Broad Street entrance, where a DeSoto idled at the curb. I got a look at the plate. It had been washed but was the same one I'd seen the day before out at the abandoned house. A valet in a neat uniform held the door open for him. The car took a right down Eighth Street and was immediately stuck in rush hour. I found my van and picked up the DeSoto as it crept west. Traffic finally relented at Malvern. Miller took a left on Commonwealth and parked on Grove near Mary Munford Elementary. Inside the school, a muted, faux-patriotic event was underway.

Bunting and balloons decorated the school's main entrance, with an American flag on one side and the Confederate stars and bars on the other. Through the open doors I could hear a brass band engaged in an off-key rendition of "Dixie." I'd heard about a Harlan Hawkins rally to be held there, but I didn't know what night. This could only have been it. I parked and got out, passing booths selling campaign buttons, yard signs, and bumper stickers. Virginia Democrats for Eisenhower had a booth there and was distributing literature as a counterpoint to the States' Rights campaign.

Men in suits and hats and women in dresses crossed Grove Avenue in the twilight, their shadows tilting in the headlights. Most appeared merely curious, as though the rally was simply an excuse to go out on a Thursday night. But Miller moved with purpose as he made his way toward a door outside the auditorium. An Admiral Security goon let him by with barely a look. I straightened my suit and lowered my hat and approached the man standing guard. If he recognized me, I was done.

"Sir?" he said. He was a kid roughly the size of Afton Mountain, and almost as dense.

"They're expecting me inside," I told him.

He stooped and picked up a clipboard holding a sheet of paper with a typewritten list.

"Name?" he asked.

"Williams."

He flicked the first page back. For some reason it took him a while to find W.

"Do you have some ID?" he asked.

I took the Klan leaflet out of my pocket and held it in front of his face. "This is my fucking ID, you dolt."

His lips moved as he took in the pertinent details, whatever they were. Then he looked at me and his eyes got wide.

"Sorry, sir!" he said.

I don't know who the kid thought I was, but I was glad it was someone important. That almost never happens. I refolded the leaflet and stuck it in my pocket as the kid pushed the door open for me. I found myself in a dimly lit area with a side view of the stage, with Miller standing in the wings. The music was winding up with one last wheeze as a middle-aged man with thinning hair approached the stage. After some light applause, he thanked all the people he was supposed to thank, then introduced the night's featured speaker, presidential candidate Harlan Hawkins. After another round of light applause, a man in his late fifties with a medium build and an outrageous blond comb-over took the stage.

"I supposed you all have heard," he began, "about Harlem representative Adam Clayton Powell. That's Harlem, New York, in case any of you got confused."

There was some nervous laughter. Someone shouted, "We like Ike!"

"I'm sure you do, sir," Hawkins said. "If you hear me out, however, you will learn that Ike doesn't like you. No sir, not at all. You see, Representative Powell is a Democrat. From Harlem, did I mention that? And he was going to support the Democrat in this campaign, Mr. Stevenson, until Mr. Eisenhower called a meeting, just the two of them. Now what do you suppose a Republican president can promise a Democratic representative from Harlem that will make him switch his allegiance to the GOP?"

The crowd was silent, so Hawkins went on.

"I am guessing it had something to do with jail terms for those in the South that defy the desegregation orders handed down by the so-called Supreme Court. Now you tell me how the Republican Party is any different from the Democratic Party when it comes to letting the states decide how best to conduct themselves."

States' Rights, cracker code for segregation. Call me old fashioned, call me naïve, but it's still shocking to hear someone spout white supremacist bullshit out loud right here in the good old. I wasn't alone in my distaste. Some in the crowd started to fidget and a few more got up and left. But many others stayed seated, eager to ingest whatever racist bilge Hawkins was selling. I myself had heard enough.

In front of me, Miller signaled and got the attention of someone in the crowd, then nodded and walked behind the stage. I tagged along as he left and walked to the other side of the school, then down a long hallway to a classroom where a couple of thugs stood guard. One of them was my friend with the gun from the hotel billiard room. A bandage poked out from under his hat, and he sported a shiner. He hadn't struck me as terribly bright, but even he would recognize me now.

I found an exit. Outside I ran into someone with a clipboard who was collecting names and addresses for supporters of the Hawkins campaign. He also had a little cardboard box full of buttons that showed Hawkins's face in front of the stars and bars. I passed on both. Once I got rid of him, I ducked into the shadows behind some shrubs outside a brightly lit classroom window cracked open for air. I peeked inside and saw Miller speaking with another man I'd never seen before. On a table in front of them was an open briefcase. It was lined on both sides with stacks of bundled cash.

"Be sure and let the candidate know how much my client appreciates his efforts," Miller said. He closed the briefcase and lifted it off the table.

"Please tell your client how much we appreciate his," the other man said.

They shook hands and the transaction appeared complete. Miller left the classroom with the briefcase. I eased away from the window and went back to my car to wait. On the way there, I stepped in a pile of dogshit on the sidewalk. I stopped under a streetlight and swore quietly as I studied the bottom of my shoe. Just my luck, and nothing to clean it off with. Then I remembered the Klan leaflet folded in my pocket and thought maybe it's not so worthless after all. I took it out and used it to clean my shoe, then dropped it in the nearest trash can. No offense to the dogshit.

Finally, Miller left the school, crossed the street, and got into his car. He made a U-turn on Grove and drove west. After a few minutes of meandering south through a residential neighborhood, he stopped outside a house on Wilton. It was situated some ways off the street and partially hidden behind overgrown bushes. I killed the headlights and pulled over as he made his way inside. Lights came on inside the living room, but then almost as quickly went out again. The front door opened, and he stepped back outside and walked to his car. I ducked behind a maple as he floored it back toward Cary and was gone.

I waited another moment. This was a ritzy area; even the quiet felt expensive. I walked around to the backyard and found a double garage with a carriage house. I smelled fresh paint. The garage let out into the alley. I gave both doors a pull . . . no luck. On one side was a window too small for me to fit through and a locked wooden door with four glass panes. Well, technically three, after I broke one with my elbow and reached in to unlock the door. I could have picked the lock in the dark with some effort, but there are times when it pays to be expedient.

Inside, the smell of fresh paint was evident. I kicked the broken glass aside and let the air clear for a moment before I lit the Zippo for light. To the left of the door was a small woodworking station. A vise was mounted to the edge of a worktable alongside an assortment of tools, nails, wire cutters, and bits of snipped wire. I flashed back to Miller and Clay putting the crate of TNT into the trunk of the car the day before. Here were all the makings of a bomb, but no actual bomb.

At the other end of the bench, some bits of paper caught my eye. It was a series of target sheets stacked on top of each other. The usual generic criminal profile pointing a pistol at you used for target practice had been replaced by a cartoonish Black male with a short afro, exaggerated lips, and bulging white eyes. The shooter had worked different parts of the body, with several different sheets showing holes around the head, heart, and groin. Top marks for accuracy, less for style.

On the other side of the garage was a panel van still wet with fresh white paint. I memorized its license number as the Zippo flickered and went out. I gave it a shake, but it was empty. As I felt my way toward the door, the crunch of gravel in the alley signaled an approaching car. Through a window, I could see a cone of headlights make its way down the alley, coming to a stop outside the garage. The passenger got out and raised the garage door. It was Clay. I hid between the van and the garage wall as the car backed in. The engine idled long enough to fill the space with a noxious cloud of carbon monoxide. Clay closed the garage door while the driver killed the engine and got out. They left through the door with the broken window. If they noticed the missing pane, I was cooked. I made a mental note to look into bringing a gun to situations like this.

My luck was in. In the darkness, they didn't even pause. They walked across the lawn and vanished into the house. A light switched on in back, then off again. The house stayed dark for several minutes. By now it was late, and I figured they had done what they were going to do. I was tired and still woozy from the fumes, and I'd seen plenty. I snuck out and found the van on the street. On the way back to my place, no one followed.

CHAPTER 32

King Ventilation

I got to my shop early the next morning and parked the van around back. I had three days to get everything packed and moved. With my sideline bringing in more business than I could handle, moving hadn't been a priority. Now, out of necessity, it was. I changed into a pair of coveralls and boxed up the front of the store first, displays and all. Knowing it was possible I was being watched, I took the first load back to my apartment and left it in a large shed out back by the alley. Sure enough, by the time I got back to the shop, an Admiral Security goon had taken up residence out front in a dark green Plymouth. He was eating a sandwich and looked like he didn't want to be bothered. I set about packing up the back of the shop as quickly as I could and took off with a second load in the van.

The sandwich thing reminded me I hadn't eaten yet, so on the way home I detoured to Monroe's at First and Grace. It was a narrow little joint, cramped, stuffy, and loud, but they made a mean omelet and bacon with enough grease in it to make me feel human again. I sat at a counter in the front window, reading the *Times-Dispatch* and rubbing elbows with a couple of other hard cases sipping coffee. The sun had come out earlier for the first time in days, and shoppers had ventured out to drop some dough at Thalhimers or Miller & Rhoads. Now they were about to get rained on again. A bored traffic cop stood in the intersection and scowled at the clouds. On the sidewalk in front of me, umbrellas popped open.

I paid up and made my way across the street to Fusco's where I'd left the van. Richmonders loved their parking lots almost as much as they loved their monuments. At Reaney's Sunoco on Belvidere, an attendant filled the tank. I asked for a receipt, just so I'd know how much I wasn't charging Darnell Washington. A few minutes later I was home again, unloading the van in the alley. Inside the shed, I took a moment to look at it all. I hadn't gotten everything, but I'd gotten a lot. I went inside and got cleaned up and changed before heading out to Virginia Union.

With traffic backed up on Lombardy, it took me fifteen minutes to travel less than a mile to campus. Finding a place to park took another ten, but I finally found a spot near Hovey Field on Brook Road. A poster outside the stadium advertised tomorrow's game at Morgan State. The football team counted off cherry pickers as I passed, their movements fluid and easy. The heaviness of my own body had never felt more palpable.

I joined a line of people streaming toward the Belgian Building. The vast majority of the crowd was conservatively dressed Black folks, some fifteen hundred teachers from across the state according to the paper. I stood out a little, but there were more white faces here than I'd have thought. Some were RPD cops in their brown uniforms, but I also saw a contingent of earnest-looking young white men in suits and ties. With them were young coeds with short, sensible hair and conservative dresses. The occasional minister or priest bobbed up here and there in modest vestment. My job was to blend in as best I could and see if any of them looked like Mick Miller.

Near the base of the steps to the front entrance stood several VUU students and faculty in suits, ties, and topcoats. A light drizzle tapped the brim of my hat and a warm breeze fell across my face. I turned and saw a large black Chrysler pull up to the curb in front.

A Black man in a suit, hat, and raincoat raced from the left backseat to open the back right passenger door. As he did, another man emerged from the front passenger seat and held a navy umbrella over the man stepping out of the right rear door, a Black man in his late twenties in a plain blue suit and tie, who was around five-eight and a 150 pounds. He had close-cropped dark hair and a thin mustache. Seeing the people gathered on a damp day, he smiled and waved the umbrella away, then moved toward the crowd and started shaking hands. I'd never seen so much as a picture of him before, but this could only have been Martin Luther King, Jr.

To even a casual observer there was something striking about him, even if it was hard to pinpoint. Neither particularly tall nor very handsome, the crowd was nonetheless drawn to him and he to it. He greeted each person warmly as though they were old friends catching up. King moved with purpose but without hurry, projecting a calm that seemed to affect those around him. Apart from an occasional shout of "Dr. King!" the crowd maintained a low, excited murmur. When he reached the top of the steps, he turned briefly to address the crowd as a flashbulb popped, glinting off his silver tie clip.

"Ladies and gentlemen," he said. "I'd like to thank you for this warm Richmond greeting, and for coming out on such an overcast and damp fall day. I'd also like to thank the faculty, staff, and administration of Virginia Union University for their hospitality in hosting this event, as well as the many fine Black teachers of Virginia assembled here for the conference. The bridge to a brighter tomorrow is built in the classrooms of today."

Some light applause broke out before King continued.

"As you know, at this very moment, the state's white teachers are also holding their annual conference at the Jefferson. Let us work together here and in the future so that one day there will be not two separate conferences, one for white and another for Negro, but rather one that unites us all. Thank you."

There was more applause as King turned toward the entrance and vanished inside. The crowd buzz grew as people began pressing their way in. In the corner of my eye, I saw Rita Kizzie, the young reporter from the *Richmond Afro-American* I'd spoken with the Saturday before. She was standing at the top of the steps, taking in the moment and scribbling furiously in her notepad. Then she turned and squeezed her way inside.

Standing in the crowded vestibule, I lit a cigarette and looked around for anything that resembled an administrative section. Off to the right rear side was a lighted hallway, but before I could make my way to it, a young Black man in a gray suit approached me.

"You Bostic?" he asked.

"Yeah."

"This way."

I followed him through a doorway on the rear left that led to a short walkway open to the elements. Outside to my left was a muddy grass courtyard rimmed with recently planted shrubs. At the end of this hallway was the section of the building that housed the tower. When we reached the door that led inside, he turned to face me and said, "Spread 'em."

I spaced my legs apart and raised my arms.

"I'm not carrying," I said.

He frisked me anyway. Hard to blame him. If I was Black, I wouldn't trust a white man either. He patted the front of my jacket and found my wallet. He took a look inside, then handed it back, unimpressed. He held the door open and made sure it was closed it behind me. I stepped into a large lecture hall where three men stood near the podium in front of a schematic of the building. They continued speaking quietly amongst themselves until one of them looked my way.

"You must be our locksmith," he said, waving a business card in my direction. He motioned me over and we shook hands. "My name is Ralph Everly. I'm with the NAACP. Darnell Washington sends his regards. I've got good news. The Richmond police have arrested the man who wrote the letters."

"I know," I said. "I was there. I think it's a decoy, and the man we want is still out there."

"What makes you say that?"

"Keen observation," I said. "Is Dr. King's head of security here?"

We walked over to the two men at the podium. "Mr. Bostic here believes the threat has not been neutralized," Ralph said.

"Just when were you planning on telling us this?"

"I'm telling you now. It's a short little shit named Mick Miller. The kid RPD has in custody is his brother-in-law; he's trying to frame him for it."

"Do you know the whereabouts of this Miller?"

"No, but I haven't seen him here. At least not yet."

"All right, good," he said. "Go out and tell the man at the door what you told us. He'll spread the word to those who need it."

This I did. Dr. King was scheduled to speak in the main lecture hall at four. I made my way back to the main building, scanning the crowd for homicidal white faces. All the ones I saw were young, earnest, and fully engaged in whatever it was that was happening here.

"Mr. Bostic," a woman's voice called.

I turned and saw Rita Kizzie standing toward the center of the floor, waving her arm. I stepped toward her.

"I see you made it after all," she said.

"The social event of the season."

"I told you it would be something," she said. "The *Times-Dispatch* even sent someone."

"Fancy," I said. "Any scoops?"

She made a disappointed face. "No. I can't even get an interview with Dr. King."

"If at first you don't succeed," I said. "I don't guess you've seen anybody suspicious looking milling around."

She raised an eyebrow at me. "In this crowd?" she said. "Just the white people. Why, is there something you're not telling me?"

"Not at all," I said. "How well do you know this building?"

"I'm a Union grad, so I know it some."

"Where would I find Conference Room D?"

She pointed to a hallway off to the right. "It's right back there," Rita said. "Across from Conference Room C. You did learn your ABC's, Mr. Bostic?"

I smiled. "Excuse me," I said.

I made my way through the crowd and peered down the hall toward the conference room, where the silhouette of a Black man in a suit and hat stood vigil outside. I went to the front of the building and stood in the damp drizzle to watch the late crowd lingering outside, shaking off umbrellas and stamping their feet on the wet mat. Traffic was heavy on Lombardy, and there was a jam-up near the parking lot entrance as more cars waited to pull into the already full lot. The whole time I didn't hear a single car horn. Richmonders were funny like that.

I went down the steps to the side of the long brick building. A narrow access road curled around back to a small parking lot filled with cars and maintenance vehicles. I walked among them checking for Harlan Hawkins stickers, weapons, racist literature, or Klan robes. There was nothing quite that obvious until I came to a recently painted white work van parked neatly in a space. It had the same license plate as one I'd seen in the garage last night. Inside, it looked a little too neat to be an actual work vehicle. Both doors were locked. On the side panels was stenciled the company's name, King Ventilation, which I didn't like the sound of.

The maintenance door beside the loading dock took me back inside. I followed a short hallway to the office of the maintenance supervisor, A.O. Jenkins, according to the nameplate. Inside was a lean Black man about my age or so, wearing gray coveralls and drinking coffee from a paper cup. The name Lewis was stitched in red on his left breast pocket, but I couldn't tell if it was his first or last name.

"You Jenkins?" I asked.

"No," he said. "Euphrates Lewis. Who are you?"

"Your first name is Euphrates?"

"Call me Lewis," he said.

"My name's Bostic, and we have a small problem," I said. "Where's Jenkins?"

"He has gone inside to hear Dr. King. Along with most everyone else in the building. Are you a cop?"

"No, but I'm working security here. Do you know of any work orders being filled this afternoon, specifically the ventilation system?"

"Lord no," he said. "All those were filled earlier in the week ahead of the conference."

"That's what I thought," I said. "Can you show me how to access the ventilation system?"

"I ain't showing you crap, man."

"Look," I said. "There could be an armed man in this building right now looking to harm Dr. King. Do you believe me now or would you rather wait until the shooting starts?"

From inside the main hall came the muffled sound of a speaker introducing King. It came to an end, followed by applause.

"Come on," Lewis said.

We walked out into the vestibule and opened the door into the main hall where King had already started his address. He stood at a podium between two long tables, flanked on either side by an assortment of religious types and conference pooh-bahs. The room was silent as his voice boomed across it.

I got Lewis's attention and pointed up at the ceiling toward the air vent openings. "How can I get up there?" I whispered.

Lewis led us out of the crowded hall toward a stairwell that led to the second floor. Once there, we passed through a wide, carpeted hallway with a series of doors on the left. No one else was around. When we reached the last door, Lewis took a key from his pocket and was about to unlock it.

"Access door," he said.

"Hold on," I told him. I crouched down for a look at the doorknob and saw a series of fresh scratches near the lock. "You're the only one with a key?"

"Mr. Jenkins has one. Otherwise, it stays locked."

The doorknob turned freely in my hand. I looked at Lewis, "I need you to find Jenkins and tell him where I am and what's going on."

"He ain't gonna like it."

"He's going to like it a lot less if the last speech King ever gives is right here in this building."

Lewis left. I opened the door carefully and quietly and slipped into the darkness. Inside the room was the metallic hum of the system working to keep the air moving. It was a warm and muggy fall day, a Richmond specialty, and the first floor was jammed with people. As I worked my way inside, easing my back along the walls and panels toward the front of the room, I could hear King's words muffled in the room below.

I reached a corner near a stack of crates and felt something give as I set my left foot down. I looked down and in the darkness saw an unconscious man in a suit sitting up against the crates as though he'd been flung there. I had stepped on his arm. I kneeled and felt for a pulse, then inspected his face in the dim light. He was a young Black man with a lump over his left eye and a bloody scrape on his forehead. He was going to hurt when he woke up, but he would wake up. Sometime. I stood to continue my search.

I could make out the curving silhouette of a large duct a few feet away. It was about chest height. As I ran my hands over its side, I found that an access panel had been unscrewed in all but one corner and left to swing. I put my ear to the side of the duct and heard nothing. I stuck my head into the open vent. There was no sound, nothing. Below me, the speech continued.

Something about this didn't feel right. If I'd been a canary, I would have sent myself into the vent to see if there was a short, murderous bigot with a rifle on the other end. But the open panel felt more like a way to lure someone into a trap where they couldn't maneuver, fight, or whistle "Dixie."

Then the click of a switchblade behind me told me all I needed to know. I spun around and saw Miler in gray coveralls lunge at my midsection with the blade. I jumped to the side as he slashed again with a backhand swipe aimed at my jugular.

"Nigger lover," he said.

I grabbed his wrist and twisted his arm behind his back, pressing with my thumb until he dropped the knife. Then I slammed him hard against the metal duct with a loud crash.

"I have had it with rednecks trying to cut me this week," I said.

I stepped on the switchblade and felt it crack at the handle. He struggled briefly but seemed to value a not-broken arm.

"Some tough guy," he said, with a laugh. "You got nothing."

"Save it," I said. "You're finished."

I grabbed him by the back collar of his coveralls and kept his arm pinned to his back. He was a wiry little guy, maybe five-three, kicking at me with his left leg. From below the speech continued.

"Not quite," Miller said.

"What's that?" I asked.

"I figure, why kill just one nigger when you can kill a whole slew of 'em?"

As I scruff-marched him toward the door, a voice outside called out from the hallway.

"Who's in there? Show yourself!"

I slammed Miller face first into the metal door of an electrical panel. "What's that supposed to mean?"

Before he could answer, the door opened against the gray daylight and I saw the crouched silhouette of a plainclothes cop, his gun drawn.

"Drop your weapon," he said.

"I'm not armed," I said. "Is Lewis out there?"

He was pointing his gun right at me. As my eyes adjusted to the light behind him, I saw that it was John Clay. Before I could react, he pistol-whipped me across the left temple, knocking me to the cement floor. I wasn't unconscious, but the signals from my brain to the rest of my body has been scrambled. He rolled me over and went through my pockets. I mumbled something and reached feebly for him, but Clay brushed my hand aside.

"He's clean."

Miller paused. "All right, we need to get the hell out of here, but we're both gonna be nice and calm. I'm your prisoner and you're taking me to jail. Got it?"

"What do we do with him?" Clay asked, gesturing at me. At the same time, more voices approached in the hallway.

"Leave him," Miller said. "He'll die in the blast."

As the other men appeared in the doorway, Miller and Clay brushed past them into the hallway, offering only a brusque "Police business!"

Someone switched on a light and the room filled with a yellow glow. The first man to find me was Lewis. He called Everly and Jenkins over. The two other men with them fanned out over the room. One of them found the man I'd tripped over earlier.

Everly knelt beside me and said, "Mr. Bostic, what happened? Are you all right?"

I blinked as my eyes finally began to focus, then sat up and tried to shake my head clear.

"We need to evacuate the building," I said. "There's a bomb."

CHAPTER 33

Art Appreciation

I got to my feet again and found my shoes with some help, then pressed a handkerchief to my throbbing left temple that came back bloody. The stars flashing in my eyes were the envy of any planetarium. On my left were Everly and Jenkins. Lewis poked around with a flashlight over by the air duct.

"I believe you're delirious, Mr. Bostic," Everly said.

"I'm not," I said. "I'm telling you, there's a bomb somewhere in this building."

"How do you know that?"

"I just do." I inspected my hankie, blood still seeping from the cut.

"Do you know where?"

"No."

Jenkins sighed. "You fail to make a compelling case, Mr. Bostic."

"How much longer is the speech is supposed to last?"

"Not much longer," Everly said.

It seemed to me that if a bomb had been planted in the lecture hall, it probably would have gone off by now. If you wanted maximum bang for your buck, why count on a long speech?

"Do you know Dr. King's itinerary for the rest of the conference?"

"Some meetings here and then a ride to Byrd Field for a seven o'clock flight."

I thought about that for a minute. Lewis came back over.

"You have to evacuate the building," I said.

"I will do nothing of the sort," Jenkins said.

"Perhaps Mr. Bostic has a point," Everly said. "Dr. King's house in Birmingham was bombed earlier this year."

"I am not going to let this man embarrass this institution," Jenkins said. "If we evacuate the entire conference over a false alarm, that makes tomorrow's paper. For all I know, you're in cahoots with whoever those men were."

"The headline's a little worse if it's about the avoidable death of a prominent Black leader and scores of teachers from across the state."

Williams eyed me with suspicion and thought about this. "All right," he said finally. "My mama didn't raise me to go weak at the knees at the first sign of trouble. I'm not evacuating, but I want every available man searching the building for anything suspicious."

The group split up. My temple throbbed as I wandered into the hallway where the glare of gray daylight nearly blinded me. I made my way down to the stuffy vestibule, looked around, and saw nothing out of the ordinary. Someone had opened a door to the main hall for air.

I went down the hallway toward the conference room. It was lined on both sides with framed pictures of the Belgium Pavilion at the World's Fair. I listened outside the conference room and heard no one inside, so I tried the handle and found it unlocked. Inside was a rectangular room filled with modern office furniture and a long wooden conference table at its center. Atop that was a tray with two pitchers of water and some glasses, along with a scattering of papers, folders, and pencils. I checked around for a briefcase or anything that might house an explosive but saw nothing. By the door, a coat rack held a variety of raincoats and hats.

Along the far wall were two smaller tables displaying ancestor statues and face masks from the Belgian Congo. Their expressions ranged from surprise to puzzlement as though they'd seen what colonization had in store for the Congo and wanted no part of it. One statue stood out: made of clay, it showed a shirtless and barefoot runner in mid-stride. He was supposed to be holding a torch in his right hand, except there was none. There was also no tiny card nearby to help explain what it was or where it had come from, unlike the others. It fit in and yet it didn't. I lifted it for a look at the heavy wooden base and found an alarm clock face that showed three minutes to twelve. Metal screws secured each corner. In a museum, they'd call it *Harrier with Time Bomb (20th Century)*.

Down the hall, the auditorium erupted in applause as King concluded his speech. I looked at the statue. My first instinct was to take the damn thing out back and chuck it in a dumpster, but just then the auditorium doors opened and people began spilling into the lobby. My path to the back entrance was now clogged with teachers, students, faculty, conference officials, and assorted religious types, none of whom had gotten out of bed this morning hoping to be blown up this afternoon.

I sat down and placed the bomb on the conference table. I'd handled explosives in the army and had some familiarity with homemade bombs from my time in the RPD. But this was unlike anything I'd ever seen. Miller had removed the minute hand and wrapped a thin piece of aluminum around it, then put it back in place. The clock's face was still encased in its plastic shell, which had been glued back on. I took out a pocketknife and removed the screws, then lifted the panel away from the bottom. The clock stayed in place, as did the circuit and the stick of TNT it was wired to. Black and red wires led away from the left of the clock, red and yellow ones to a tapered fuse on the right. I checked the battery under the clock face but didn't dare touch it. That was the extent of my expertise. I had about two minutes before it turned this part of the Belgian Building into a smoking crater.

"Could you use a hand, Mr. Bostic?"

I looked up and saw Euphrates Lewis, the assistant maintenance supervisor, standing in the doorway.

"Depends on how quickly you can clear the entire building before we kiss our ass goodbye."

He walked over and took a look at what I was doing. Calmly, he took a pair of bifocals from the pocket of his coveralls and peered in at the device.

"Interesting," he said.

He mumbled something and traced the wires leading away from the clock, then produced a pair of wire cutters from his tool belt. He snipped the black one and the ticking clock stopped dead.

"Neat trick," I said. "Where'd you learn that?"

He smiled and stood up straight and put the reading glasses back in his pocket. "Where else?" he said. "The army. I served with the 549th Engineers in Europe."

I barely heard him. I was sweating and my hand was shaking as I let out a deep breath. "Jesus, I need a drink."

"If that's an invitation," Lewis said, "I'll have to pass."

Outside the conference room, muffled voices headed our way.

"We might want to smuggle this out of here," I said. I stood up and put my hat on, then draped my jacket it over the statue. The door opened and King's bodyguard stepped into the room.

"Who are you?" he asked.

"I'm Euphrates Lewis," Lewis said. "I'm the Assistant Maintenance Supervisor in this building. And this is Eddie Bostic. He's been helping out around here today."

"And what's that?" the man asked, gesturing at the coat-covered statue in my left hand.

"Art," I said. "We're collectors."

I handed the statue back to Lewis. Behind him, other men pushed into the room. The only one of them I recognized was the NAACP man, Everly. The scene upstairs in the mechanical room seemed to have been forgotten. Everly spoke quietly with King as they entered the room, then stopped to address me.

"Bostic," he said. "I trust you have everything in hand here."

"With some help from Lewis here, yes."

"Fine, fine," he said. "Bostic, this is Dr. Martin Luther King, Jr."

King looked at me and we shook hands. There was a warmth and charisma to him you didn't encounter often. "Pleased to meet you," I said.

He smiled but seemed distracted by the bundle Lewis was holding. "I hope we didn't put you out too much," King said.

"Not at all," I said.

King turned his attention to another man who'd come into the room. Lewis made for the door, and I followed.

"Everly," I said.

"Yes, Mr. Bostic?"

"If you happen to see Darnell Washington," I said, "tell him he owes me."

CHAPTER 34

Job Offer

Out in the lobby, the crowd thinned. I gave Lewis one of my cards, which required the usual explanation. I liked him though and told him to contact me if he ever needed a locksmith. He looked at the card like he wasn't quite sure what service I was offering, but then we shook hands and I left.

It wasn't yet six o'clock, but already dark out. When I got to the van, I made sure Cleo's Beretta, or rather her dead brother's, was still in the glove box. I'd thought about taking it with me into the Belgian Building but was glad I hadn't, as Miller would have relieved me of it when I got knocked silly. I remembered the bullets rolling around inside Cleo's purse and knew the weapon needed cleaning. But that could wait. With a round in the chamber, I put the safety on and stuck it in my jacket pocket.

My head ached, but the cut on my temple had stopped bleeding. I swung back by the house on Wilton; it was dark and deserted. I went around back and checked the garage. Neither the car nor the stolen van was in it. A nearby trash can in the alley was empty. At the residence, the front and back doors were locked. I wanted a look inside, but it was clear Miller & Co. had decamped. By now, what I wanted more than anything else was an easy chair and a stiff drink. I decided to go home, since that was the only place I knew where I could find both of those things.

The neighborhood was quiet when I pulled the van into a spot on Floyd. On the walk to my place, I heard that voice in my head, the one that warns me when something is off. It was a voice I'd first heard on Saipan, and later in my days with the RPD. Not listening to it could be hazardous to my health. I looked around for the DeSoto that Miller drove, but it wasn't parked nearby. The Beretta was in hand as I approached the front door and opened it slowly, leaving the light off. As I closed it quietly behind me, another light came on at the desk across the room.

In its chair sat my old buddy Teddy Janus, white hair and all. Loitering in the shadows by a corner bookcase was Mick Miller. He knocked a hardback book to the floor that landed like the blow of a hammer.

"You always did have a hard head, Bostic," Janus said.

Miller brandished a revolver as I kept the Beretta trained on him. Janus did not appear to be armed.

"You figured out where I live, congratulations. Now what do you want?"

"Just to talk some sense into you."

"About what?"

"The future."

"I've got my hands full with the present."

"Yes, well. At present, there are some very powerful people who are upset with you."

"So what else is new?"

"Mr. Miller here was given an assignment for this afternoon, one he'd been paid to carry out. Unfortunately, you came along and unraveled it. He's upset, and so is his client."

"Let me guess: his client is a local candidate for higher office, right? If he paid to have a man murdered this afternoon, that's tough shit."

"I don't know what would make you think such a thing. The candidate would have no part in any such scheme. Besides, Miller here had a private stake in the outcome, given his personal dislike for Blacks. I mean, it's visceral. Everything is 'nigger this' and 'nigger that.' I harbor no hatred toward them myself."

"You could have fooled me," I said.

"You and me, Eddie, we're from up North. We weren't raised in it like they were here. It's different in the South, they're steeped in it. Miller himself is from Richmond. What part did you say, Mick?"

"Penitentiary Bottom," Miller said.

"Fascinating," Janus said. "A part of the city named for its prison. And the area where your shop is, that was the center of the old slave trade."

"Done your homework, have you?"

"'The Devil's Half Acre' they used to call it. Slave jails, traders, auction houses. Men buying and selling flesh right out in the open, all that happened just blocks from where you work in Shockoe Bottom. Bell's Tavern, the Exchange Hotel. Hard to picture these days."

"Is it?" I said.

Janus smiled. "I have to admit, Bostic. I admire you a little. You can think on your feet. Admiral could use a man like you—tough, not afraid of a little dirty work . . . smart, but not too smart."

I kept an eye on Miller stationed in the corner. He knocked another book to the floor.

"Tell your yapping little dog over there he's about to get kicked," I said.

Miller's eyes narrowed as he tightened his grip on the revolver.

"Easy Mick," Janus said. "Believe it or not, Bostic, Miller here is a good employee. He isn't in it just for the money. No, he hates from somewhere down deep inside. What is it they say? The North loves the race but hates the man, while the South loves the man but hates the race?"

"The worst of both worlds," I said.

"What Miller did today at the college he would have done for free. Plus, he's loyal. That's what I prize more than anything. Would you describe yourself as loyal, Eddie?"

"I'm loyal to whoever's paying me."

"From the looks of it," Janus said, looking around, "nobody's paying you for much of anything these days."

"At the moment, I'm looking into the death of Casey Lloyd. How about it, Miller? Casey Lloyd found out Admiral Security was knee-deep in human trafficking and tried to extort you, didn't he?"

"Never hustle a hustler," Miller said.

"Maybe, but the hit was a rush job. You had to kill him in the car, then dump him at the tracks because you couldn't get caught with a bloody corpse in the back seat."

"Clay's idea," Miller said. "He panicked. Said he could cover for it."

"What did you expect?" I said.

"Admiral Security could use a man like you," Janus said. "Provided you still know how to follow orders. You used to be good at that, Eddie."

"The war was a long time ago."

"The war," he said. "Do you know how I got into security and shipping?" Janus said. "The war. I got the idea from all those troop ships coming into and out of the country."

"You shoulda joined the navy," I said.

"I would have if I'd known. I'd never been on a ship before or even seen the ocean until the war. After it, I did some traveling in Texas and Mexico and began to make the connection."

"You need ships if you're going to traffic in people," I said. "I mean in numbers. Not just a handful at the Mexican border, but by the boatload from Central and South America. That's some living you're making, Teddy."

"Given the choice between some shithole country and the USA, most would rather be here. We're giving them a better life when you think of it."

"Sure," I said. "The woman I saw on the slab at the morgue last week looked like she was having a grand time."

"An unfortunate accident, was it not Mr. Miller?"

"Janus," I said, "I doubt your client would appreciate you importing more brown people into the country. He doesn't like the ones that are already here."

"All he cares about is the color of my money and how much of it I can donate to his campaign. He never asks where it comes from."

"Why here?" I asked.

"That's what I've been trying to tell you," Janus said. "The Turnpike. The future. That highway bill Congress passed calls for forty thousand miles of road stretching from coast to coast. Soon there will be interstates across the whole country, but the Richmond-Petersburg Turnpike is in the vanguard. And anywhere an interstate is being built is where Admiral is going to be providing the highest quality worksite security."

"Sure," I said. "Along with lots of cheap labor and ways to keep it going."

"We have offices up and down the Eastern Seaboard; soon we'll be nationwide. It's a real growth opportunity I'm letting you in on."

"Are you serious?" I asked.

"Dead serious," he said. Janus stood and straightened his jacket, then covered his white hair with a hat. "Think about it, Eddie. If nothing else, it will get you out of Podunk. Travel, money, adventure. Isn't that right, Mr. Miller?"

Miller said nothing, staring at me like he was trying to burn a hole. Janus turned and motioned him to the door.

"All for just a small part of my soul," I said.

"So small you won't even notice," Janus said.

CHAPTER 35

Lamar Clemons

I locked up after they left and finally poured that drink. I set up a card table in the living room and refilled the Zippo, then lit a cigarette and cleaned the Beretta. I disassembled the weapon and inspected it, cleaned and oiled everything. The design was simple, few moving parts, and the simpler something was the more I liked it . . . generally speaking, of course. I reassembled it, loaded the magazine, and chambered a round. If any other visitors showed up unannounced, I'd be ready. I found a sling and holster. The draw was smooth enough.

I stretched out on the couch and turned the TV on with the volume low. I'd gotten it from Montgomery Ward, the first set I ever owned. The reception was terrible. I hit the Old Stagg until it was empty, then fell asleep. The last thing I remembered was the "The Star-Spangled Banner" followed by the Indian chief test pattern.

* * *

I awoke the next morning unmolested and in one piece. The TV was still on, showing some kids' puppet show called *Johnny Jupiter*. I cleaned up and checked the bathroom mirror. My left temple was bruised and there were bramble scratches on my neck and a cut across my chest from the woods on Wednesday. The shave could wait. I'd had enough sharp things near my face for the time being.

I dressed in coveralls for a locksmith job, then made my way in the van to the King Carter. I turned into an alley behind the hotel and drove to the service entrance, which was underground next to the loading dock. I told the maintenance supervisor I had to rekey six locks in the Admiral Security offices by Monday morning. I wasn't on his list of approved vendors, but I was carrying a full toolbox and looked convincing enough. I put him off further by name dropping Teddy Janus, who would surely not want to be bothered about something so mundane as a work order. The supervisor handed me a clipboard and told me to sign in, so I did.

"Valentine?" he asked. "The name on your van says Bostic."

"He's the big boss man," I said. "I work for him."

Someone had signed in just above me on the list. The handwriting was remedial, but the name was clearly Mick Miller. Inside, the offices were quiet. The empty reception desk contained a typewriter with a vinyl cover and some neatly arranged steno pads and pens. The offices behind it were dark. From the first wood-paneled conference room came the sound of muffled voices just behind the door. I ducked into the empty conference room next to it just as the door to the first one opened and three men stepped into the hallway. Miller was the last to leave.

I snuck into that conference room as soon as they were out of sight. Atop the conference table was a model of the stretch of land from south Petersburg to north Richmond. According to a placard in the lower left corner, it was dated Fall 1958 and featured the completed length of interstate that was only now beginning construction. Colorful little cars headed north and south along the clean ribbon of road sweeping north, leaping the James in an arc past Main Street Station and through Jackson Ward into Northside.

Red push pins lined the route at various spots along the model's terrain. According to a legend near the placard, these pins were designated as "Areas of Opportunity." One of them was placed very near the house I'd seen out in the sticks Wednesday, but there were others scattered along the route as it wound its way north. Richmond's shipping hub, Deepwater Terminal, was set out in some detail. It was the start of the river's flatwater, and at its farthest point north it was deep enough to accommodate shipping. The kid had done some detailed work on the capitol building and Tobacco Row, as well as the bridges linking north and south. Richmond, City of Tomorrow.

Someone came in through the reception area. I ducked down under the table and stayed low as a man in a suit came in and went to the mini-bar, where he poured himself a drink and downed it in one gulp.

"Fuck it," he said.

It was an older man with close-cropped gray hair. It was the same man I'd tussled with a week ago outside the trailer. Buford. He took the bottle of vodka with him when he left. I went to the door and watched him walk toward the office area. When he reached the one on the corner, he stepped inside and closed the door. I followed in his footsteps until I reached Mort's office. His nameplate was gone. I tried the knob and found the door locked tight, so I set about picking it. In less than a minute, I was in. I closed the door quietly and set my toolbox on the floor beside the desk.

The filing cabinet I'd seen the other day was gone, leaving a square depression in the carpet. The desk still contained papers and notebooks, but generic, the sorts of things all executives receive their first day on the job. I took one, and the first page opened with a list of corporate officers for Admiral Security. Mort was listed as General Counsel, which likely wasn't true anymore. I saw a picture of the briefcase man's face listed beside another. Mick Miller again. It was at the very bottom, though, and he was listed only as ombudsman. I'd always wondered what an ombudsman did. Now I knew. At the top of Admiral Security's corporate ladder was Teddy Janus, President and CEO.

The rest of the notebooks contained marketing information. I picked one to take with me when someone in the hallway tried the door.

"Mort? You in there?"

I ducked under the desk and rolled the chair in close. With my frame, it wasn't easy. The door opened and someone stood there, scanning the dark office and breathing quietly. It sounded like Buford again, but I couldn't be sure. It sounded like he took a swig off the bottle, and I could smell the vodka. He stayed near the door for a few seconds and let out a breath.

"Fuck it," he said again.

I always did appreciate a man of few words. He turned and closed the door, so I unfolded myself from beneath the desk. As I did, I kicked my toolbox. Not only did it hurt like hell, it also raised an ungodly racket. If Buford hadn't noticed it on the floor in his first pass, he couldn't help but notice it now.

The office door sprang open, and I squared to meet him. He staggered for a moment then lunged forward, swinging the vodka bottle at my head. I dodged and it hit the wall without breaking. Then it came at me from the right and missed again. While he was off balance, I caught him with a left jab and then a right that snapped his head backward. He steadied himself and tried to hit me with the bottle a third time. This time I caught his wrist and squeezed until the bottle tumbled to the carpet with a slosh. Then I got him with two more rights that knocked him against the wall and down for good.

I wanted to credit my own skills for taking him out so quickly, but it was more likely the alcohol. He was drunk and I wasn't. I picked up the bottle and took a swig that I nearly spit out. I turned on the light and checked the label. I'd never had vodka from Paraguay before, but I was glad to know it could double as lighter fluid. I set it aside and searched Buford's pockets. Inside his wallet, his operator's permit told me he had an address on Pine Street in Oregon Hill and was fifty-seven years of age. Give it up, old man.

I peeked out into the hallway to see if anyone had noticed. The floor was quiet, so I left Buford where he was and grabbed my toolbox. I closed the office door behind me and made for the exit, but as I reached for the handle, the door opened in front of me. I looked up expecting to find myself well and truly screwed. Instead, it was the maintenance supervisor who'd let me in earlier.

"Ah, Valentine," he said. "Have you made any progress?"

"Yes," I said. "All done. Do I need to sign out?"

"As a matter of fact, yes," he said. "You changed six locks in half an hour?"

"Rekeyed," I corrected. "I work fast."

"I see," he said, dubious. "I don't have the sheet with me, I'm only here to let these two men in. They're here to pick up a model. You didn't happen across it, did you?"

Behind him, two Black workmen in gray coveralls appeared with a flatbed cart. One of them was quite large, the second lean and slim. The latter sported a pink scar on his right cheek—the same kid I'd tried to catch last Sunday in the Ward. He didn't seem to recognize me in my work duds, so I led the three of them to the conference room where the model was. A few minutes later, they were on their way out again with the model loaded sideways on the cart. I left the Admiral offices with them as they made their way to the loading dock.

"Can I get a look at your work order? I need a number off it."

The larger man looked at me like I'd sprouted antennae. "They ain't one," he said.

I was hardly one to preach. But without a destination address, I'd have to tail them to see where they were taking it. I found my van where it was parked by the loading dock. There the two workmen gently loaded the model into the back of a Studebaker van painted primer red. It belched thick smoke as it eased past me on the ramp heading into traffic up Eighth.

The vehicle's hideousness and exhaust fumes made my job pretty easy. So did the short trip. I picked them up as they turned right onto Broad and then left on Ninth. I kept a couple car lengths behind, but apart from some dump trucks, traffic was scarce past Leigh. By the time I reached Turpin and Ellett streets, I might as well have been in another country. The road was empty, desolate, and mud-streaked. The intersection with Abigail Street was blocked off entirely with barrels and rope, compliments of the RPTA. I rolled the van to a stop, got out, and walked the long block.

The dilapidated wreckage of east Navy Hill surrounded me on both sides of North Ninth. Vacant lots strewn with trash and debris darkened the landscape like missing teeth. The remaining one-and-two story houses leaned unsteadily, their outlines tilting and stark in the gray horizon. Porches sagged, their front doors gone. Broken windows were boarded up, or else hastily covered with dingy metal signs from Royal Crown, Lucky Strike, and Gulf Gas. Leafless trees stood vigil at the curb, their trunks rain-blackened.

In front of an abandoned corner store, the Studebaker drove onto the sidewalk around the blockade, then lurched back onto the road and came to a stop a half-block away. The passenger got out and walked north toward a row of nearly demolished houses and vanished around a corner. He might have walked off the edge of the earth, but some minutes later came back with a stocky Black man in a hard hat, work jacket, and jeans. He was smoking a cigar. He went to the driver's side and there was a heated exchange. This man seemed familiar, so I moved in closer. When I saw his face, I saw the large strawberry on its right side. It was Lamar Clemons.

He stepped back and gestured angrily for the Studebaker to turn around, then started back the way he came. As they passed me heading the other way, I got out of my van and followed him through the mud toward a large open construction site on a hill.

"Clemons," I called out.

He turned around slowly and glared at me, then took a puff off the cigar. The two-face effect was unnerving, and he knew it. "What?" he said.

"Remember me?"

"Should I?"

"You had your goons kick the shit out of me outside Neverett's a week ago."

"Looks like the message didn't stick."

"I'd love a rematch. But for now all I need is to ask you some questions."

He looked at the name stitched on the front of my coveralls and smirked. "Get out my face, *Eddie*. You ain't no fucking police."

A fair point. Clemons turned and started walking.

"Maybe not," I said, "but that could be arranged. The cigar alone is reason enough to bring you in for questioning."

He stopped and looked at me again. "Bullshit."

"It's the same brand as a chewed-up stub found at a crime scene last month," I said. "I'd show it to you myself except it's locked up in the evidence room at RPD headquarters." That wasn't true but he didn't know it.

"Same brand don't mean shit," Clemons said. He took the cigar stub out of his mouth and looked at it. "A lot of men smoke these."

"Actually, they don't. That's a Mohawk Chief you're chomping on. Those are pretty rare around here."

"Yeah, well, I haven't murdered anybody," he said.

He walked away again.

"I don't think you have," I said. "But I do think you've been set up to take the fall for one. There was a Mohawk Chief stub found near a body in the Seventeenth Street train yard just down the hill. Miller probably planted it, but the cops might not think so. In fact, if they come out here and find some of your cigar stubs, not only will they arrest you, they'll enjoy doing it."

He stopped. "Look, man, I'm just trying to run my business. What do you want?"

"Do you know Mick Miller?"

"Yeah, I know him. So?"

"You might want to pick your friends a little more carefully."

"He's not a friend, he's a business associate."

"What business is that?"

"I deliver trailers for the Turnpike Authority. I'm a contractor, a legitimate businessman. They need 'em and I deliver them, that's what I do."

"Yeah, well, your associate is trying to frame you for murder. You know Casey Lloyd, right?"

"I don't know no damn Casey," he said.

"Then why did I find a picture of you when I searched his place?"

"Damned if I know, man," he said. "What place? What picture?"

I pulled the photo out of my pocket and showed it to him. He shrugged.

"I went to some weird party one night, so what? Doesn't mean I killed anybody."

I sighed and shook my head. The lead looked like a dead end, not exactly a surprise by now.

"Happy now?" he said.

I kept staring at the picture. "Do you at least know who took it?"

"Actually, yeah," Clemons said. "Some dude named Simkins."

Then he turned and slogged his way down the hill.

"Sam Simkins?" I asked.

Clemons paused and looked over his shoulder at me. "I think so, yeah. Always taking pictures. Dude gave me the creeps."

"Do you mind if I ask how you remember that?"

"Easy," Clemons said. "Motherfucker owes me money."

CHAPTER 36

Suspect

I'd met Simkins one afternoon after I agreed to help Mike Wells look for Jane Wynant. Her parents were paying Simkins a small fortune to help her overcome a stammer. The therapy was helping, and Jane was becoming more confident speaking in class and among her friends. Then she went missing during the Tobacco Festival Parade on the night of October 12. Her father was an aging skinflint from Detroit nicknamed Daddy Warbucks who, legend had it, had made his money profiteering off aluminum during the war. He didn't think much of the progress RPD was making and decided to go private. The old chiseler wanted control more than he wanted results, so Mike got the gig the following Friday. While they negotiated the nice price, the trail went cold. No ransom note, no sightings, nothing. Shortly after, Mike called me.

At the time, I wasn't so sore about Daddy Warbucks's negotiating tactics that I wouldn't take some of his money under the table. Mike had set up interviews at St. Patrick's. I told him they were a waste of time, but he had gone to some trouble setting them up and didn't want to hear it. The school was up in Church Hill at Twenty-Sixth and Grace. We held the interviews in two classrooms with members of Jane's social circle. This included her friends and teachers, as well as her speech therapist, Dr. Sam Simkins.

In my interview with Simkins, something had seemed off. He smoked a pipe that he fiddled with constantly. He was in his early forties, medium height and build with a full head of hair, but his mottled skin and gray temples had made him look older. His offices were in Cary Court, where Jane Wynant went three days a week for therapy.

Simkins had brought some reports regarding her progress. He didn't have much to say that was helpful, but I got the impression there was something he wasn't saying. But then Daddy Warbucks had gotten wind of my involvement and blew his stack. He threw me off the case and made sure I stayed off. I collected my fee from Mike and left a note in the file to follow up with Simkins. Then I had tried to forget the whole damn thing.

I left Clemons at the worksite and drove home. There I changed out of my coveralls and into civilian garb—suit and hat, a loosened red tie. The Beretta was holstered under my jacket. I got back in the van and drove to the shop, but I stopped at Sardi's for a sandwich first. Out on the sidewalk, I passed City Diner, now closed for good. Someone had smashed the glass front door with a cobblestone; jagged shards littered the ground. At the Sock Shop, Roger Viola was locking the front door for the day and muttering to himself.

"You know how many sales I had today?" he asked.

"A pair?"

"Not one," he said. "Not a single one."

There goes the neighborhood. It might have been a small mercy if the Authority had taken his building. I wouldn't have wanted to stay. I got to the shop and checked my messages, went through the *News Leader* classifieds, packed, and made a few calls. One of them was to Vince at Old Market Auto to check on the Mercury 8. I was told he was in Norfolk on a family emergency. Swell. My next call was to a real estate agent named Abe Fronek. By five o'clock, I'd arranged to see a vacant building at 108 N. Seventh Street. It was a brick two-story with parking around back, and close enough to the financial district that no interstate would be built through it anytime soon. The rent was a little more than I could afford but I took it on the spot. The payday from the RPTA would help. I got the keys from Abe and brought some boxes and tools in from the van. Then I took a few minutes to look the place over in the dark.

* * *

I wanted to go home but decided to swing back by the shop for a box I'd forgotten earlier. The trip back into Shockoe was quiet until I brought the van to a halt at the intersection of Fifteenth and Cary. On my right down the sidewalk, the red and white lights of two RPD squad cars lit the night in front of my shop. At least one cop stood loitering out front. Whatever this was, I didn't like the looks of it. On a bench outside the train station, a couple of winos watched me in the idling van. As far as I could tell, they were the only ones who'd spotted me. One of them raised a brown paper bag in my direction and took a deep drink.

From Fifteenth I took a left onto Main and traveled west. I didn't peel out, I didn't speed off. I drove like normal person whose name wasn't plastered all over the side of his vehicle and was definitely not suspected of anything. Thanks, Vince. I kept to side streets for the most part and blended in with what little traffic there was. It took a while, but somehow, I arrived safely back in my neighborhood with no squad cars, sirens, or cops. My building was dark and quiet, which was fine since I wasn't planning to stay. I just needed enough things to live somewhere else for a few days. They might have known about my old shop and my apartment. But they didn't know about the new building on Seventh.

At my place on North Morris, I let myself in and found the light. I was alone for all of two seconds when I heard a knock at the door. Actually, it was more of a pounding, followed by some shouting. I opened the door a crack and found John Clay on the other side pointing his revolver at my forehead. I noticed the revolver first—it was chrome and loaded with real bullets. I stood back from the door as it swung open. Clay was accompanied by a patrolman I recognized, Officer Evans, who'd helped me with the house on Grove the day before. Through the open front door came the static chatter of a police radio from a car in the street. I heard my name in connection with an APB. Evans frisked me and took the Beretta, handed it to Clay.

"Evans," I said, "whatever this is, you shouldn't be mixed up in it."

The kid drew his gun on me, a regular Matt Dillon. I couldn't even imagine the hours that had gone into practicing that in front of a mirror. I try to do him a favor, and this is what he does.

"Hands up," he said.

"Easy, kid," I said. "Clay, I don't guess you have a warrant."

He holstered his gun, then reared back and gut punched me. Just north of a low blow, it still dropped me to a knee. Then he produced a folded piece of paper from his jacket pocket and waved it in front of my face. "Signed and sealed," he said.

I snatched it from him and read it. "Premeditated murder?"

"We have reasonable suspicion to believe that a felony has been committed on the premises, specifically in your bedroom upstairs."

"Doesn't sound reasonable to me," I said, "but congrats for finding a judge at this hour."

I managed to stand. The kid motioned me aside with his revolver while Clay went up the stairs. After a minute, he called out for us to join him. I went first. The overhead light was on in the bedroom. On the near corner of the bed, I could see a woman's bare foot tied to the post.

"You pissed off the wrong people yesterday, Bostic," he said.

"What is this?"

"Why don't we go ask your lady friend?"

"You'll have to be more specific. I keep a harem."

"Well, one of 'em is all cozied up in your bed. Something mighty familiar about her too. If I'd known what kind of pervert you are, I would have kept her away from you."

Clay shoved me forward into the open doorway of my bedroom. Atop the bed was a deceased, naked woman purple in the face, hands and feet bound to the posts. It was Lila Cummins, tongue swollen, blank eyes fixed on the ceiling. Around her neck was a slim belt cinched at the buckle. I recognized it as the belt from a St. Patrick's uniform, the same one I'd found at the abandoned house in Colonial Heights. I'd brought it home as evidence but never secured it.

"You may fry for two murders, Bostic."

"Planting corpses, John? Is that what got you kicked off the Jacksonville PD?"

"She ain't planted, bub. Not 'til the coroner's done with her."

"This looks more like Mick Miller's handiwork. You don't have the sand for something like this."

"Doesn't matter now. A dead woman in your bed strangled with a belt found in your apartment. A little incriminating, wouldn't you say? We can't have a killer sex maniac like that running the streets. But let me guess: you have an airtight alibi and a slew of witnesses who will swear to your whereabouts this evening."

I had nothing of the sort. "You know damn well I didn't do this," I said.

"Prove it, you Yankee piece of shit. Officer Evans?"

"Yessir?" the kid said.

"Would you say the prisoner is being uncooperative?"

"I would, sir."

This time I saw the punch coming and bobbed left as his fist flew past my head. I popped him with a right hook square in his big, jowly hog jaw. His hat flew off, and he wobbled for a second but never went down. By this time, Evans had quick-drawn his weapon again and had me dead to rights.

"Freeze and place your hands in the air, sir," the kid said.

The order was problematic, but I put my hands up just the same. Clay straightened his tie and gave me a look I didn't like. He fished a pair of handcuffs from his coat, then spun me against the wall and slapped them on.

"By the power vested in me by the Commonwealth of Virginia and City of Richmond, I hereby arrest you for the crime of murder in the first degree."

CHAPTER 37

Tunnels

Evans dropped us off in front of the station and went to park the car. Clay led me through the lobby to the elevator and pressed the button.

"So, how long have you been corrupt?" I asked. "Is that what got you run out of Jacksonville?"

His face reddened. "It was nothing like that," he said.

"Every crooked cop in history has a good reason for doing what they did. Still doesn't make it right."

"Like you're so pure," he said.

The elevator door opened.

"Did you get the RPD gig through Admiral Security?" I asked him. "Otherwise, I don't see how you qualify."

He wasn't in a talkative mood, so I pressed.

"I'm guessing you applied to work at Admiral, but when they saw your police background, they figured out another use for you. They needed a man on the inside at RPD and fixed it so the incident in Jacksonville magically went away. They fooled just enough of the right people here to get you the spot."

We came to the interrogation room and he threw me inside. The other day, he and I had questioned Lila Cummins in here. Now she was dead, and I was on the other side of the table for it.

"I've been meaning to ask, what's the going rate in Jacksonville for a cop who covers for a pedophile priest?"

He hit me hard enough to knock me to the floor. As luck would have it, that was where he'd pistol-whipped me the day before and it hurt. The cut reopened. I stayed down on the black and white tile floor and closed my eyes against the trickle of blood already starting to sting. I blinked. The chair and table legs came into focus as Clay moved toward me. He grabbed my jacket by the scruff and threw me back down in the chair. He drew his weapon and pointed it directly at my head.

I closed my eyes as the pounding in my temple took over like a drum. Part of me was ready for him to pull the trigger. It would end the pain, end everything. There was a pause, so I opened my eyes and blinked at him.

"Well?" I said.

He held the gun on me for another second, then drew it back as a knock at the heavy wooden door startled both of us. From the hallway, Evans asked for permission to enter, which Clay granted. By the time Evans got inside and closed the door, Clay's gun was back in his holster.

"Keep an eye on the prisoner," Clay said to him. "I need to make a call."

He stepped outside and closed the door. Evans stood there in his brown RPD uniform, arms crossed.

"Look," I said. "You don't seem like a bad kid, but there's some crooked shit going on around here. I don't want to see you caught up in it."

Evans remained silent.

"At the very least, Clay is dirty. He or someone he knows is responsible for the dead woman in my apartment."

Evans didn't move.

"So I guess some aspirin is a no?"

I set my head down gently on the table and closed my eyes. I kept it there while Clay came back into the room.

"Evans, have you finished processing the paperwork for this prisoner?" he asked.

"I have, sir."

"Good," Clay said. "It's late and the prisoner is being uncooperative."

It wasn't until he slammed his hand on the desk next to me that I lifted my head.

"Evans, you may go about your business. I will remand the prisoner to city jail myself."

"Are you sure, sir?" Evans asked. "My watch isn't over for another hour."

"I've got it, Evans," Clay said. "You are dismissed. Leave the door open."

Evans gave the scene one last disappointed look, then opened the door and left.

"City jail," Clay said. "Such a welcoming place. Too bad we're not headed there. Come on."

He stood me up by the collar again and shoved me toward the door. I stumbled into the corridor.

"Any chance I could have the Beretta back?" I asked. "It was kind of a present."

"Sure," he said. "Let me undo those cuffs while I'm at it. They look so tight and uncomfortable."

He did neither. We took a back way out, down a staircase that let out onto North Eleventh. We trudged north, nary a cop in sight. At Twelfth and Marshall, the DeSoto pulled up and stopped, Miller himself at the wheel. Clay gave me a shove toward the car with the sole of his shoe. As he reached to open the door, I pinned his wrist to the handle with my foot and pressed as hard as I could. He let out a yelp and bent forward. I regained my balance, then brought my knee up and caught him in the face. His nose cracked and he fell to the curb. I took off up the street, both hands still cuffed behind me. Miller yelled something at me and fired two shots that missed.

With a squeal of tires, the DeSoto raced up the block. Its headlights caught me crossing the street near the White House of the Confederacy. I raced past it up the sidewalk toward East Clay. The MCV Library was locked up tight for the night, but the entrance to the Capitol tunnel system just below it wasn't. The car screeched to a stop as I raced down the concrete stairwell beneath the library's main entrance. Beside a gray metal door was a black and yellow Fallout Shelter sign. I turned my back to the door, found the handle, and yanked it open.

The tunnel greeted me with a rush of warm, humid air. Its concrete passageways were seven feet by seven feet, but still felt claustrophobic thanks to the array of pipes and ducts that snaked along the walls on both sides. Lightbulbs in metal cages lined the ceiling to provide what little light there was. It seemed like every third one was out or flickering. The air was damp and stale. I plunged ahead through a spiderweb and reached the first turn. The door opened behind me and another gunshot blasted through the tunnel. I followed the chamber southeast and passed under MCV's power plant on Thirteenth Street.

I stopped briefly to move my cuffed hands to the front, looping them through my legs. From behind me came the sound of someone trying not to be heard, so I pressed on toward the section beneath a nurse's dormitory, St. Philip Hall. After a twist that took me under Hunton Hall, the tunnel forked between the two buildings. This was the likeliest place to get lost if you didn't know where you were going.

I heard the sound of squeaky wheels on concrete ahead of me. I stopped and listened for another minute as steam hissed through the pipes along the wall. I knew it was not uncommon for med students to use the tunnels. I turned a blind corner and ran into a young Japanese man in green scrubs. He was pushing a gurney in the pale light. As I stood opposite him with a dead man between us, he pulled the sheet up to cover the face of the corpse. He shook his head as he looked at me.

"God damn," I said. "Are you real?"

He looked surprised. "I think so."

"Is there anyone behind me?"

We were both quiet for a moment as he listened.

"I don't think so," he said. He noticed the cuffs on my wrists. "You don't look so good, mister."

"I don't guess you have a key," I said.

"If I was you," he said. "I'd be more concerned about that cop hanging out by the tunnel entrance to MCV. It's about thirty yards straight ahead."

"Did you get a look at him?"

"Somebody busted his face for him."

"Good. The man back there that's after me," I said, "he's armed, so steer clear."

I moved ahead steadily, keeping low. Outside the MCV tunnel entrance, the silhouette of John Clay stood inside a triangle of yellow light. He produced a flask and took a deep, long pull, then slouched against the wall. By this time, I was close enough to hear him trying to light a cigarette. He turned his body against the tunnel's warm draft, but the lighter still wouldn't work. I moved up quietly behind him and made both hands into a large fist.

"Need a light?" I asked.

Clay turned and I smashed into his face, catching him flush on the nose again. Any part of it that wasn't broken before was broken now. Blind with pain, he cried out as he landed on the tunnel's concrete floor. I pounced on him and slammed his head twice against the floor, knocking him unconscious. After a quick search, I found the keys to the cuffs in the front pocket of his jacket. I dragged him into a shadow and found the Beretta tucked into the back of his waistband. It was warm and sweaty, with a round still chambered. I shook my head.

"I told you it was a gift," I said.

CHAPTER 38

Gold Star Society

With the Beretta back in hand, I paused to listen for noise in the tunnel behind me. It sounded like Miller had given up. I made my way through the tunnel entrance into the basement of the MCV building and closed the heavy door behind me. It opened onto a long, wide corridor tiled in green and white. I passed through an area of abandoned IV's, wheelchairs, stretchers, and other hospital equipment. The first men's room I came to had a sign outside that read "Colored," but I didn't think they'd mind. Inside, I took a minute to work the cuffs free.

My wrists were bloodied and bruised, so I ran some cold water over them and washed my face. It had the desired effect of making me look slightly less terrible, so I straightened my coat and tie. My hat was long gone. I still looked like a man on the run, but all I needed to do was find Broad Street and vanish. I took the freight elevator to the lobby, doing my best Claude Rains. As I headed for the exit, I saw a familiar head of blond hair sitting in a chair at the admission window. I didn't think it could be her, but the closer I got I saw that it was.

"Daisy?" I asked.

She turned and looked at me. Even with her eyes red and swollen with tears, she was still beautiful. "Eddie!" she said. She stood up and hugged me. "You got my message?"

"No," I said. "I just happened to be here." A lie would have sounded better but she didn't seem to notice.

"It's Mort," she said. "He's had a heart attack."

"Jesus," I said. "When?"

"This morning," she said. "I was in Atlanta when I got the news, but I got back as quick as I could. He's on the ninth floor."

I wasn't in any condition for a hospital visit, unless I was the one being visited. Sweat from the tunnel dried cold on my skin. My hands shook and my temple ached, but I didn't see much choice. Mort had been like a father to me when I first came to Richmond, had gotten me a spot with the RPD. He and his family were the whole reason I'd stayed. Now I had failed each of them in turn, starting with Archie back on Saipan. I'd have to gut it out. With the police and Admiral Security thugs looking for me, I moved us quickly through the lobby to the elevator. As the doors closed, Daisy looked up at me and noticed the cuts and bruises on my face and neck.

"Your job looks a lot more dangerous than it sounds," she said.

It was the first time we'd seen each other since the train station, and under the circumstances it was hard to tell if she seemed different.

"How did you find out about Mort?" I asked.

"The Thompsons next door. Dad didn't look well when I left, so I told them how to reach me in Atlanta."

"Does anyone else know?"

"I don't know. If dad was working, some of his co-workers might know. He works too hard for that company."

"I couldn't agree more. It's funny though, since this is the first of Admiral Security I'm hearing from either of you. Mort never mentioned his new gig, and this is the first time I've heard about it from you. If I didn't know better, I'd say you two didn't want me to know he had unretired and gone back to work."

"How am I supposed to know what you two talk about?"

"Then let me ask you this: Is there going to be an armed man waiting for us when the elevator doors open? Short little guy?"

The elevator dinged to a stop. As we waited for the doors to open, Daisy apologized. "He made me do it," she said. "Told me I couldn't see dad unless I did what they asked me to do."

The doors parted and Miller was standing there holding a gun on me. Daisy sidestepped him on her way out of the elevator. Miller waved the gun at me to step forward.

"Let's have the pistol," he said. "Slowly, left hand."

I stepped off the elevator and handed him the Beretta, which he stuck in his coat pocket. "I oughta dust you right now," he said.

"Check your man down in the tunnel first," I said. "He wasn't looking so good the last time I saw him."

"Forget him. Move."

I went down the green and white tiled floor under the glare of fluorescent light. Down a hallway, I spotted a man standing guard outside one of the rooms. We went in past him and into room 910, which was unoccupied by anyone in need of medical attention. Instead, the man waiting for me there was none other than Teddy Janus.

"Bostic," he said. "What a nice surprise."

"Wish I could say the same."

"Oh, come now," he said with a thick country accent. "How about a little of that Southern hospitality for an old friend?"

"Dry up."

"You know, you might want to watch how you talk to a potential employer."

"I'm just here to see Mort."

"Yes, poor Mr. Williams. That is unfortunate."

"Nice to know his employer is so concerned."

"We're not," he said. "Mort can be replaced."

"Can't we all?"

"I'm beginning to think you might not be taking my job offer seriously."

"Some offer." I glanced at Miller. "I'm not used to job interviews with a gun pointed directly at me."

Janus looked over at him. "Mick, put it away. And while you're at it, give him back his piece."

"Boss," Miller said. "This guy's a pain in the ass."

"Just do what I tell you."

Keeping his gun trained on me, Miller put the Beretta on the floor and kicked it across the tile toward me. "Choke on it," he said.

"Now then," Janus said, "the hard sell. This is your last chance on the job offer. What do you say?"

"Janus, until one week ago you hadn't seen or talked to me since 1944. I promise you I'm not the right man for much of anything."

"From what I've seen and heard these past few days, you are the exact sort of man we'll need. Think of it. Travel the country and make more money than you ever thought possible. After her divorce, you might even be able to afford Daisy Williams and a nice castle on the James where you can both live happily ever after."

"When do you need an answer?"

"Tomorrow."

I got the impression that saying no right then could be hazardous to my health, so I told him he'd have an answer in twenty-four hours. Then I turned and got the hell out of there.

Down the hall, Daisy was speaking with a nurse outside Mort's room. I walked past them without a word and went to his bed. He was hooked up to a machine and looked ghastly. His face drooped beneath gray skin, and his eyes blinked at the ceiling. I pulled a chair to his beside. He reached out with his right hand and grasped mine.

"This is a real mess, Mort," I said.

A tear escaped his right eye. "I thought I could help."

"Help who?" I asked.

"Casey," he said. "He needed help if he was going to escape that life."

"He escaped it all right. In a box."

"Don't," Mort said. "I couldn't save Archie, but I thought I could save Casey."

I closed my eyes. "How did you even know him?"

Mort swallowed. "Some time ago, I started to attend these gatherings I'd heard about for parents who'd lost a son in the war. The Gold Star Society. The meetings were small and hosted in different houses around the city; people took turns. Anyway, we'd sit in a circle talking about what had happened, how our lives had changed. It helped, it really did."

He motioned for a glass of water on the table by the bed, so I reached for it and bent the straw to his mouth. He finished drinking and continued.

"One night, a meeting was held in this little neighborhood off Jeff Davis. I'd had a breakthrough of sorts when I finally realized Archie was gone for good and there was nothing I could do about it. But I could take the energy I would have put into Archie and channel it into something positive. I could find someone, anyone, who needed help and make a difference in that one person's life.

"On the way home that night, my car broke down. I was alone, it was dark and late, and I didn't know the area. That was when I met Casey. He happened by and offered to help with the car."

Daisy came into the room with a doctor, who told me I needed to leave. I was desperate to learn more from Mort, but it would have to wait. I stood and Daisy took the chair beside the bed.

I went to the room's entrance and looked down the empty hallway, then walked to the room where I'd spoken with Janus. It was empty too.

Back in Mort's room I found Daisy speaking softly to him and holding his hand. I sat down in a corner chair and closed my eyes. After a few minutes, I heard them say good night to each other. I stood as she walked over to me.

"Catch a lift?" I said.

"Sure," she said. "We need to talk."

"About what this time?"

"The contents of dad's safe," she said.

CHAPTER 39

Long Distance

On the way to Mort's house in Windsor Farms, Daisy and I had a chat. Given the stress she was under, I took most of what she told me with a pillar-sized grain of salt. I know she did the same.

She'd known for a few months that Mort had gone to work for Admiral Security and that he'd been secretive about it with her too. He had unretired sometime last year, less out of choice than necessity. Mona's cancer treatments had been long, expensive, and ultimately fruitless. When she died their savings was gone, and at sixty-one Mort was a widower and nearly bankrupt. He took the gig at Admiral Security as their General Counsel just to put food on the table. If the swimming pool out back was any indication, it did that and more. His employer had money to burn.

We found Mort's safe inside a wall in the den. It held some papers and files, a box of jewelry, and an old pocket watch.

Daisy spoke up. "Dad told me he asked to inspect the operation so that he would have some idea of the activity he was supposed to defend. He brought his camera along to document what he saw, but clearly he was not supposed to. He had to develop them himself. No one else could see them."

An envelope was nestled toward the back next to some old family documents and labelled Ad. Sec. in Mort's neat cursive. Inside it was a series of pictures of people coming off a ship at night, shackled at their ankles with a length of chain. Others showed them in their bunks aboard what appeared to be a ship. The effect of the photos was that they had been taken surreptitiously, hastily. Some were blurred or taken at odd angles, while others were cut off with a piece of coat fabric or thumb, as if taken from a pocket camera. But enough of them were clear that the story they told was no less horrifying. Janus, Miller, and Clay were in many of the pictures. Mort had written a brief description of each picture on the back. The envelope also contained some shipping invoices I would need to look at more closely.

* * *

I took the envelope with me before we went upstairs and sat down at the kitchen table. Nearby stood the grandfather clock Mort had assembled some years back. It had seemed a sort of therapy for him in dealing with Archie's death. He took no small amount of pride at having assembled it himself in his woodshop and he'd point out its craftsmanship to any and all who asked. Winding it involved a complexity of metal chains to calibrate the pendulum. As Daisy and I sat there exhausted, it chimed 1:30 a.m.

"So what now?" she asked.

"Sleep," I said. "I'm beat."

"And what are our sleeping arrangements?"

"I was curious about that myself," I said, "after that stunt in the elevator."

"They said they wanted to see you about a job offer and asked if I could get you there. I couldn't see Mort until I at least tried to reach you. It sounded harmless enough."

"Forget it," I said.

I went to Mort's room and clicked on the light. After a minute, Daisy joined me and started rooting through the nightstand. She found Archie's letter.

"This must be it," she said. "The famous letter." She sat down on the side of the bed and examined the battered envelope, saw the brown blood stain faded in the corner.

"You've never read it?"

"I never could make myself," she said. "How long did you carry it around?"

"From July '44 to April '46. It's what brought me to Richmond. I took the train all the way from Troy."

"I remember that day," she said, "out in the garden." She turned the letter over in her hand. "This is his blood on the envelope?"

"Mine."

Daisy just stared at it.

"It's open, go ahead and read it. That's why I carried it with me from hell and back, so his family could see and have it for themselves."

Daisy just held it in her hand and wiped away a tear.

"Have you ever heard that when you give someone a gift, you give up control of whatever they choose to do with it?"

"I guess."

"What I want to do with this is tear it up into so many little pieces that I can forget it ever existed and go back to being the person I was before any of this ever happened."

"Back before we knew each other. Can't blame you there."

"Not like that," Daisy said. "If he never writes this letter, he never dies." Then she looked at me. "I've always wanted you in my life, Eddie. You know that."

"Go ahead and rip it up. If you're comfortable making that call for Mort. It's nothing to me but old paper."

I lay flat on the bed and let out an exhausted sigh. Daisy quietly placed the letter back in the nightstand and closed the drawer.

"No," she said. "Don't fall asleep. Not here."

She grabbed my hand and pulled me down the hall to the guest bedroom, which had once been hers. It had a musty, closed-door feel. It also had a made bed, which we crawled into. Inside a minute, we were both out cold.

* * *

The next morning gave me a glimpse of the life I'd missed out on. I awakened to the smell of bacon and eggs wafting up from the first floor, followed by a slight burning smell. When Daisy came back up to the room wearing a man's dress shirt, she was carrying a tray of food and a glass of orange juice. I sat up and started in on the food.

"You remember how I like my eggs."

"Don't remind me," she said. "That information is taking up valuable real estate in my brain. If it weren't for things like that, I might be able to learn something valuable, like a second language or the theory of relativity."

"Are these key concerns of yours?"

"No, just some examples."

"The glamorous Hollywood lifestyle of Daisy Williams. Are you this gracious at home, or are you too busy rushing around from studio to studio?"

"I wish I had that problem," she said. "I spend more time at home than I do working."

"And you've used the extra time to brush up on your domestic skills?"

"Some," she said. "But I'm not completely predictable yet."

"I'll say. What do you have planned for today?"

The phone rang. There was no extension in the guest room, so Daisy took the call in Mort's room. I could only hear her side of the conversation, but that was enough to know it was her husband back in L.A. She filled him in on what was happening and told him he might need to be ready to bring their son to the East Coast. They spoke of a few other matters, and Daisy asked him to put their son on. She spoke with him for a bit. I could hear how much she loved him, how her voice went soft and sweet. Then her husband came back onto the line, and they spoke some more. By the time she got back to the room, I was already half-dressed.

"I knew there was a reason I hated myself more than usual today," I said.

"Stop it," Daisy said. I watched her reflection as she checked the mirror and fixed her hair. "I couldn't just let it ring. And don't give me that look."

"Do you still love him?"

"I married him, didn't I?"

"That's no answer."

"Then I guess the answer is no, not much." She turned to face me, her lipstick artfully applied. "Did you know I see a shrink in L.A.? Of course you don't, why would you? My husband pays for it, which he believes gives him the right to speak with my therapist behind my back. And I found out not long ago he's been reading my diary."

"So leave him already."

"And come back to Richmond? I can't do that without an answer."

"I already gave you one."

"You'll help provide for me and my son if I do that?"

"I already said."

"That I'll be Mrs. Eddie Bostic?"

"Say the word," I said. "I can't undo the past, but the future is ours."

I sat down on the side of the bed. We were quiet for a few seconds, then she found a small suitcase and packed some clothes for an overnight stay. She took out a full-length white cotton nightgown and threw it in on top, then zipped the bag closed.

"As for your original question," she said, "I plan to spend the rest of the day at MCV with Dad. If I have to stay the night, I'll be ready. What about you?"

"I need to go home and feed the goldfish," I said. "Mind dropping me there?"

"What time?" Daisy asked.

She peeled the dress shirt over her head and cast it aside, then moved toward me in all her naked glory. She tugged on my tie and looked up at me.

"I never did like you in this one very much," Daisy said. "And I don't believe you own a goldfish."

She undid the knot and threw it into the corner with her discarded dress shirt. The two went surprisingly well together. She kissed my chest and looked up at me as she straightened a lock of hair on my forehead. Hating myself for it would just have to wait.

CHAPTER 40

Julian's

She dropped me off that afternoon on Plum, a few streets away from my apartment. It was a typical sleepy Sunday in the Fan District with few people out. I took extra care with the cars parked nearby, last night's failure at this very task still fresh in mind. Again, though, nothing suspicious. No RPD cruisers, no DeSoto. The yellow tape across the front door was a helpful reminder that my apartment was now a crime scene. The neighbors must have loved that. I went in through the back and made sure the place was empty.

Inside the bedroom, the mortal remains of Lila Cummins had been removed, along with my mattress, my address book, and a few other things. That she had ever been there at all was deeply disturbing. I wanted to call Herb Ivor to see if she'd been through yet, but it was Sunday, and I didn't have his home number. If she'd been processed, that would tell me this was being done by the book. If she hadn't, it told me Clay and Miller had taken care of it personally.

I went to my desk and examined the yellow shipping invoices from Mort's safe. They were for cargo delivered to Admiral Security at Deepwater Terminal beginning in early July and going through October. The deliveries were made by a shipping company I'd never heard of named Rex Nautical. I studied the dates and realized each shipment fell on the first Sunday of the month at 11:00 p.m. No specifics as to the cargo, just numbers. There was no invoice for November, which made me realize today was the fourth, the first Sunday of the month. I cleared my calendar for the night just in case.

The phone rang. The list of people I wanted to talk to was pretty short, so I let it ring itself out. It took a while. Things were quiet again for a few minutes as I gathered enough belongings to survive a few days away. I also changed into some fresh clothes and found a suitable hat. The phone rang again; this time I picked up.

"Eddie? It's Mike Wells. What the hell is going on?"

"You tell me."

"Word is you murdered a woman, assaulted a police detective, and escaped custody."

"That sounds about right," I said. "RPD doesn't seem terribly interested in finding me at the moment, but that's subject to change."

"I saw John Clay at the station earlier. He didn't look so good. Bandaged nose and raccoon eyes that kept watering up. You wouldn't know anything about that, would you Eddie?"

"Not a thing," I said. "Is that why you called?"

"Not entirely."

"Let me guess," I said. "The St. Patrick's girl?"

"I'm at a dead end," Mike said. "I think I'm about to get fired."

"So this wasn't a welfare check. That's hurtful."

"Well, I figure while I've got you. You know how it is."

"I've been kicked off that case once already. And besides, I have plans this evening. But if you care to part with few of your client's dollars, we can talk."

"How can you think about money at a time like this?"

"Easy," I said. "The rent's due."

"I'll cut you in if you help me."

"Up front," I said.

"Fine. Where can we meet?"

"Well," I said, "I have some things I need to do first, but it shouldn't take long. Meet me at Julian's at six. You're paying. Bring the case file."

***

Among the things I had to do was make one last trip down to the shop. To my amazement, I had managed to move almost everything from the building, still mine until midnight. It was where I'd worked for almost two years, where I'd learned a trade from a decent man and straightened out my life. All that was left of that was a couple of boxes and some tools. This was my last chance to retrieve it before the wrecking ball arrived.

When I got close, I used back alleys to reach my building. The whole area felt different. Sunday afternoons around Main Street Station usually bustled with traffic and pedestrians, but such was not the case now. A ripple effect, maybe, from the condemnation notices and construction vehicles parked nearby. Outside the First Market building, produce vendors stood idle. The buildings on either side of mine were already vacant. Nearby, empty restaurants and darkened storefronts greeted visitors. I loaded up the van, left the shop unlocked, and drove off without a look back.

* * *

I dropped the stuff off at the new place. On the way, an indicator light on the van's dashboard came on, accompanied by an ominous noise from the engine. Just what I needed. I should have pulled over for a look, but I was already late and just wanted to get where I was going. A few minutes later I eased into a booth at Julian's, an Italian place on Broad across from Union Station. The restaurant was busy and I was hungry. Mike had already ordered; he got the cheapest thing he could, spaghetti in butter sauce and a glass of water. Since he was paying, I ordered the most expensive thing: beef tenderloin with green peppers and a glass of red.

"Live a little, man" I said. "Life is short."

"Mine will be if little Janie don't turn up," he said.

"Let's have the file."

He slid it toward me across the crimson tablecloth; it was thick with papers and notes. Where case notes were concerned, Mike favored quantity over quality. There was lots of duplicate information, much of it in his messy scrawl. I reviewed my notes from the interviews—they weren't half bad for a locksmith.

"How's the missus?" I asked.

Mike's wife, Enid, was Jewish, while he himself was not. The marriage wasn't an easy thing for either of them, but they seemed perfectly happy being miserable together.

"Perpetually pregnant," he said.

"Sure they're yours?"

"So far as I know."

"Mazel tov," I said. I flipped through a few pages in the file and found the note I'd left him about Simkins. "Did you ever follow up on the speech therapist?"

"Yeah, he looked okay to me. Why?"

"Something squirrelly about him."

"Not that I saw," he said.

His food arrived. I read the file while he ate and asked a few more questions. Mike was a slow eater and got sauce on parts of the pages. My food arrived before he could finish his.

"Stained case notes," I said. "And you call yourself a professional."

"C'mon, Eddie," he said.

"Follow up with the speech therapist."

"What for?" he asked.

"I just would. Something tells me he's in it up to his elbows. If you'd put a tail on him before now, we wouldn't be having this discussion."

I pushed the file back across the table and started eating.

"I'll do that," Mike said. "Except I kind of need to get home. Enid hates me working late on Sundays."

"That's funny, I hate *me* working late on Sundays."

"How would you feel about having a look yourself?" he asked.

"Later this week, sure."

"There might not be a later this week. It has to be tonight."

"Tonight isn't great," I said. I thought about Deepwater Terminal, and about Daisy and Mort down at MCV. I checked my watch. "I'd need to get paid first. You know my rates, but they go up if it's urgent."

"Payment isn't a problem," Mike said.

He fished an envelope from his jacket pocket, part of the retainer Daddy Warbucks had given him. The last time I'd seen it that day at St. Patrick's, it was considerably thicker. Mike took out double my usual fee and placed it on the table with his palm on top of it. He kept it pinned there as I reached for the cash.

"Tonight, right?" he said.

* * *

After leaving the restaurant, we got caught up in the crowd just leaving *Private's Progress*, a WWII British comedy playing at The Capitol. We passed several people trying out an English accent, seemingly for the first time. We got to my van first, but naturally, it wouldn't start. I told Mike to hang on, and we both took turns looking under the hood. He was no more useful than I was. It was dark and getting late.

"Look," I said, "if you want me to do anything about this tonight, I'm going to have to borrow your car."

"This isn't my car," he said. "It's Enid's."

"I don't care whose car I borrow, but I can't do shit without wheels."

I grabbed my toolbox from the van and placed it in the back seat of Enid's Packard, then climbed in to drive. I dropped Mike off at his place on Robinson and checked in on the therapist's office in Cary Court. It was very much closed this late on a Sunday—most everything was as the city tensed itself for another work week. I pulled the Packard into a spot on Sheppard and took a metal flashlight from my toolbox. A cobblestone alley led to the back entrance of Simkins's office. The door was locked, but I made quick work of it.

Simkins kept his client files in a filing cabinet beside his desk. I found Jane Wynant's file, which I'd first seen during the interviews at St. Patrick's. Her sessions were three days a week after school. I put the file back and thumbed through the ones in the front of the drawer. The one marked "Clay, Cynthia" was new information. John Clay's daughter was also a client; she had a lisp that Simkins was helping her with. Her appointments were three days a week as well, just one hour before Jane Wynant's. They might not have known each other at school, but John would have seen her in this office. Maybe not all the time, but sometimes. The connection might not hold up in court, but it was worth a look.

I got the good doctor's home address from a piece of correspondence in his desk. It was on Addison between Main and Stuart. I left the office and drove to his building and found a spot across the street with a view of the porch. The place was quiet, but there was a light on inside. I wanted a closer look, but first I checked at the cars parked nearby. Miller's DeSoto was parked two spots ahead. Something was up.

I sat quietly for a few minutes with the brim of my hat down. Waiting around for something to happen is most of what investigators do—it's not glamorous or exciting. Most PI pulp covers show a sneering gunman in a doorway firing at a woman inside a room, or a sneering woman inside a room firing at a gunman. It's all so exhausting. No one ever buys a pulp with a cover showing a guy sitting in his car with his hat over his eyes.

About fifteen minutes passed as a light drizzle blurred the windshield. The area was still quiet, so I sat up and rolled down the window. Under a streetlight up the block, a tree lost some yellow leaves in a gust of wind. I was giving those leaves a whole lot of thought when the shot rang out. Just one shot, unmistakable, muffled slightly but still quite sharp. It had come from inside Simkins's apartment.

After another minute, the front room light went out and the building went dark. When the front door opened, a man in a raincoat and hat stepped outside dragging a rolled rug behind him. As he approached the streetlamp, I saw to my surprise it was not Miller but Clay, his nose bandaged. He slung the rug over his shoulder and brought it out to the DeSoto, then popped the trunk and threw it inside. A car passed as he closed the trunk and went back indoors. Clay emerged a minute later leading a barefoot young woman by the arm. She wore tattered clothes over her slight build and her head was covered by a burlap sack. They crossed the street together, then got in the car and drove off. A few seconds later, I followed with the headlights off.

We turned east on Grove through the RPI campus. After a series of turns, we ended up on the Ninth Street Bridge, a narrow wooden span with just one lane in each direction. Each had a pair of metal slats you had to guide your car onto. The noise of tires going across earned it the nickname "The Singing Bridge." Yeah, it sang all right. With no divider between the north- and south-bound lanes, head-on collisions were common. My introduction to it was in 1946, my first day on the job with RPD. A crack-up on a muggy July morning left two dead and traffic tied up for hours in both directions.

The bridge had poles stationed at intervals to support the meager lights strung across. They swayed when there was wind off the James like there was tonight. I drove under the last of these, south into Manchester where the route got tricky. Richmond being what it is, the Ninth Street Bridge let out onto Seventh Street, then hooked east toward Hull. Through the open window came the greasy reek of fuel as we passed the Army Diesel School, which shared the train yard with Southern Railway. The road shifted south a few miles through a rural area running parallel to the James. We took a left toward the river and I checked my watch. The slow boat to China had taken us finally to Deepwater Terminal, and we were right on time.

CHAPTER 41

The Boat

I peeled off and parked between a couple of warehouses facing the James, then followed on foot with the Beretta in hand. Each warehouse was dark and deserted, save for the third and last one. Atop it was a bank of stadium lights that shone out onto the water where a freighter was moored. At its garage bay, two doors stood open. Clay stopped the DeSoto and killed the engine, then went inside and made a phone call. He came back out to the car and stood watching the ship, as if waiting for someone or something. Soon enough, a figure appeared on the deck of the freighter. It was a man in white pants and a blue-and-white striped shirt wearing a captain's hat. He placed a foot on the railing and lit a cigar.

Clay opened the passenger door of the DeSoto and yanked the girl out violently by the arm. She landed hard on the concrete but didn't cry out. Clay threw the car door shut and pulled her to her feet, then took her up the gangplank to the deck of the freighter. He spoke briefly with the man at the railing, who stayed there smoking a cigar after Clay and the girl vanished. I aimed the Beretta at him but didn't have much of a shot. It had been a while since I'd fired a weapon of any kind, and I'd never fired this one at all. The most likely scenario was that I'd miss and give myself away. It didn't help that my hand was trembling.

A few minutes passed and Clay reemerged, alone this time. The two men had another brief exchange, followed by some laughter, before the captain disappeared below deck. Clay stood at the railing and smoked a cigarette, staring down at the dock. At last, he flicked the spent butt into the night and casually strolled down the gangplank to the warehouse.

I could have gone after him but wanted to get to the girl first. Crouched low, I bolted across the dock and up the gangplank. They had gone left and vanished into the ship's interior through an iron door. As I reached for the handle, a muffled thumping noise came from my right. In the shadows I could make out a large wooden cargo crate covered with a heavy oilcloth tarp. I listened again and heard more thumping coming from the crate, followed this time by the sound of voices inside.

I crept over to it and caught a whiff of raw sewage. Either the city's treatment plant wasn't up to snuff or the stench was coming from inside the crate. I checked under the tarp and found the box unmarked. Waste seeped from its base onto the deck and puddled with the rain that was now falling. I knocked lightly on the rough wood.

"*Hola!*" said a voice inside. "*Ola, agua por favor!*"

"Hold on," I said.

The thumping increased and a woman's voice spoke. "Agua, señor!"

I set the tarp back down. As my eyes adjusted to the darkness, I looked around for a crowbar but came up empty. An infant inside the crate began to wail. I went over to the crate and tried to cobble together what little Spanish I could remember.

"I'll come back for you," I said, and then repeated in my halting Spanish. "*Volvere para usted.*"

At the moment, that felt like real hubris. I went to the iron door and listened at it for a moment. I heard nothing, so I opened it and found myself at the top of a narrow stairwell painted gray. When I reached the bottom, I was in a long hallway with a series of rounded metal doors on each side. I put my ear to the first one and heard nothing inside, so I pulled the heavy handle and found it unlocked. The door creaked open to a large, dimly lit chamber filled with rows of wooden bunks. As far as I could tell, the room was empty. Along the end of the closest line, I could make out a series of shackles held together through loops on a long chain. I opened the door on the opposite side of the passageway and found the same setup.

Above each door was a metal lightbulb cage. Most of the bulbs were clear except for one that glowed red farther down the hallway. I approached it and heard a man's voice inside speaking Spanish in low, reassuring tones. I checked the handle. The door wasn't locked, so I gathered myself and opened it.

Inside the room, a single metal bunk was bolted to the middle of the floor. On top of the thin, dirty mattress, the girl lay naked and gagged, her hands and feet bound to the bedframe. Kneeling between her legs was the man I'd seen earlier in the striped shirt and captain's hat. His dirty white pants were pulled down around his knees, and he was trying to get his dick hard enough to do something with. In his concentration he hadn't noticed me and maintained his low patter with the girl as she wept, her eyes glistening. In his left hand he held a Bowie knife.

"Hey!" I shouted, loud enough to startle them both. I advanced on them as if I belonged there, the Beretta trained on him. He looked at the gun with wide eyes.

"Drop the knife," I said, "and get the fuck off her."

In halting English, he responded, "They said it was okay."

"It's not," I said. "Nothing about this is okay. Now drop it."

The knife hit the floor with a clatter. His striped shirt was covered in dark stains, and the cap he wore had an anchor stitched on it in yellow thread. I pointed the gun at his head as he climbed off and pulled his pants up. He had an enormous member, which he had used for the last time.

"¿Eres el capitan?" I asked.

He looked at me. His oily, unshaven face had the stub of a cigar stuck in the middle. "*Sí*," he said.

I lowered the gun and shot him once in the chest. He dropped to the floor in a spasm, so I put another one in him to end that. Inside the narrow room, the gunfire was impossibly loud and set my ears to ringing. I shook my head to clear it, then found a sheet on the floor to cover the young woman. Her hair was dyed black, but I knew exactly who she was. I looked her in the eye.

"Jane Wynant," I said. "You'll be all right."

I found the Bowie knife on the floor and used it to cut her loose. Her body was scraped and bruised, her hands and knees bleeding. None of her injuries appeared major, but what the hell did I know? She sat on the edge of the bed and covered herself in the sheet as I untied her gag. She was reluctant to move, like this was some fake rescue she'd seen before. She pulled her elbow away when I placed my hand on it.

"Can you walk?" I asked. I stood up and offered her my hand. She looked up at me and nodded but didn't speak. Her eyes focused on a spot behind me, then opened wide.

"Y-Y-NH!" she said, pointing behind me. Reflexively, I turned around and reached into my jacket for the Beretta. In the doorway stood Clay, a bandage covering his pulverized nose. His gun was already drawn.

"Uh-uh," he said. "I'll take that."

"You don't look so good, John," I said. I didn't hand the weapon over, hoping to stall him. "How's the family?"

"I'm going to enjoy this," he said.

"Christ, man. She's almost the same age as your daughter," I said. "How can you stomach this?"

"It was never my idea," he said. "I'd never seen her before today. I was told to bring her here, so I did."

"Bullshit. She went to the same speech therapist as your daughter. And you worked security at the Tobacco Festival. You were the one who took her."

"After tonight, none of that is going to matter."

"And Simkins. Was he a loose end?"

"Just following orders."

"Come on, John. Do what's right and help me get her out of here. I'll ask the judge to go easy. I'll tell him we were both looking for her and got here at the same time."

"There's too much else," he said. "Sorry, Bostic. Now let's have the weapon."

I was the only thing standing between him and the girl. "The captain's dead." I said.

"Tough break," he said. "We'll figure something out."

"This boat isn't going anywhere without him."

Navy men hated that. Clay relaxed for a second and gestured with the gun. "It's not a boat," he said. "It's a ship."

In one motion I drew the Beretta, leveled it at his eyes, and pulled the trigger once, striking him in the forehead. The impact blew his hat off in a pink spray as he squeezed off a single shot that ricocheted off the floor. Clay stared briefly at the ceiling as if trying to remember something, then staggered backward and fell heavily, blood gushing across the tiles.

The ringing in my ears was deafening. I took Jane's wrist and led her carefully past him to the door. We went down the deserted and dimly lit corridor toward the staircase that led topside. At the landing I opened the iron door slowly and saw no one on deck. I looked toward the crate and it was quiet. I took Jane to the gangplank and helped her down onto the dock.

Inside the open garage was a phone on a large metal desk. I picked up the receiver and dialed Mike Wells at his house. I didn't know what time it was, but it took a while for him to pick up.

"Get Daddy Warbucks on the horn," I said.

"Geez, Eddie."

"Don't geez me," I said. "I've got your girl at Deepwater Terminal. She's alive. Get down here now. She needs a doctor."

"You have Jane Wynant? How?"

"I'll tell you later," I said. "Just get here. She'll be inside your car. It's parked between the first two warehouses."

"Can't you just bring her yourself?"

"No, you lazy bastard. If you want the headlines, you get your ass down here."

"All right already," he said. "What about Enid's car?"

"You're driving it out of here," I said. "I'm taking yours."

I hung up and took Jane through the open garage door. Clinging to the boxy shadows of the warehouse, I led her to the Packard and put her in the backseat with my coat over her shoulders. She put it on and bunched the sheet around her legs. She trembled and stared vacantly into the darkness. On the river, a passing tugboat blew its horn.

"You're safe here," I said. "There's a man coming for you, his name is Mike Wells. He'll be here in a few minutes to take you to the hospital."

I went to close the door, but she grabbed the arm of my shirt with her fingernails and haltingly tried to speak. Whatever good her speech therapist had done for her was long undone by the trauma. I didn't blame her for being terrified. It was cold and dark and eerily quiet in the alley between the two warehouses, and the air was heavy with river smells.

"I'm sorry," I said. "Keep your head down and wait."

She tightened her grip on the sleeve of my shirt and looked at me through bulging eyes.

"All right," I said. "I'll wait."

I got in behind the wheel as she curled into a ball in the back. Around us the night was quiet and we sat without speaking, though at one point I could hear her sobbing lightly. After a few minutes, a car passed in front of us, speeding toward the dock. More company was the last thing I needed. I kept an eye on the rearview mirror for Mike, who seemed to be in no hurry. I smoked a cigarette. Finally, a pair of headlights appeared in the rearview. I opened the door and got out as he pulled up beside us.

"Take this one," I said, handing him the keys. "She's in the back. Don't stop for anyone or anything."

I opened the back door and looked at Jane, huddled up in the seat. "You're going to be fine," I said, "but I need my jacket back."

She wrapped it tighter around her. I turned to Mike and told him to give her his. Grudgingly, the exchange was made. I shrugged mine back on and straightened my tie.

"Take her to the nearest hospital," I said. "You got that?"

"Yeah," Mike said. "Which one?" He gave me the keys to his car, an old Plymouth.

"Richmond Memorial, wherever. Just get her out of here as fast as you can. Don't use your lights until you hit the road. And for Christ's sake call RPD as soon as you can and tell them to get out here."

"What are you doing?" he asked.

"I'm going back to the ship," I said.

CHAPTER 42

Cargo

The Packard turned around and vanished down the alley. I wished I had gone with them; anyone with any sense would have. All I really wanted to do was go home and sit down with a drink and not think about any of this. I checked the glovebox and then under the seat in the vague hope there'd be a flask of some sort, or maybe a bottle of Manischewitz. No dice. I wasn't surprised; Wells was no fun.

I reloaded the Beretta and chambered a round. The army wasn't good for much, but knowing how to handle a weapon in the dark came in handy sometimes. I made my way back to the freighter rocking lazily in its moorings. Outside the gangplank sat the DeSoto. I ducked down and listened for a moment to the quiet night. Miller may have gone up for a look-see below deck, or he might still be in the garage bay. All I knew for sure was that whoever was stuck in that crate was no closer to freedom if I did nothing.

I ran as quickly as I could onto the deck and took cover behind a large pallet carrying paper bound for Philip Morris. I knelt down at one corner and caught my breath. The night's silence was broken behind me by the click of a pulled hammer.

"Give me one good reason why I don't blow your brains out right here," a voice said.

"Too messy?"

"Hands up," he said. "Stand up slowly and turn around."

When I did, Miller was standing there pointing a .22 at me. "Put the Beretta on the deck. Now."

He had me cold. I placed it on the deck and took a step back.

Miller picked it up and stuck it in his jacket pocket. "You've been busy tonight," he said. "Turn around and start walking."

I did as told. The crate under the tarp was illuminated by the warehouse lights. It was silent.

"Hold on," Miller said.

I stopped walking and looked back to see him pointing the Beretta at the crate.

"Stinks like shit over there," he said. "I think it could use some ventilation. How about six nice, neat holes with your signature on 'em?"

"Your boss won't like that. Damaged cargo costs him money."

"What do I care?" he said. "We've got more money coming in than we can spend."

Miller closed one eye and aimed, then held the pistol there for another second before he pointed it at me again. "Maybe you're right," he said. "Can't make the boss mad. Say, here he comes now."

Miller gestured down the dock at a car racing toward the ship. Since there were no sirens involved, this likely wasn't the cavalry. The car screeched to a stop in the light of the open garage bay. After a moment, Janus got out and stepped forward to look at us, his shadow long as a blade. Then he walked up the gangplank to the deck and over to us. He took off his hat, revealing that ridiculous white hair. He did not seem pleased.

"What in the hell is going on here?" he asked.

"The girl's gone," Miller said. "Clay's dead, so's the ship's captain. I moved the bodies into the hold, but there's still some cleanup to do."

Janus shook his head and studied the surface of the deck. "Goddamn it," he said. "I had a buyer all lined up."

"And there's this," Miller said, producing the Beretta and handing it to Janus. I had now armed them both.

"Swell operation," I said. "Modern-day slave trade. It's been tried in Richmond before, you know."

"Southerners," Janus said. "They had the right idea but didn't think big enough. Why supply slave labor to just the South when you can supply it to the whole goddamn country?"

"For starters, the many laws against it."

"Sure," Janus said. "A nation of laws, not men. Don't believe it for a second. There are some men the law doesn't apply to. And when it tries, they simply bend it."

"It is fun," I said, "catching up like this. I guess I got the job?"

"Consider the offer rescinded."

"In that case, I'll just be on my way," I said.

Miller jabbed the gun in my ribs. "What do you think, boss?" he asked.

Janus thought for a second. "Did Clay bring Simkins?"

"Still in the trunk," Miller said.

"Good," Janus said. "Let's go out to the island."

CHAPTER 43

Footing Pour

I led the way down the gangplank, hands in the air. On the dock I was nudged toward the DeSoto and told to get in the back.

"You'll never guess who I found in Mort's room," Janus said.

I looked over at Janus's car and could see a figure on the passenger side. He went over and opened the door and Daisy emerged. Her hands were tied behind her, and she was dressed only in the long white cotton nightgown I'd watched her pack the night before. Janus led her to the DeSoto, opened the front passenger door, and shoved her inside. He went back into the garage and made a short phone call.

"Daisy, what the hell?"

"I was staying the night in Mort's room when he showed. He must have known they'd find me there. I had no choice."

Miller got in beside me, .22 at the ready, likely the same weapon he had used to kill Casey Lloyd. Janus came back and got behind the wheel. He looked back at me as he adjusted the mirror.

"Miller, cuff him," he said.

Miller rooted around the floor of the backseat and produced a shackle attached to a length of chain and round lead weight. In their line of work, they probably kept a bunch of these just lying around. Before I knew it, the shackle was around my right ankle and held in place with a padlock. The shackle and chain glinted in the dim light, shining as if newly forged. But the padlock was familiar to me. Janus started the car, and we sped north out of the complex toward the city.

"It's funny," Miller said. "I've got the only key for this thing." He rolled the window down and showed me the skeleton key before he pitched it out of the moving car. "Now where's your carry?"

"You already have the Beretta," I said.

"Not that," Miller said. "The lockpick set you carry on you. Let's have it."

"Upper right pocket," I said. I'd moved it from its usual place to accommodate the holster.

Janus spoke up. "Don't sweat it, Bostic," he said. "You're hardly the first man to roam the port of Richmond in a shackle. And you won't be the last."

Miller found my pick set and relieved me of it, then threw that out the window too. We rode without another car in sight for some minutes until the intersection with Maury. I remembered the strange bruise on Casey Lloyd's right leg and knew I was in a dead man's seat.

Janus took a right and kept straight half a mile, then slowed as the road became clogged with construction vehicles along the muddy shoulder. The area was desolate, heavily wooded, and marshy. A hand-painted wooden sign indicated this work was for the relocation of Brander Street, part of Turnpike construction on the south bank of the James.

We stopped as the headlights came to rest on a cement mixing truck idling in the road, its noise and fumes fouling the air. It was ready to move in the same direction we were, headlights on with a little yellow siren on top. Janus rolled down the window. A man in khaki work overalls and a blue cap walked over to the car.

"All set, Mr. Janus," the man said. "Fresh cement as ordered, sir."

"Good," Janus said.

The man took a quick look at me and Daisy. "Can't recommend you use the pier for the car if the mixer is on it," he said. "It's a weight issue; the bridge needs some shoring up. We'll have a crew out in the morning."

The man turned away and was gone. Janus rolled up the window, then turned and looked at us.

"Mr. Miller," he said. "Drive the mixer out to the footing pour. We'll be along shortly."

Miller got out and walked over to the truck, then climbed into the cab. Amid a gnashing of gears, he finally found first and started rolling down the worn and mud-caked road. We followed him to a muddy path that led to the temporary work pier being used to construct the support column for the interstate. Here the truck continued ahead while we rolled to a stop.

Janus killed the engine and turned to look at me. "One last thing, Bostic," he said. "Let's get some air."

"I'd love to," I said, "without the shackle."

"Oh yes, that," Janus said. "I think I have just the thing in the trunk."

He got out of the car and ordered me to do the same. I picked up the round lead weight attached to my left ankle and got out. Janus motioned me to the back of the car, then opened the trunk. I let the weight drop to the ground and the chains clanked. We looked in the trunk and found the body of Sam Simkins rolled up in a rug. At some point in his long journey, he had bled out, and his bowels had shuffled off their own mortal coil.

"Complete this one task for me, and we'll call it even," Janus said.

"I'll need the chain cutters first," I said.

Janus motioned toward the body with the pistol. "You're going to have to move him," he said. "It'll be just like burying dead Japs. I wouldn't know myself; I was smart enough to get out of that detail."

"Wouldn't want to get your hands dirty," I said. With some effort, I lifted the stiffening body out and dumped it on the ground with a thud. Blood and viscera had seeped into a blanket lining the trunk. I moved it around and eventually found a long-handled chain cutter. It was slick in my hands, which were covered in gore. I looked at Janus standing back with the Beretta on me. There was just enough distance between us that he would get me before I could get him.

"You were there when Archie Williams got it," Janus said, loud enough for Daisy to hear. "Right, Eddie?"

"You know damn well," I said. "And you sure as hell weren't."

I took the cutters and broke the chain. A few links trailed behind me, but the weight was gone. I got a better look at the lock that still bound the shackle to my leg. It was a brass Honesty padlock about the size of my hand, thick and bulky, with a sliding cover over the keyhole. They looked intimidating, but Irv used to call them Dishonesty locks. Often, they boasted eight, ten, or twelve levers, but all they really had was two. Easy enough to pick with my regular set, which was sitting by the side of the road a good ways back.

"Word is he got it that night because you cut and run."

"Bullshit," I said.

"Don't be so sentimental, Eddie," he said. "We don't all get an open casket. And besides, that's no way to address your potential employer." He motioned at Simkins's body on the ground. "Pick him up and start walking."

I glanced at Daisy and saw she was crying softly.

"Now," Janus said.

I bent down and lifted the damp and reeking body over my shoulder like a sack as Janus continued.

"It seems odd to get worked up about one death, doesn't it, Eddie? I mean, after carnage on such a mass scale in the Pacific, even on one little island, who can get worked up over one more?" He looked over at Daisy. "Or two more?"

"I'm glad to see you've retained your humanity," I said. "I was afraid you might have lost it during the war."

I started walking into the dark in the same direction as the cement mixer, its exhaust lingering in the heavy air. The hard road soon gave way to a path that led to the river, heavily rutted with the tracks of construction vehicles.

"I never had much use for humanity," Janus said. "There's only winners and losers. I'm a winner. You're not."

Under the circumstances, his point was hard to argue. Halfway down a short hill, we came to a clearing where the city's low, pale skyline came into view. We had reached the south end of the same temporary work pier I'd been on a few days earlier. Farther across, Miller had stopped the cement mixer under a large industrial floodlight beaming bright light on a work area in the riverbed. Simkins wasn't getting any lighter. I stopped for a moment to catch my breath and started going through his pockets.

"Keep moving," Janus said.

Our footsteps echoed across the rough timbers of the pier. To our right, as we walked in darkness above the current, I could see that the first T-shaped support pillar for the interstate had been completed. It was a stout concrete column reaching into the sky, pale enough to glow. Another one nearly completed stood beside it. Farther out into the James, others were mere concrete stumps jutting out of the water. One day they would brace the ribbon of interstate running through Richmond, but for now they stood mute like some inscrutable emissary.

We walked past a series of cranes stretching high into the darkness, then came to the idling cement mixer, its drum revolving smoothly in the floodlight. It was backed up to one of the cofferdams recently driven into the riverbed. The shackle on my leg weighed half a ton, and my legs were brittle as glass. I dropped the body onto the pier, then dragged it by the collar into the light at the edge of the cofferdam. My search of his pockets had yielded a pipe smoker's tool made of brass. I remembered how he kept fiddling with it during our interview. It held a tobacco tamp, a snuff spoon, and a long pin used to clear the stem. The pin and tamp interested me, so I snapped them apart.

"What are you waiting for?" Janus asked. "Dump him."

I pretended not to hear. Given the racket of the cement mixer, it wasn't exactly a stretch. I bent over the dead man and worked the lock on my ankle. In the light of the worksite and shielded by the body, the hardest part was finding those two levers amid all the empty space inside it. Using the tamp as a makeshift tension wrench, I tripped the first lever all the way in the back. I found the second one toward the front and with a click, was free of the shackle and chain. Neither was much of a weapon, but heavy enough if I needed it. I dropped them onto the pier.

"Throw him in!" Janus shouted.

I rolled the dead man over to the corrugated edge of the cofferdam and peered down inside. It was about twenty feet deep and watertight, with a rebar floor large enough for a team of five or six workers. At its center was a cylindrical rebar column that jutted into the air. I peered into it and pretended to see something other than dry riverbed.

"You're going to want to see this," I said to Janus.

Janus fired once and splintered a chunk of the pier three feet away. Miller leaned out of the cab and looked back to see what was happening.

"Everything okay back there, Mr. Janus?" he asked.

"Yes," Janus shouted. "Lift the drum."

Miller went back to the truck's cab and closed the door. With a lurch, the mixer's hydraulic lift sprang to life and raised the drum into pouring position. The noise was now considerable as Janus approached me holding the gun in one hand and Daisy in the other.

"It's a shame this is how you wanted it," Janus shouted over the din. "You could have gotten very rich."

I stood at the edge of the cofferdam, staring into it. Janus pointed the gun at me and squeezed the trigger. The Beretta jammed. Before he could clear it, I tackled him and knocked Daisy free of his grasp.

"Run!" I told her.

She froze for a moment, her eyes wide with terror, then turned and vanished back down the pier. I grabbed Janus's wrist, and we grappled for the weapon. After a moment, it tumbled from his hand and landed in a shadow beyond the floodlight. I brought my fist down into his face twice before he counterpunched and knocked me backward toward the cofferdam. I got to my feet and circled right, looking for any sort of weapon. The shackle and chain sat near the dead man; Janus noticed them as well. As he leaned down to pick it up, I kicked him in the head and knocked him backward. He stumbled over the body and lost his balance, then tumbled headlong into the cofferdam.

Miller sprang out of the cab, gun in hand. Inside the cofferdam, Janus shouted and tried to scale the high steel wall. As Miller advanced, I scrambled to the other side of the truck and crouched near the rear tires as the mixing drum spun on. I looked for the jammed Beretta that had fallen to the pier, but it was nowhere to be seen. I noticed the anchor from the slave ship that I'd seen the other day, now sitting on its side. Miller paused briefly and looked down at Janus and told him he would be out soon. Janus cussed him furiously.

I climbed onto the side of the truck as Miller came around the back, then launched myself into him feet first. The impact sent us sprawling onto the pier as his gun skittered away. Miller hit the back of his head on the rough wood. I landed on my back near his feet. Beside me, the silver shackle and chain glinted in the floodlight. I clamped it tight to his ankle and clicked the padlock shut.

"What the hell?" he said, looking down at me.

Miller lifted his shackled leg and kicked at me as the chain clanked against the wood pier. He scrabbled around and reached for his weapon. I grabbed the end of the chain attached to him and looped it through the rusted hook at the top of the anchor. By now Miller had found his .22 and was aiming it at me. I kicked the anchor off the pier, jerking his leg as he squeezed the trigger. The shot flew wide, and the anchor splashed into the James, back into the past where it had lived for so long. The chain rattled like a saw against the wooden edge of the pier, then dragged Miller screaming into the murky current below.

I waited for him to resurface, but he didn't and never would again. I found the Beretta nearby and cleared the jam, then chambered a round. Janus was where I'd left him, trying to find a handhold on the cold, steep wall of the cofferdam. The drum of concrete continued to rotate under the floodlight, its contents sloshing. The hold on the bottom of the discharge chute that controlled the flow of wet concrete was a simple handheld device. I looked down at him.

"Bostic," he said. "Get me out of here."

I thought about the kid I was back in Troy, the one before war, what he might have done in this situation. God, I hated that kid. I know what my father the minister would do, and what he would have wanted me to do. Look within myself, show compassion, show faith in something, anything. The person I was back then would have done the right thing. Turn the other cheek and help this man, let justice take care of itself. Whatever his crimes were, they were not for me to judge. It was for the Almighty to judge, as He does to all of us eventually.

"What was that you were saying earlier about getting worked up over just one death?" I asked.

"Be reasonable, Bostic," Janus said. "I'm just a businessman. Get me out of here, and I'll hire you to help me make Admiral a legitimate company and get rich doing it."

"Sure," I said. "Tell me some more about Archie Williams. You seem to know an awful lot about him."

"Forget all that," Janus said. "It was twelve years ago. Forgive and forget."

I gave the flap attached to the discharge control a tug, and a torrent of concrete splattered into the cofferdam, enough to cover the rebar floor. Janus swore at me as I staunched the flow. With his shoes covered in wet concrete, he fled for the safety of the rebar cage in the center. He climbed the metal skeleton that held it in place.

"How about his father, Mort? He's in the hospital because of you."

"You're crazy to think I had anything to do with that," Janus said. "Miller did that, he did all of that. Bostic, where is your humanity?"

"I left it on the boat," I said.

I gave him another burst of wet concrete, then looked down at him. How many had died up to this point? I could be sure of the two men in the woods who'd tried to kill me, but that was self-defense. More recently, two men tonight on the freighter and Miller just now. If the cops put that all together, they might conclude I'd gone on a rampage. And they might be right.

"Bostic," Janus said.

I remembered him cutting that man in half with a BAR right in front of me. Like it was nothing, like he enjoyed it. And here he was trafficking in humans, one of them a kidnapped local girl. This was how he'd chosen to live his life after the war, building another slave trade. I could shoot him now and bury him in concrete, and no one would be the wiser.

But that was murder, plain and simple, and I'd had enough of that for one evening.

There was some rope coiled on the pier. He didn't deserve it, but I picked up one end and threw it into the cofferdam. I tied the other end around one of the support pilings and told him to pull himself up. I kept the gun on him as he scaled the steel wall. It didn't look easy; there was a lot of grunting. He'd put on a few pounds over the years and was covered in dirt and wet concrete. As he neared the top, he reached for the pier and his foot slipped. Out of instinct I reached for him and he grabbed my hand, but the sudden weight pulled me off balance. The Beretta fell to the pier as I reached for the rope with my other hand, but before I knew it, I'd lost my balance and was falling. I kept hold of his arm, and he lost his grip and tumbled back into the cofferdam with me. We each landed hard on the slick rebar floor. Janus got up first. I tried to lift myself up but could barely move.

"You're weak, Bostic," Janus said.

"Not too weak to put you away."

"It'll never get that far," he said.

With some effort, I steadied myself against the rebar column and rose to one knee. Before I could stand, Janus was in front of me. He landed two gut punches. As I doubled over, he drove his knee into my forehead and nearly knocked me into the next dimension. I could hear the noise of the cement truck up on the pier as Janus's blurred figure towered above me, blocking the floodlight. He checked me for a weapon, but there wasn't one to find.

"I appreciate the hand, Bostic," he said. "But I really do have to go."

He stepped away from me and toward the rope. I shook my head to clear my vision, but by the time I could focus, he was halfway up the wall. I wondered why he didn't finish me, but I realized it would involve doing it with his bare hands. And he wasn't about to do that if he could watch me squirm from safety instead.

I lost sight of him when he reached the top, and I could only assume he was looking around for the Beretta. I prayed he didn't find it; I knew it wouldn't jam a second time. When I saw him next, he was looking down at me and holding the device that controlled the flow of wet concrete. He gave me a splash of it in the cofferdam.

"How does it feel, Bostic? The cement shoe is on the other foot."

I blinked again and figured he was about to bury me right there.

Just then, behind him, I could make out a ghostly figure on the pier, clad in white. When I heard the voice, I knew it was Daisy. She was holding the Beretta in her outstretched hand.

"Daisy, no!" I shouted.

Janus lunged for her, and I heard a single shot. He clutched his stomach and staggered backward on the edge of the cofferdam, then fell and landed heavily just a few feet from me. His shirt was bloody from a hole in the stomach, but he was still very much alive. At the same time, I realized he'd released the hand controller, and the cofferdam was filling with wet, slippery cement. Janus was semi-conscious and trying to speak, but there was no saving him. I had to get up that rope if I wanted to live, and there was no way I could carry him at the same time. With concrete lapping at my heels, I pulled myself up as fast as I could. When I reached the top, I looked down and saw the wet concrete engulfing that white head of hair.

I looked over at Daisy. Her arm was limp at her side, the pistol still in her grasp. I went over and eased it from her, then turned and threw it as far into the James as I could. Daisy stared down into the cofferdam, where the concrete was settling with a few last drips, smooth and even. The worksite was still lit by floodlamp and awash in noise. I went over to the cab and climbed inside, took the key from the ignition. The sudden quiet was eerie.

"You could have been killed coming back like that," I said.

"Lucky for you I did," Daisy said. She had a point. "Where's that other man? Miller?"

"In the river."

"What do we do now?" she asked.

"We get the hell out of here."

CHAPTER 44
Hollywood

Two days later, I met with Malone and Gettle in the RPTA's offices in the Southern States Building. I still didn't have a car, but I could walk there now from my new place, just a couple of blocks downhill. We met in the same conference room as before, and at the same table. I may have even worn the same suit.

I placed the typed copy of my report on the table in front of them and gave them a few minutes to digest. Gettle stopped reading about halfway through, a look of disgust on his face. When Malone reached the last page, he took off his reading glasses and looked at me but didn't speak. I cleared my throat.

"Obviously," I said, "there will be charges and a trial. One of your contractors was a front for a human trafficking ring."

"We had our suspicions," Gettle said.

"Then why didn't you do something about it?"

"Hiring you," Malone said, "was us doing something about it."

"Now you tell me."

"As for a trial," Malone said, "it won't come to that."

"How's that?"

"For starters, this man Janus has gone missing. It's very difficult to prosecute someone you can't find."

"He and Miller were the drivers, but the other executive officers of Admiral Security must have known something. Mort Williams knows about it and is ready to talk. But he'll want a deal."

"What kind?"

"A reduced prison sentence. He knows what he did was wrong, but in fairness he hadn't been with the company long. They hired him to cover it all up and make it look as legitimate as possible."

Gettle smiled. "I don't think prison time is of any real concern," he said.

I was stunned. "What about human trafficking? Is that not a concern?"

"It was," Malone said, "but now it's not. If Janus and Miller were behind it, and no one can find them, then it sounds as though our problem has been solved."

"And the people they've already imported here to use as slave labor?"

"They will be ably compensated and invited to stay on."

"In return for silence?" I asked.

Malone and Gettle put their heads together briefly and whispered, then nodded in unison. Neither spoke as they looked at me, so I pressed them.

"And the people on the freighter last night, what happens to them?"

"Deported. They've been freed and given hot food and clean clothes. But at the moment, they are on board the ship you saw last night, steaming down the James and back to whatever godforsaken country they come from."

"You're only now seeing my report. How did you know about the ship?"

"We have a source inside the police, just like you."

"Great," I said. "So none of this happened."

"As far as we're concerned," Gettle said. "Case closed."

"What if this isn't all the evidence I have?"

"If there's more," Malone said, "it's our property. You see, among other things, I am an attorney. Any and all information you found in the course of your investigation is covered under attorney-client privilege."

"Interesting interpretation."

"It'll hold," he said. "Unless you'd care to revisit Mr. Williams's role in all this. And I don't think you would."

* * *

Later that day, I went to visit Archie's grave in the Williams family plot at Hollywood Cemetery. With everything that had happened, I felt like his birthday had gotten short shrift. Mort and Mona had repatriated his remains in 1949. I wasn't a fan at the time but kept it to myself. I figured Archie was happy enough where he was, on Saipan with the men of the Twenty-seventh. But as these things go, the ceremony was pretty moving. Honor guard and everything. A couple of years later, Mona had joined him there. Mother and son together again, or at least that's the hope.

The view from this particular part of the cemetery wasn't much, but on days like today it wasn't bad. The rain earlier had stopped, an overcast sky in its wake. The wind had picked up, swaying the tops of the trees between me and the river.

"I haven't been out here since mother died," said a voice behind me. I heard a woman's footsteps and turned, saw Daisy coming up the walkway.

"You've got a good excuse," I said. "You don't live here anymore."

She laced her arm through mine, and we stood in silence as some cool air kicked up around us. Daisy held me a little tighter, and I knew I should enjoy that one final time. We hadn't coordinated the meeting, hadn't even spoken since the night on the pier. What was there to say? I could think of a lot of things to base a marriage on, but murder wasn't one of them. We were done and we knew it. I caught a whiff of her perfume and flashed back to the first time I ever saw her. The spring of 1946. It was a million years ago and it was yesterday. Daisy spoke up.

"I remember seeing his death notice in the paper," she said. "His death year, 1944. It didn't look real to me, like some future year that hadn't happened yet."

I nodded but was finding it hard to concentrate. A short wrought-iron fence surrounded the plot. There but for the grace of God and all that.

"I don't get out here much myself," I said. "I'm never quite sure what to say or why I'd say it. I mourn him in my own way but not everybody notices."

She was quiet for a minute, then said softly, "You should come out to California sometime."

"I'll stay in the guest room," I said. "How much longer are you in town?"

"The house in Windsor Farms will be on the market soon. Dad has some more packing to do, but he's ready to go."

"So he's really going?" I asked.

"It's best that I have him out there. I can't look after him here, and I can't ask it of you."

"That's fine," I said. "I just can't believe he's leaving Richmond. Everything he's ever known has been here. His whole life is here."

"The agent's going to handle all that. In this case, I think a change of scenery will do him good. Blue skies, warm weather."

"Yeah," I said. "Not a bad idea at that."

"We're flying out Friday if you'd care to see us off."

I looked at her, taking in her face one last time. "You keep leaving, I keep staying. Yet every time, I'm still surprised. Almost like I expect it to end some other way."

* * *

On Wednesday, I finally got my car back from Vince. It still drives like shit but at least it starts. He even gave me a discount because it took so long—heckuva guy. Now, the van is in the shop, and it's not looking good. Something in the engine, but I probably won't find out what until next year. On the bright side, I won't be needing it anymore. Sometimes you have to bet on yourself.

Wednesday afternoon, I drove the Mercury 8 to Southside and met with JW Coulson again, but not at Model Tobacco. Instead, it was a few blocks away at a place called the Hi-Z Grill, which is exactly where you'd go to get news like this from a guy like me. We sat in an uncomfortable booth with a sticky tablecloth and torn red vinyl seats. Over beers, I told him his younger brother had been killed in an extortion scheme gone wrong, and his killer was now dead. I told him it was Simkins who'd called to tell him about Casey, and he was dead too. JW didn't seem shocked or sad or surprised about any of it. Mostly he was relieved it didn't make the paper. Now he could forget his brother had ever existed apart from innuendo and gossip. If any of his kids turned out like their Uncle Casey, I wished them luck.

On my way back into town I got stuck in traffic out front of Main Street Station. Outside my old building, a bulldozer idled in a low growl. I waved a vendor over from his newsstand and bought a fresh copy of the *News-Leader*. Jane Wynant's rescue was still the big story, at least the agreed-upon version of the truth. Tragically, an RPD detective named John Clay had been killed in the valiant effort to free her. Clay was now a hero who left behind a wife and two kids. But wait, it gets better. The article singled out local investigator, Mike Wells, who'd cracked the case. Sure, sure, wide open. No mention of Eddie Bostic, locksmith extraordinaire, who still got paid anyway. I folded the paper in half and threw it in the back.

The bulldozer revved its engine, spewing a cloud of gray exhaust. The driver lifted the blade and crashed it forward into the brick storefront, shooting shards of broken glass across the sidewalk. Traffic finally thinned so I quit rubbernecking, relieved to be moving again. Back at the new place on N. Seventh Street, the sign man had finished his work. I was now the proud owner of RE Bostic Investigations, licensed and bonded, though the paperwork hadn't gone through yet. They say a leopard can't change its spots, but that's not entirely true. It can change them and keep them that way for as long as it takes to survive.

But in the end, for better and for worse, they always change back.

THE END

AFTERWORD

Although populated largely with fictional characters, this book references a handful of real people. Cerelia Johnson, the secretary at Sixth Mt. Zion Church, is among them. She did what is described herein and is among the heroes who saved John Jasper's historic church from the wrecking ball. Mrs. Irma Thompson was the president of the Virginia Teachers Association in 1956. In the time of massive resistance to *Brown vs. Board of Education*, she had her hands full.

The Jesse Woods case in Wildwood, Florida was real, but had a happier ending than most because Woods wasn't killed. In fact, he lived until 2007 when he died at the age of ninety. The Klan's tactics in the Woods case were used to far deadlier effect in 1964 Mississippi, ending with the murders of civil rights workers James Chaney, Andrew Goodman, and Michael Schwerner.

Dr. Martin Luther King, Jr. did appear at Virginia Union University in November 1956 at a conference for the VTA. There he gave a speech titled, "Facing the Challenge of a New Age."

Daisy is a composite of a handful of postwar actresses: think Cathy O'Donnell, Lizabeth Scott, and Peggie Castle. Cleo Nichols is a B-movie mashup of Cleo Moore, Barbara Nichols, and Janis Paige (among others). Likewise, Paul Eggar is an amalgam of several fifties actors whose public persona was often at odds with their private life.

Izzy and Moe were Isidor "Izzy" Einstein and Moe Smith, a pair of Prohibition agents who were weirdly famous in the early twenties. Harlan Hawkins is based on a real Virginia politician who did run for president in 1956 as a States' Rights candidate. The idea that this man had anything to do with an attempt on MLK's life in Richmond during this time is completely fabricated.

The Battle of Saipan was fought from June 15 to July 9, 1944, and was a joint operation between the US Army and Marine Corps. Its culmination saw the largest Banzai charge of the war, in which a desperate group of Japanese soldiers with improvised weapons briefly overran American positions. Saipan was also the first Pacific battle to involve a civilian population, some twenty-two thousand of whom were killed. Many of them perished via mass suicide in the battle's last days by jumping into the sea from the rocky cliffs of Marpi Point.

The Richmond-Petersburg Turnpike was built from 1956-58. Although now part of I-95 that stretches from Maine to Florida, its construction pre-dated the National Interstate Highway System and used no federal money. To this day, it's still possible for Richmond residents to get into arguments about the route its planners chose and the gutting of Jackson Ward.

Recommended Reading

Battling for Saipan by Francis A. O'Brien. An indispensable account of the battle from the army's side, with insights from veterans who were there. Pairs nicely with Capt. Edmund G. Love's *The 27th Infantry Division in World War II*, which provides a macro view of the division's deployments in the Pacific from Pearl Harbor to V-J Day, replete with maps and photographs.

Twentieth-Century Richmond: Planning, Politics, and Race by Christopher Silver. Most histories of Richmond dwell on its role as capital of the Confederacy during the Civil War; one could be forgiven for thinking the city's history stopped there. Silver's book is an antidote to that way of thinking and depicts a city in need of change that it's also desperate to stop. *Richmond's Unhealed History* by Benjamin Campbell shows a city hobbled by the wounds of its past as it takes on the twentieth century.

Richmond: The Story of a City by Virginius Dabney sheds light on Richmond's role in the slave trade. His depictions of the hotels where traders stayed, the jails where slaves stayed, and the auction houses where they made their deals are required reading for anyone interested in the barbaric minutiae of trafficking in humans.

Lesbian and Gay Richmond by Beth Marschak and Alex Lorch, an invaluable guide into the gay underworld of post-WWII Richmond.

Virginia State Penitentiary: A Notorious History by Dale M. Brumfield. It is inconceivable to most modern Richmonders that the state penitentiary once stood in the middle of the city. Yet from 1800-1992, there it stood in plain sight on Belvidere Street, a stark brick edifice that housed the Commonwealth's most wanted and feared. The electric chair was also housed there. Death row inmates spent their final days here in often squalid conditions.

Acknowledgments

This book wouldn't exist if not for the efforts of many talented people. The Brandylane Crew: Ceci Hughes, who sent the email that changed my life; project manager Andrew Holt, who kept me on task and off the ledge; editor Mary-Peyton Crook, who helped me turn a misshapen lump of clay into something real; editor and fact-checker Ashley Barnhill, who made several key saves; designer Sami Langston, for a killer cover; Robert Pruett for his wisdom and forbearance. Elsewhere: my friends Don Semmens and Cynde Liffick, who looked at the first fifty pages back in the day and offered helpful criticism and support; author Bill Blume, for his input on a later draft; author Craig Terlson, for shining a light in the dark; Thomas Crew, Kevin Shupe, Jennifer Huff, and Cassandra Farrell, Archivists at the Library of Virginia, who held my hand through the research to the very best of their ability; my friend and advisor, E.G. Allen, who always comes through in the clutch; and especially my wife G, who didn't kick me out of the house when she learned I'd lost my job and wasn't going to look for a new one until I'd finished the first draft. Why any of you have anything to do with me is part of the everlasting mystery. Thanks, y'all.

Author photo by Lauren Okes Photography

About the Author

Neal Savage has called Richmond, VA his home since 1974. He received a BA in English from James Madison University ('87) where he studied creative writing under Mark Facknitz. He is a member of James River Writers, and Mystery Writers of America. He lives in Richmond with his wife and just enough cats.

Socials:
Facebook: Neal Savage, author
Twitter: @NealSavage_